# BROKEN

### BOOK ONE OF THE

### WARWICK COOPER THRILLERS

## DONNA SIGGERS

# DEDICATION

For Tracey, my dear friend: you faced
your battle with such courage.  May
you rest in peace.

# ACKNOWLEDGEMENTS

To my family (and friends considered family) I owe a special debt. Your love, patience, understanding and the fact you've been there for me every step of the way since my head injury in 2014 means the world to me. Thank you will never seem enough in my eyes. Our warped humour has helped see me through the toughest of times in what has been a life-changing experience.

Vickii, my eldest daughter, was brave enough to be the first to read this novel – and brave enough to suggest to her mother where she needed to elaborate. Her annotations on my manuscript will always bring a smile to my face. Thank you sweetheart, for all your hard work.

Finally, to the talented professionals at SpiffingCovers, I thank you for your incredible support, an awesome front cover and logo and for your editing. Without you guys this would still be a dream.

# CHAPTER ONE

Returning to the city had put me on high alert. Old anxieties returned without warning, acting as a reminder of why I'd moved so far away. Streets that once felt familiar and comforting now seemed alien. My senses were working overtime, each little sound screaming its warning to me. With a palpitating heart and an overwhelming need to gain control, I made my way through the streets of London. I longed to return to the tranquillity of my new home, the little Cornish fishing village I'd fallen in love with four years ago.

Each time a hooded figure came into view – and they were in abundance – fear engulfed me. In my mind, each carried a knife and placed me in danger. My stomach clenched in anticipation of attack. Realistically, I knew these people had no interest in me and that my reaction to them was my own; unfortunately my brain was having trouble keeping up with this concept and my anxiety levels continued to climb. Making a mental note to contact my therapist on Monday morning, I continued to stroll the pathways of London.

The three or so hours spent with two of my closest friends at our favourite restaurant had been a long time coming. Busy lives meant that shared time was scarce these days. But we'd made the effort. Wine had flowed and laughter had filled the air as news was shared, memories recounted and new ones born. For just one evening only, the three detectives were back in the city. We'd made a good team back in the day. Mel, Jen, and me.

Hugs, tears and promises that next time we'd not leave it so long saw the three of us going our separate ways and back to what had become very separate lives. Unbeknown to us, our lives were destined to become entangled in a way that would haunt my very existence.

The cases we worked together were tough ones. The sort that either ripped friendships apart, or bonded them for life. The three of us had had a unique way of coping with the stresses that came with our job and it had got us through some very tough times: our humour was dark to those who didn't understand. Our last case was particularly harrowing. Despite us getting a good result, we lived with the daily guilt that solving this one sooner would have saved many women from their fate. How these women lived with the consequences of their ordeals was beyond me and I didn't think I could ever have their strength of character. Each of them had begged for him to take their lives before he had released them. Even then they weren't free from his grip – they had begged the medics to put them out of their misery. Now living an assumed life, with their mental and physical scars, these women were somewhere within the witness protection programme.

If I had gone through their ordeal I am convinced I would have taken my own life; I know at least one of them had. There wasn't a day that passed when they weren't in my thoughts and I'd had to factor that into my routine to prevent it from controlling my life. I wondered what had become of each of them. Some had wanted to stay in touch with the three of us but it was not allowed: professional distance for us and protection for them.

That case had changed each of us. Jen had hit the wine in a big way, she took sick days too often and was seriously not coping with the psychological impact of viewing so much devastation. Mel had struggled to remain in relationships since the case, drifting from one to the next. When she finally settled it was with a no-hoper type that she'd never have given herself to before. For me, I started taking unnecessary risks. Eventually our boss, Phil Andrews, had called us into a meeting. He had arranged for us to be separated, for Jen and Mel to be moved to a different station. They would remain in London but we would never work a case together again. It had been the end of a very successful era and, in my humble opinion, such a shame that we hadn't been able to continue as a team. I remained at Paddington Green, where Phil had partnered me with a man who seemed grounded and where, I was about to learn, he could keep a close eye on me. He had taken me under his wing, promised Phil he'd take good care of me, and led me directly into the risk-taking I had learned to love. Our risks got results. Sometimes they got us hurt. We both had the scars to prove it.

Having spent longer with the girls than expected, I hoped I wasn't going to miss the train. There would be others of course, but none with the connections I needed closer to home. As I rushed through the streets the coolness of the air chilled me. The tiny hairs on my arms were standing to attention and I cursed under my breath at not picking up a jacket when I left home this morning. I had been rushing about and running errands before I'd left and had felt the warmth of the early autumn sun. It had lulled me into a false sense that it was warmer than it was. What had I been thinking? October in England is hardly the time to forget your coat.

Turning into Paddington station, I glanced at the clock and was immediately annoyed with myself. With moments to go, I broke into a jog and headed towards my platform just in time to watch my train slowly build momentum as it drew away. I hadn't even reached the ticket gate. Anxiety rose like bile from the pit of my stomach as I realised I was stranded in a city in which I no longer belonged.

Suddenly sensing something wasn't quite right within my world, a cold shiver ran along my spine. Unable to place what was wrong, I felt the muscles tighten in my shoulders. Tension was beginning to build in my body and if I wasn't careful I would end up with a migraine. This was the last thing I needed. With no other choice than to place my fear to the back of my mind and focus my energy on finding somewhere safe to spend the next few hours, I turned to leave.

Stranded in what had become such foreign terrain, I looked towards the exit and into the darkening sky, cursing under my breath once more. The tension in my shoulders was now beginning to creep up my neck and behind my eyes. Rolling my shoulders, first forwards and then backwards, I attempted to loosen them. Although people were milling about, the station wasn't busy. I wished it was because quiet stations unsettled me and I wasn't sure how much more anxiety my mind could cope with this day.

Unsure what to do, I started walking towards the exit. Ahead of me were three hooded youths, who did nothing to help my mood. They were walking with purpose straight for me. Each of their black sweatshirts had, what looked like, two yellow owl eyes on the hoods. Fear surged through me as easily as the blood in my veins and my heart rate intensified. There was no choice other than continuing my planned path and pretending that I hadn't noticed them, nor that they bothered me. It took every single piece of remaining self-control to place one foot in front of the other. One of them bumped shoulders with me as we passed one another and his shrill laughter filled the air, the sound penetrating my eardrums and seemingly bouncing around in my head. My heart rate soared but I fought every instinct to turn around and run.

Their trainers were squeaking on the floor as they walked and when the sound pattern changed I was convinced they'd turned around to follow me. My pace automatically quickened. Hurrying through the exit and on to the street, I could sense them closing in on me. Their footsteps now sounded hollow as their trainers made contact with the paving slabs. I knew they were running. Instinct was telling me that my survival depended upon reaching a taxi before they caught me up. Rarely were my instincts wrong. Acting quickly, I broke into a sprint and made haste for the line of taxis waiting, opened a door and clambered in.

"Please just drive. Now!" I said with urgency in my voice. "Paddington Green Police Station. Please hurry." Anxiety hung in the air and I had no intention of making any apology for my rudeness.

As the driver pulled away, I turned around and took a look at my pursuers. All I glimpsed was the three of them pulling their hoods over their faces; these individuals did not want to be identified. I wondered what business they had with me. I checked my bag and, to my relief, I still had my purse. During my moment of distraction at missing my train, it would have been easy for them to have robbed me as they brushed shoulders with me. They would have read my body language and could have easily seen how intimidated I had been because of their presence. Being away from the city had softened me.

"Is everything alright, lady?"

"Please hurry," I said.

"Those boys giving you grief? Not seem them about before. Some kind of new gang I expect." He pulled away and started to negotiate the traffic.

Not in the mood for chatting with a cabbie, whose company I would keep for just five minutes, I forced a smile that he saw through his rear-view mirror and stayed quiet. It seemed absurd to get in a cab for a journey that would take me less than ten minutes on foot, but I didn't feel safe on the street. In fact, I was sure that right now, it was fair to say, I was unsafe on the street. As we approached the station, I glanced at the fare. Because of the late hour, it was nearly ten pounds, so I handed the driver fifteen.

"Thank you," I said as I opened my door.

Half walking, half breaking into a jog, I hurried away from the taxi towards the door of my old workplace. Fumbling with the door, I barged my way through into the building where I hoped to find someone on duty that I knew. It had been over four years since I'd last been here and I wasn't sure how I felt about that. A wave of nostalgia swept through me as the familiar smells and sounds hit my senses.

Hearing a familiar voice from behind a collection of people brought me to a standstill. I felt my lips tighten as they curled into a broad smile. My heart also started to beat a little faster but for reasons other than fear or anxiety. Excitement and anticipation now surged through my veins as I pulled myself together and started walking again, watching and listening as this officer went about a job he was far too qualified for. Somehow, through the noise and the business at hand he met my gaze, looking genuinely pleased to see me. Feeling a surge of energy travel through my body, instinct told me that time apart had done nothing to suppress my feelings for this man.

Just over four years ago, my partner and I had been in pursuit of a suspect. We'd chased him, on foot, into a deserted train station late at night. Unbeknown to us, our suspect had had help waiting in the shadows. I was stabbed in the back with a knife and lost a lot of blood. The two men escaped leaving my partner, Sam Cooper, to stem my bleeding until medical help arrived. He saved my life that night. After recovering, I couldn't face returning to work. It was a combination of things really, but mainly, I felt that I just couldn't remain in London. Selling up and moving so far away, I'd put physical distance between my old life and my new one, hoping that emotional distance would follow. There was no doubt that Cornwall had been good for me: I'd chosen a busy tourist area, so always had plenty of people staying who needed my attention. I'd made new friends too.

Not one of my colleagues had made the journey to Cornwall to see me though, despite how close we'd become over the years, which had hurt in all honesty. They all seemed to have had the same response, that they respected my need for space. Each of them had invited me to stay with them instead, which I'd politely declined. We were stuck in this catch-twenty-two situation of complete stubbornness and denial of just how much we needed to get together.

In our modern world of mobile phones and social media, however, we made our friendships work. Let's face it, there really is no excuse not to stay in touch these days! Not many weeks passed without contact between us all on our group chats and the banter flowed as if the geographical distance didn't exist between us.

Jen and Mel had moved on too, to the Midlands and Norfolk respectively. Unlike me, they hadn't left law enforcement, but had opted for quieter areas in which to operate. They saw my change of occupation and location as running away from my past and the truth. I couldn't blame them for thinking this way, to be honest. Despite my public denial, I had run as hard and as fast as my tired legs would carry me. My two friends had seen right through me. To say I hadn't looked back would be a big fat lie, so I won't say it. The very reason for my departure was now standing before me, the pull on my heartstrings as strong as ever. Yet he was as out of reach as ever before.

Married.

Just my luck.

# CHAPTER TWO

"No way. Get out of here!" Sam Cooper exclaimed, ignoring the two young officers stood before him and the mouthy drunk they were booking into a cell.

A feeling of warmth suddenly swept through me as old attractions bubbled to the surface; not that they had been buried too deeply. Sam Cooper had not changed one bit. As if the physical distance of the last four years hadn't happened, there was an intense reaction in my body and, briefly, I felt like I might cry. Forcing composure, I responded to my old partner against crime.

"Book him in Sam, so you can make me a cuppa," I said as I sat in the waiting area and anticipated, smiling to myself, Sam's response.

"Katie-Anne Warwick. What drags your sorry ass all the way back from Cornwall?"

Sam, now grinning, tried to hurry through the paperwork, but the drunk was giving him a hard time, especially now he knew Sam had other business. Watching this struggle was entertaining me, but it was also reminding me just how much I missed my old life.

How much I missed Sam. I'd loved my job before the knife attack. Having suppressed the impact of having my career taken from me during the past four years, it returned with an almighty thud and, once again, I found anger building towards my attacker. This day seemed to be one for regression with regards to my psychological recovery and I had to wonder just how healed my therapist thought I might be. Right now, it was questionable and a large part of me was regretting having made the journey.

With the i's dotted and the t's crossed, the man was transferred into the care of the cells. The two young officers disappeared back on to the streets; I hadn't recognised either of them and wondered just how young and new to the job they might be. Sam's attention turned to me. As he approached I stood and took a couple of steps forward. We hadn't seen each other in over four years but we'd spoken on the phone a lot. His smile broadened and I felt my cheeks flush.

"Sam, you don't look a day older," I said and I meant it. He looked no different to me and I wondered if I was blinded by my feelings.

Wrapping our arms around one another, we embarked on an embrace that neither of us seemed willing to break away from. Every feeling I'd ever had for this man engulfed my very existence in that moment and I felt a single tear escape and run down my cheek. As our bodies touched I physically ached for his affection. His large hands seemed to cover my entire back and I could feel their welcome warmth through my thin blouse.

"It's so good to see you Kate," Sam muffled into my neck.

I was too overwhelmed to speak, so I clung on to him with all my might.

Eventually, we allowed our grip upon one another to loosen. Lingering in the air however, was a slight awkwardness that had never been there before. In this moment, I knew something had changed between us but had no idea what that something could be. We'd always flirted and messed about, and the banter between us had had the whole station gossiping about what might be going on. Truthfully though, nothing had ever happened, nor had it come close. Sam was a married man. Neither of us crossed those lines.

"Cuppa?" he asked, raising his left eyebrow.

And I was reminded of how quirky he could be, as if raising an eyebrow was needed to punctuate his question.

"Thought you'd never offer," I smiled. "I'd love one."

The small room behind the desk was mainly unchanged. The kettle had been replaced with a hot drinks machine and a water cooler. The small table, chairs and the colour of the walls were just as I remembered.

Sam busied himself with making our drinks and I quietly sat, suddenly exhausted. I could feel his eyes on me and felt the warmth seep into my face as my cheeks begun to flush again.

Placing two steaming cardboard cups between us, Sam took the other chair. The moment of awkwardness already long forgotten, our conversation began to flow.

"It's really good to see you too, Sam." And I struggled to keep my eyes to myself. He really was looking good.

Picking up the flimsy cup, I was grateful for the warmth in my hands. As I took my first sip, Sam's right eyebrow raised.

"What?" I asked, because his quirkiness also preceded an impending question. I took a large gulp of tea.

"So, anyone significant in your life I need to check out?" he asked, as I inhaled my tea.

"No!" I replied, through chokes and gasps of air. "How's Lauren?" I managed to croak.

"No idea actually. She remarried last year."

"No way. How many times have we spoken on the phone? You didn't even mention you'd split up." And I was truly shocked and feeling hurt.

"I have my reasons," he said, holding my gaze before continuing. "And anyhow, how could you be in the city and I know nothing about the visit?"

Okay, so he had me on that one. Guilt turned my cheeks scarlet and silence fell between us.

Realisation was, perhaps, a little slow to catch up with my tired mind, but when it arrived I wasn't too sure how to react. Sam and I were both available and here we sat. The awkwardness I'd felt a few minutes ago had reappeared and it now hovered in the air between us. What had shifted between us was now clear, it was his big fat divorce. Why would he keep something like that from me? Was there someone else? No. I couldn't think about that right now. As my thoughts started to run away with me, I became acutely aware that Sam was staring at me. When I looked up our eyes met and he was smiling.

"A penny for them?"

"I'm just processing the fact that you're divorced. Partners are supposed to share that sort of thing, Sam. I can't believe you went through that on your own."

"I know. I wanted to tell you so many times but there was something stopping me from telling you. Something important."

"What could that possibly be?" I asked.

"Your move to Cornwall was your way of coping with what you were going through. My staying here and keeping quiet was mine. Phil is the only one that knows. There's more to it than that though, but that's no convo for here."

Privacy had always been important to Sam. It took a lot for him to let you into his private life. I knew his previous partner had never met his wife or son. To my knowledge, there were only two of us that had made the graduation from colleague to friend. One was me. The other was Phil, and he'd had a head start as they'd been childhood friends, had joined the army together and had eventually joined the police force together. They had worked undercover cases together too. Phil had been Sam's best man when he'd married Lauren and was the couple's only choice for godparent when their only child, their son, Charlie, had been born.

It had been Phil that had put Sam and me with each other when he'd decided that Jen, Mel and I shouldn't work together any more. Apparently, he'd be a good influence and would calm the risk-taking attitude that I'd developed.

Would he ever?

That hadn't been a shift in logistics I'd wanted, but Sam had made a massive effort to make me feel good about the changes. Within one week I had met his family without realising what an honour it had been. Colleagues that had worked closely with Sam for years had not earned that privilege and so the rumours had begun. To have been let in so quickly, when so many hadn't been let in at all, must have meant we were sleeping together, right?

Wrong.

Lauren and I had become great friends too. But looking back at things now, with my new knowledge, she had become distant a year before I was attacked. Had this been when their marriage had started to fade?

The sound of Sam's voice brought me out of my thoughts.

"My shift finishes in an hour. Where are you staying?" Again the raised eyebrow.

"I hadn't intended to stay actually, but I missed the train I needed. If it's okay, I'll hang about until I need to head back to the station?"

"No way. You can kip at mine. No argument," he smiled.

"I don't want to impose," I replied, but am not sure if I meant it.

"Nonsense. I'll enjoy the company and it'll be good to get the gossip started all over again," he said with a broad smile and a little too much excitement. Standing, he left the room in time to man the desk for the next arrested man to enter his care.

Samuel Robert Cooper was five years older than me. The instant we met we had clicked. The night of my stabbing, it had been Sam's bare hands that had pressed against my bleeding body until the paramedics arrived. It had been Sam who travelled in the ambulance with me, stayed at the hospital throughout my operation and who was there when I came around from the anaesthetic. When the doctor came to tell me that he had been unable to save my kidney, it had been Sam who had been there to hold my hand throughout that consultation. And, yes, it was Sam who collected me from the hospital, took me home and camped out on my sofa until I was fit enough to look after myself. I hoped I hadn't cost my friend his marriage.

Our complex friendship had run that deep for many years. Before Sam saved my life, I had saved his. The fact that we had each experienced this intense connection meant a rare bond existed between us that no one else around us understood. Sam learned early on in our partnership that he could depend on me to watch his back because I had quite literally held his life in my own hands. During one of my many hospital visits with him he had asked that I take a leap of faith in him; that he would always have my back too. We made a deal that day. And it paid off. I would walk to the end of the earth for this man and I knew he would do the same for me.

# CHAPTER THREE

As I stood outside Sam's new flat waiting for him to unlock the door, any sense of calmness vanished and my emotions swept over my skin like sweat. Feeling like an excited teenager, my nerves were starting to get the better of me. Somehow, by stepping over the threshold of his home, I knew that our relationship would shift. Certain events were destined to unfold and where that would leave us, with me living so far away, was impossible to tell. My life and my business were many miles from the city. How could we possibly make this work?

There had been no one in my life, romantically, for eight years. Not even a one-night stand. Quite simply, once I had met Sam, no man had any chance at holding my attention beyond a first date. Eventually, even those had stopped. Trust was also a huge issue for me. My ex had cheated on me twice and I hadn't forgiven him the second time. When he walked away from the life we'd build together: from our house, the cars and our healthy bank balance, and wanted nothing, I wasn't sure if it was out of pity or because of his guilt. I didn't need his pity and I no longer believed he was capable of feeling guilt. I concluded that it must have been out of pure embarrassment that he'd walked away from his half of our shared fortune. After all, his second affair had been with my adoptive mother.

Sam almost had to pull me through the door because I was so lost in thought.

"Sorry, I was miles away," I said through a smile.

Sam proudly showed me around his flat, the whole time talking me through a timeline of events and decisions he had made during his renovations. The design was so very different from the seaside feel of my bed and breakfast, with its overstuffed chairs and driftwood trinkets. This space was modern, minimalistic, stylish and beautiful. It gave me great pleasure in telling him so.

We ended our tour in the kitchen, where I was now glancing at a floating shelf. On it were three framed photos. The largest was of Sam and Charlie, and it startled me at how mature Charlie now looked. The second was of the team taken sometime last year. Some familiar faces looked back at me. I noted that the two young officers from earlier were not here and again I wondered how new they were to the force. The third photo was of Sam and me. It had been taken by one of my nurses on the day I had left hospital. I reached up and gently grasped its frame. Bringing it to eye level, I was taken back in time and remembered the pain.

"I look so ill in this."

"I know. I love it though. It reminds me of how fragile life is, but also that was the first day of the rest of my life. It was the day that Lauren announced she'd been having an affair for two years."

"I'm so sorry." I didn't know what else to say and I made eye contact with him.

"Don't be sorry. Yeah, I was shocked at first. Angry even. Do you know how hard it was for me to keep my hands off you all those years?" he joked, before continuing. "I was physically loyal to my wife, but I was definitely not emotionally committed. And I'd never admit that to anyone but you. When Lauren announced she was gay it really was the best thing that could have happened at the time."

"Wow. She left you for another woman? I didn't see that coming. How did Charlie react?"

"That's a long, long story my friend!"

"So, in my absence, I'm wondering if you may have found someone else I need to check out?" I said with a cheer in my voice I didn't feel.

"There is this one woman who I've been plucking up the courage to ask out for dinner," Sam replied, as he took a couple of steps closer to me. He reached up to the cupboard beside the shelf to collect two wine glasses.

"Details!" I demanded, as my heart plummeted towards my stomach. Watching him fill glasses with red wine, a heaviness swept through me and I wondered if I had missed my chance with this man because I was getting mixed messages. I couldn't agree more that we shouldn't have taken things further while he was married, but I'd have been there for him if I'd known. Was there a hidden message in what he'd just said? Was he glad we hadn't taken things further because he had found someone more suited to him? Feeling tired and cranky, I wasn't sure if my mind or my body could cope with much more emotion this day. I was now seriously considering leaving and a part of me was tempted to run out the door – running away, it seemed, was what I did these days. The other part of me wanted to stay, to rip the shirt from his back and to feel his skin against mine. What to do?

"Thanks," I said as he passed me my wine.

"To freedom," he said, holding his glass in the air.

"Freedom and independence!" I replied through a forced smile, clinking my glass against his.

We both drank and were both aware of him avoiding my question.

"So, come on... Details. I hope this woman is deserving of such a decent bloke."

"Well," he said, taking my wine from me before I had a chance to take a second sip. He placed it beside his own on the worktop.

"She is beautiful, witty, amazing and I've waited many years to be able to tell her." The back of his fingers touched my cheek, my heart soared and my stomach seemed to flutter, as if it contained a dozen butterflies.

As our eyes met, I felt a wave of emotion sweep through my entire body. Gradually leaning into the moment, I was aware that Sam cupped my face in his hands. We kissed, gently, tenderly, softly; savouring the special moment. Sam's hands started to move away from my face. One found the back of my neck and gently caressed it. The other found the small of my back and pulled me in closer. My hands found his chest and I extended them slowly upwards. One slid around his body and the other over a shoulder and around his neck. I pulled him even closer. I didn't ever want to let go.

Our kisses became deeper as our passion intensified and I felt my eyes well up. Tears escaped and cascaded down my cheeks. I could taste their saltiness as we continued to kiss.

Sam moved his attention to my neck. He kissed me there before nestling his head into my hair. With his face buried we held each other tightly. I could feel his heart beating against my body.

"Wow!" he said.

Unable to speak I let out a contented groan.

"Come on beautiful. Let's go and snuggle up with our wine."

Collecting both glasses, Sam led the way into the lounge, settled himself into the corner of his sofa at an angle and I settled into the gap he had left. As soon as I'd taken my wine, his free arm worked its way between the sofa and my body and wrapped around me. We both sipped at our drinks, apparently lost in our own thoughts. Our silence was a beautiful, cosy moment – the awkwardness that had lingered earlier, gone.

Sam finished his wine before me and placed his empty glass on the coffee table. His second hand now fiddled with my hair, my shoulder, my arm and came to rest over my stomach. My right hand was free, so I reached towards his hand. Our fingers entwined as he began to kiss my neck.

In a flash of movement, Sam took my glass and drank the wine. My mock protest was a feeble attempt at restraint. I was giggling almost uncontrollably, which didn't help, but mainly I was so very out of practice. In the struggle, I ended up straddling his body. He had me right where he wanted me! Somehow, and I was under no illusion other than he had allowed it to happen, I had trapped his hands above his head. Our eyes locked and the giggling stopped as the moment became more serious. Lowering my face to his, until our noses touched, I lingered there for a few moments to catch my breath. Sam raised his head slightly and our lips touched, sending electricity through my entire body. I released his hands and they were fast to relocate to my body, pulling me in close to him. I needed access to Sam's body, so I gently slid my upper body over to one side and propped my head on one hand. The other hand, now free to explore, followed the firm contours of his muscular body.

Passion was building and, although fully dressed, there really wasn't much imagination needed as to what each of us had to offer the other. One of his hands found its way to my hips and then worked its way back up. As it reached my blouse, I felt a rush of material and cool air against my skin. When Sam's hands made contact with bare skin, we both let out a groan.

"I'm going to take a shower, then I'm all yours," he said.

Without hesitation, I was suddenly on my feet and holding out my hand. I could very much do with showering too. Sam took the hint, leapt off the sofa and took hold of my hand. Running like excited teenagers, we headed towards his bathroom.

In one move, Sam turned on the water, scooped me into his arms and started kissing me deeply. I worked on his shirt buttons, very tempted just to rip them open, but I managed contain myself. Once finished, his shirt cascaded to the floor and my hands met skin for the first time, his muscular body felt incredible. Sam was struggling with the buttons on my blouse, so I pulled away from our kiss, stood on tiptoes and whispered in his ear.

"They're poppers!"

Holding me at arm's length and with a broad smile across his face, he took hold of the bottom of my blouse, one side in each hand, and with an outwards movement, each popper gave way in turn.

"God that was sexy," he said, pulling me in close again.

The rest of our clothes started to fall, in turn, into a crumpled heap around our feet. The moment the last garment hit the floor, Sam started walking us backwards, edging us towards the water. Closing the cubicle door, we allowed the steaming water to caress our bodies. We continued to kiss and our hands explored one another as our hunger grew. Sam reached up to a shelf and introduced shower gel to water and steam.

The shower door kept springing open because there really wasn't enough room in here for the both of us: each time cool air gushed in, Sam extended his arm to close it. Through water and steam our eyes met. I raised my arms, wrapping one around his neck and the other around his shoulder. He lifted me into the air with ease, my legs immediately wrapped around his body and he held me close. Our noses were touching and our eyes were still locked in an intensity I was reluctant to break away from. I felt like I was melting from within. Leaning in slightly, Sam gently nipped my top lip and every cell in my body wanted to respond at once. As we began kissing deeply the door reopened and we were blasted with another shot of cool air. Sam hit the power button and attempted to carry me through the door.

"There's no way this will work!" We were both laughing and he tried a different angle.

"Breathe in," he said as he took a huge breath.

I allowed my legs to slide over his and, as my feet touched the shower tray, I took his face in my hands, stood on tiptoes and bit his lip back.

"You step out first and I'll follow."

There was no time for drying: as I stepped through the door Sam scooped me up and ran into his room with me in his arms. Water streaked down our bodies and on to the floor. Our laughter was shrill as he leapt and we flew towards his bed, collapsing in a heap on top of it.

Within moments our bodies pressed against one another and we started to kiss. Sam pulled away slightly, our eyes locked and our bodies became one – we made love.

As we lay in each other's arms, his hand found my scar.

"I already knew I was in love with you but when we were on that platform, and I had my hands pressing into your wound and your blood was still pumping through my fingers, that was the day I knew how much I loved you, Kate. Losing you would have devastated me."

Tears filled my eyes and he held me close, kissing the top of my head. I pulled away slightly so I could see his face. Tears filled his eyes too.

"Sam, have we just wasted the last four years?"

"You needed to get away from London, right?"

"Yes and from your marriage, Sam. That was the main reason I left."

"Oh. Jesus Christ! No! By the time you'd gone, she'd left me."

"I wasn't to know that."

"I should have listened to Charlie. He told me to chase after you. I should have listened to Charlie."

Sam was getting himself worked up. I sat up on the bed and turned my body to face him. It didn't matter that I was naked. Reaching out, I took his hands in mine.

"Sam, listen to me," I said, as I lifted his hands to my lips and kissed his fingers before continuing. "I did need space, but not from you. I needed to escape London's violence, the pressures of work and my insistence at placing myself in danger. I was making unhealthy life choices and that needed to change. It nearly cost me my life. I'm gutted I wasn't here for you when you needed me and I'd have dropped everything to be here had you told me. You do know that, right?"

"I know all of that. I didn't tell you in the beginning because I knew we'd have ended up in bed. I didn't want us to be just about sex. You mean too much to me, Kate. The longer I left it, the harder it got, because my feelings for you just got stronger and stronger. You, walking into the station tonight felt so overwhelming. Look at me: when do I cry?"

He broke away from the grip of my hands and held out his arms for a hug. Emotions were running high for both of us.

"I'd be lying if I didn't wish you hadn't moved away, but I should have come to visit; I know that now."

"Sam, I couldn't stay and not act on my feelings any longer. I refused to be responsible for ruining your marriage, and I would have ruined it. I couldn't have done that to Charlie, or to Lauren. I thought that the physical distance would dampen my feelings over time."

"If this is your dampened feelings, I can't wait until they intensify again," he joked, lightening the mood.

"I was kidding myself, Sam, no one could ever come close to winning me over from you."

\*\*\*

Sam raided Charlie's room for a hairdryer and I took my time to make myself look presentable. Sam rummaged through his wardrobe and selected one of his smaller shirts for me to wear, which he was finding sexy. He couldn't keep his hands to himself, which I was loving. Our flirting was continuous. He was wandering about in nothing but boxers, and I was having trouble keeping both my eyes and my hands to myself too.

Sam disappeared, soon to return with renewed glasses of wine – setting them down on each side of the bed. He snuggled under the duvet and watched me as I finished drying my hair. When I was done, I turned to face him and started to unbutton the shirt.

"Leave it on."

Smiling and laughing, I climbed into bed. Our hands were quick to find one another but we were taking our time now. Our touches were sensual as we explored the contours of one another's body through touch and taste. Tenderness had replaced urgency: when we made love from now on it would be less urgent, have a deeper meaning and would be more about love, passion and growth as a couple, rather than a release of pent-up hunger and frustration of unimaginable proportions. We could take our time now and relish learning about what each other enjoyed.

Having waited so many years for my time with this man, going home tomorrow seemed so very cruel. Despite not wanting to waste a single moment, it had been a long day and my eyes were feeling heavy; I knew

I wouldn't keep them open for much longer. Sam sensed this too.

"Hey. I've put a toothbrush in the bathroom for you."

"Hmm. Thanks."

"Come on. Before you fall asleep."

Reluctantly I emerged from under the cosy duvet and headed to the bathroom with Sam following. As I cleaned my teeth he peed and I allowed myself a smile. Apparently, we were that relaxed with each other that our bodily functions did not embarrass. I'd never felt this comfortable with someone before, yet I felt no hesitation in doing so now. When we'd finished our little bathroom routine we returned to the warmth of the bed, kissed, snuggled into each other's arms and drifted into sleep.

# CHAPTER FOUR

Alec Johnson didn't have a great start in life. At the tender age of nine months his parents didn't come home from work: they had been involved in a car crash and had been killed at the scene. His grandparents were elderly and were his only surviving relatives. Having opted to give him up to the mounting number of American families willing to open their homes to fostering orphan children, the infant was bundled into the arms of a stranger and was never seen by them again. It had been heart-wrenching, but what else could they have done? Better for the child that they did it now than in three or four years.

Alec hadn't been an easy child. He had moved from home to home and it had been more and more difficult to place him for any length of time. Couples just didn't want him around their own children and with his complex behaviours, who could blame them?

It hadn't been until he was ten that a sweet couple, unable to have children of their own, took Alec in and they seemed to take to him. They gave him the attention he needed and he seemed happy. The freedom that rural life gave Alec appeared to suit him: for the first time in his life, it appeared, he was staying out of trouble. The sad truth was he was more skilled at not getting caught. On the surface, it appeared that progress was being made so visits from the authorities stopped.

Alec Johnson was slipping through the net.

As the years passed and Alec reached his teens, it didn't go unnoticed by the neighbours that nothing bad ever happened to Hank and Mary Johnson. Their house didn't get broken into and their pets didn't go missing, or get killed. It didn't go unnoticed to Hank and Mary either, that their neighbours' houses were targeted and their pets turned up mutilated. They discussed this at length: especially when Alec turned up with bloodied clothes. Neither of them ever discussed their thoughts with Alec. Although they knew his background and the difficult life he'd had, they just assumed it was a phase he'd grow out of, so didn't contact the authorities either. Instead they prayed – they prayed at home and at church every Sunday. Through their choice to remain silent they had actively encouraged and inspired their son, and they had to live with the consequences of that. They had quite literally nurtured a monster.

Of course, realisation came too late. Like it often does. Mary had seen, from an upstairs bedroom window, the trail of blood and her heart had sunk. Darting down the stairs and out of the side door, she'd made her way along their shared path. When she turned the corner on to the neighbour's back yard she could hardly believe what she was seeing. Nancy lay slumped against the back door. Rushing to the girl, she took hold of her shoulders and gently squeezed.

"Nancy, Nancy, can you hear me?"

The girl didn't respond. Blood soaked through the girl's dress and Mary knew she had to assess the damage. She lifted her skirt expecting to find a cut knee. Nothing could prepare her for the mutilation she saw. The colour drained from Mary's face and she vomited.

"Dear God, no."

It was obvious the young girl had been mutilated in her private area and there was something still sticking out of her. Blood still trickled from her wounds on to her thighs. Somehow, this poor girl had dragged herself across the yard from the woodshed ten feet away, the trail of blood was evident.

Mary pounded on the house door and opened it.

"Dorothy! Dorothy!"

"Come in Mary, I'm upstairs. Stick the kettle on."

"It's Nancy, come quick."

Mary heard heavy footsteps on wooden stairs as her overweight friend made her way towards them.

Tears filled Dorothy's eyes at the sight of her young daughter and she wrapped her arms around her dying child. Mary held them both in her arms. There was a heaviness in her heart, somehow she knew, her son was responsible for this.

"I will find him and I'll kill him with my own bare hands for this," she said aloud, with a malice she hadn't known existed within her.

Still in the woodshed, Alec, hearing the hatred in his mother's voice, burst into the warmth of the sun and sprinted between the two houses, down the street and off into the distance. He never returned. The words of his mother hadn't really mattered to him, it was the tone she'd said them with. They haunted him to this day.

Everything that he did from that day on, he blamed on the hatred in her voice. He'd even convinced himself that she'd been the one that had twisted right from wrong, in order to transfer the death of little Nancy on to him. He'd liked Nancy, but she'd seen something she shouldn't have and things got out of hand. He'd only wanted to scare her away.

Now on the streets, his tough childhood was standing him in good stead; being homeless in New York City had only been difficult for the first few weeks. Adjusting to the coldness at night was probably the hardest thing. Cunning and resourcefulness were key to survival and it hadn't taken him long to master both. With a gift for picking pockets, he never went hungry. But he knew he couldn't live like this forever. So, on his eighteenth birthday, he decided to join the army – maybe he could make a difference in Vietnam.

What a difference a year made. On his nineteenth birthday, he was with his platoon at their base camp in Vietnam. Life was good. He was content. There was even a girl in his life, Cai. A local. He wasn't supposed to have sex with the local women of course, but what were the point of rules if not for breaking?

When the time came to move on from the camp the platoon marched into the unknown. The jungle took its toll. Alec and his fellow Americans weren't used to the subtropical climate: the heat, humidity and monsoonal rain meant waterlogged ground. Uniforms were constantly drenched with either sweat or rain. Marching through thick jungle was difficult at best, the vines cut at your skin, the swamps threatened to swallow you alive – and they took many. The steep climbs and descents took men too. Terrain and war aside, the battle against wildlife was also a struggle. The mosquitoes carried malaria, there were leeches in the water that secreted an anticoagulant, preventing your blood from clotting and causing you to bleed out. There were fire ants and Alec recalled the panicked look on a comrade's face when he'd stumbled into a nest and had been stung hundreds, probably thousands, of times. He'd reacted dreadfully and had gone into anaphylactic shock. Vietnam also boasted thirty kinds of venomous snakes; the thought or sight of snakes made Alec cringe to this very day, the sight of one caused shortness of breath, heart palpitations and a cold sweat. In the jungle, this was a massive limitation for Alec and he had struggled to keep it under control and hidden from the others. If someone noticed he'd pretend he was coming down with a fever.

Five months of jungle warfare passed before Alec returned to his base camp and he did so because of injury; drifting in and out of consciousness within the makeshift hospital before finding the strength to fight back. He had, to a certain extent, behaved himself whilst overseas because his soldiering had quenched his need to hurt things. But being confined to the hospital, he could feel the hatred building up inside his head. The first time he acted on his urges he'd grabbed a nurse's wrist tightly, leaving red marks. She'd fought with a strength he hadn't expected and he'd been sedated after that, he was sure.

As soon as he was cleared to be out of bed they attached him to a new platoon. His new sergeant had an agenda of his own and Alec had felt an instant connection with him. This man would feed Alec's hatred for women to such an intensity that it would spiral out of control. Alec would develop an attachment and a deep dependency towards his sergeant, and the two men would become inseparable. They would bully the other men into complying with their orders. Standing up to them and refusing to conform ended one way: it got you shot – but not before a humiliating showdown in front of the platoon, where they would strip, tease, poke you with sticks and burn you with cigarettes.

This happened to two men before the rest fell into line. They went into each village with the intention of murder, rape, mutilation, pillage and carnage. When they'd finished, they posed their victims with burning cigarettes in their mouths, placed bodies in sexual positions and carved images in their flesh. It was the sergeant who had placed the first ace of spades playing card on a body, and when he had explained its relevance it had excited Alec – he felt himself going hard. Nothing had made him feel this powerful before, not even when he'd killed little Nancy, from next door, back home.

The two men used the cover of war to fuel their own mission of hate: but America was pulling out. Troops were being rallied together and flown home. By March of 1973 everyone – the sergeant and Alec included – were back at their base camp, being herded like cattle. The other men in the platoon were mingling and stories were starting to circulate. A few fights were breaking out. Somehow a snake got into the sergeant's bed and by morning he was dead. Alec was convinced it was the platoon's revenge on what the two of them had made them do and he was paranoid that he'd be next. He learned, too, that other platoons had been doing similar things across Vietnam: that there were other soldiers who hated as much as he and the sergeant had.

Mainly, with his sergeant now gone, Alec felt alone in the world once again. So, on what had turned out to be the last night at the camp, Alec had vowed to seek revenge on every member of the platoon for the death of his friend – America would regret bringing Alec Johnson home.

True to his word, his personal mission had begun within three weeks of his return to America. He absconded from the army as soon as they'd arrived home and headed for New York: covering the distance by walking long stints and thumbing lifts where he could. He found that his fellow country folk had hated America's involvement in someone else's war, so he chose not to speak of his involvement. Sometimes they asked anyway and, somehow, they knew he was lying when he denied any involvement and gave him a beating anyway. He found it best to just say he was forced to go, hated that America was involved and he was now on the run, that way he got a free ride and they thought him a hero.

He hadn't thought the homeless man would be missed and it was one less the soup kitchen would have to feed. How wrong he'd been. The homeless man had a celebrity status within the city, he entertained those that chose to stay and watch his acts, and he had many regular visitors. It had been his choice to live on the streets despite his family's pleas for him to return home. The body was found quickly and this man made the national news. Alec had learned from the television screens in store windows that the homeless man was called Hank Williamson.

Hank. This reminded him of his father and that, of course, reminded him of his mother, Mary. Momentarily a moment of sadness entered his mind, for what son wouldn't miss the tenderness of his mother? Then he remembered the tone of her voice that day and that she wanted to kill him with her bare hands. What mother speaks such words? Shaking this emotion aside he pulled himself together, he could not afford for emotions to hinder him.

Alec had already placed a healthy distance between his crime scene and his new location. Almost immediately, he'd boarded a train and was making his way towards Washington. He estimated arriving in about half an hour.

Alec moved across America, tracking down the families of those he'd served with – picking a family member from each. He'd left no doubt in the minds of his fellow soldiers who had been to visit, but he knew they wouldn't be able to speak out without implicating themselves, and their careers, and highlighting what they had been involved in back in Vietnam. His actions were safe if he was careful and moved on quickly.

Some families had moved from the areas he'd recalled speaking about with his comrades, perhaps as a direct response to his actions, perhaps not. He'd never know for sure. They had taken longer to track, but that had given him the opportunity to work and save for longer towards his long-term goal. The cash in his pocket was building nicely and he would be able to afford the ticket to London once his American mission was complete. He'd given himself a time limit of two years, for he had no intention of renewing his passport.

Alec perfected his routine. Relocate, find work, visit the local churches (he'd found that most army families were religious and loved their routines), stalk his potential victims for a few days, select a specific victim and stalk them for two more days, and then select a location, day and a time. He'd then have his getaway planned with precision.

Easy.

Despite using the same knife, the same mutilation techniques and leaving the same calling card, the ace of spades, on each victim, the incompetent police did not seem to link the murders. At least not publicly. Either, they didn't want people to panic that a mass murderer was on the loose, or one state didn't share information with the next. Another possible scenario was that the army was putting a block on things. This had amused Alec no end and he often caught himself smiling at himself when he saw his reflection in store windows.

Alec had found it easy to find cash jobs and had been careful not to use his bank account once. The only time he would use his identity would be to board the plane, he needed to be careful until then. All his purchases were cash and he had become an expert at moving around in the shadows.

There were two military connections to be made. The families he was targeting for starters, and his calling card. If either had been established he was unaware of it. Alec had been sure that someone with knowledge of the events in Vietnam would have made the connection by now and he wondered several times if he should cut his mission short, but each time he pressed on with growing sureness and an increased speed.

Despite allowing two years for his mission, he'd completed it within six months. Not only that, he'd earned enough cash to return to New York, purchase a ticket to London and had chanced using his passport.

Nobody had questioned him at passport control. The authorities, it appeared, were not searching for him.

# CHAPTER FIVE

England had been Alec's destination of choice and it hadn't disappointed him. His vacation was supposed to have lasted just three weeks, but he'd never intended showing up for his flight home. Within two days he'd befriended a man with a remarkable resemblance to himself, who drank in a pub near to where he was staying. After that it was simple. It hadn't taken Alec long to discover the man was homosexual; his flirting had made that obvious. Playing along, he had allowed him to think he was interested and agreed to go back to his house. The thought made him feel sick, but he had no intention of his man touching him.

The two men continued with their flirting, the other man stole affectionate shoulder brushes where he could during the walk back to his house. In public, he didn't try anything more and Alec was relieved about that. Suggestive whisperings were one thing, but an actual public display of affection was quite different. They had only walked two streets from the pub when the man stopped and unlocked a door.

"This is it," he announced.

Alec had wished they'd had to walk further. He would have been more comfortable with a more remote location for the task at hand. This evening was only going to end one way, in murder. Alec entered the house and was temporarily taken aback that the space was shared by other people. Hiding his face, he gently touched the man's arm.

"Can't we just go straight to your room?" he requested quietly.

By the time the two men reached the bedroom, Alec was wearing leather gloves. Within two minutes Alec had the other man gagged and bound, and was working silently, searching through his belongings, until finally, he had found what he was looking for – a birth certificate. That was enough. A passport would have been an advantage, but he'd take what he could get.

"No passport?" Alec asked, as he turned to look at the pathetic heap on the bed. The man shook his head anxiously, tears filling his eyes.

From his inside breast pocket Alec retrieved a pocketknife and flicked it open.

"Sit up, I'll untie you." He gave false promise.

The man obeyed with renewed hope in his eyes

With precision and speed Alec slit the arteries in both wrists and gave the man a smile as he pushed him back on to the bed. Alec sat on the edge of the bed and watched the life drain out of the man, until he knew it was safe to cut the ties he'd used to bind him. Removing a tobacco tin from his jacket pocket, he opened it. Cutting the twine from the man's ankles first he stuffed this into his pocket. The bloodied twine from the wrists he placed in the tin with care, for he didn't want to get blood on his own clothes. He placed the knife beside the lifeless body.

He had set everything up to look like a simple suicide. He left his own passport on the bedside table and placed the stolen birth certificate in his breast pocket. From that moment, he had taken the identity of Carl Ashbeck. And, it appeared, he had got away with it.

As Ashbeck, he began fitting into the English way of life and he worked on losing his American accent – it was the only thing left that would give him away. Within a few months he spoke with a fluent East End dialect and had created a backstory of his life thus far. If anyone asked why he had a limp, he made out that he'd been injured fighting gypsies and that he'd won. No one knew he'd fought and been injured in Vietnam. No one knew he was American.

"You should 'ave seen da uvver guy! I sorted 'im awright mate," he'd brag.

Carl Ashbeck, as he was now known, was working hard and staying out of too much trouble. For a while, his urges seemed to settle. He had avenged the death of his friend, the sergeant, and for the first time in his life he was feeling content. For some reason, the sight of the water seemed to have a pull on him, so he worked at the docks. It was hard work but nothing compared to marching through the jungles of Vietnam. Nothing compared to the harsh reality of that.

Two years passed before some of the old feelings started to bubble to the surface. It didn't matter how many hours he worked, or how tired he felt, they wouldn't pass: the feelings were too strong. He missed the sergeant more and more and that got him thinking. When America pulled out of Vietnam and everyone had been gathered, sharing stories while they were waiting to go home, it had emerged that the sergeant and Alec hadn't been only two doing those things, others had been too. What if there were people like that here? Like-minded people, here in England.

It didn't matter that Alec Johnson didn't exist on paper any more, he was still inside. Carl Ashbeck was about to evolve.

Ashbeck's house was small and midterraced, but it would have to do for now. He would start with two women that he would take from the street. He would give them a bed, feed them and they would work for him. If things went to plan he would increase the numbers.

Within one year he had places all over the city. Demand was high. Men, and the occasional woman, from all walks of life paid high prices for his women. Within five years he was shipping women in from Europe and had places across East Anglia. His legitimate enterprises had hidden depths that would make the authorities cringe. These businesses were lining his pockets and making him a very powerful man. Not only were they enabling him to feed his own urges, he had quickly learned that some high-up, powerful people in

England needed a similar release too. And for that he was a protected man.

There was, for example, a special branch of his operation, that remained hidden away and undiscovered, that still earned him millions each year, despite the predicament he now found himself in. Top names were involved. Not just because they were using the services it provided, but because they were involved. Some were so wrapped up in their own needs they covered it up from a high level, protecting their part of the action. High-ranking police officers were up to their necks in it, but they had no idea who was right at the top pulling their strings and making profits from them.

Ashbeck's other activities continued to thrive too. His incarceration was inconvenient, yes, but business continued to thrive. Only one had been closed down and that had soon been replaced. In his absence, his right-hand man had purchased property all over Essex, Suffolk and Norfolk, and he had kept the women flowing. These women paid to escape a hard life back home, wherever that may have been, for a better life in England. They had a roof over their heads and food in their stomachs, but that was where their perks ended. They were in the UK illegally but were expected to be grateful they had somewhere to sleep, with little or no concept of the language, what alternative did they have? They cleaned and cooked and couldn't possibly work any harder. At night, they were exposed to people who beat and raped them.

At night, people would visit their shared rooms and choose which one they wanted. There was no hiding from this fate. The house manager would grab and drag them to another room, where they were locked inside. Sometimes they were taken to a different location: when this happened they never returned. Within a day or so, they were replaced with a new woman.

There was no family to report them missing, no legitimate reason for them to be in the country. No investigation. On and on it went – an endless supply of vulnerable women who had paid for and been promised a better life.

***

Despite never having been named for the murders back in America, or for the man whose identity he had stolen when he had arrived in London, Alec Johnson had found his way into the English prison system. But not as himself; as Carl Ashbeck. Just over five years ago, Katie-Anne Warwick and her team had arrested him for murder. His passion for rape, torture and mutilation had been uncovered. Warwick had been clever, but not clever enough. She had manipulated a little bit of his past from him, but she hadn't put the pieces together. He remained living under an assumed name and she hadn't even scratched the surface of his operation. Customs and Excise had been working closely with the team too and they'd charged him with people trafficking. But the operation still continued without him, and he had two very special people on the outside making sure it was covered up.

Warwick and her team had given him a hard time during the interviews and he'd taken a particular dislike to her. Their dedication and attention to detail had cost him dearly on a personal level and he didn't like that. Having ensured he remained in custody prior to his trial, he hadn't had the opportunity to kill the bitch so he'd had to make those arrangements from his cell. His contacts remained loyal and eager to please, except this useless idiot got it wrong. Warwick survived her stabbing – yes it left scars, physical and psychological – but she was still alive. And now he would just have to have the pleasure of killing her himself. Personally.

Having had two important, high-up individuals help his escape from prison, Ashbeck was feeling invincible. He'd spent the last few years being the model prisoner and had earned their trust. They'd be regretting that now. He'd have loved to hang around and see the terrified look on their faces, but there was too much to be getting on with. Time was short.

His network of people now rallied to his side and were eager to lend a hand. They were under strict orders that Katie-Anne Warwick was his challenge, and his challenge alone.

It had been easy, making his escape. People seemed to bend over backwards to help him. He had become educated, learned new practical skills and was now an accomplished manipulator. The deputy commissioner of the Met himself had requested Ashbeck's leave to visit his dying mother and the judge had approved it. For now, the deputy commissioner was alive and had some hope that he would see his family again. Ashbeck, however, had plans for his family and wanted him alive just long enough to learn of their fate. For now, Smith was along for the ride. He was bound and gagged, and once he was dead he would be abandoned somewhere remote.

Ashbeck truly believed that God had been on his side that day. That God had given him the power and he would give him the glory of success. For the first time since his escape he looked up into the sky, raised his arms and spread them wide. Taking a deep breath, he closed his eyes and prayed thanks before dropping to his knees.

# CHAPTER SIX

Rachel Smith didn't notice the Ford Focus parked halfway along the street when she returned home with her two daughters. Why would she? They had stopped on the way home from school to buy a few groceries for dinner and some treats for their film night. They were squeezing one more in before the new baby arrived in two weeks. The little fella hadn't been planned and it was, perhaps, a little late in life to make such dynamic changes to family life, but it was happening and he was a most welcome addition to the family.

Max was working late tonight; he hadn't mentioned why. He usually did and she thought it a little strange that he hadn't. She was tired, so perhaps she'd just forgotten. No big deal. The three of them often planned girlie nights together when he worked and she would miss that when they started to leave home and live their own lives.

Laughter filled the air as the family unloaded the car. As soon as the bags were on the kitchen table the youngest daughter, Maisey, headed upstairs – their routine was well practised. Jane would help her mother make dinner, while Maisey showered and made a start on homework. They would eat together. The two girls would clear the table, while Mum showered. Maisey and Rachel would prepare the snacks, while Jane showered and then they would settle down together to watch their film. Once everyone else was asleep, Jane would start on her homework. It was how it had always been. It worked.

When Jane settled next to her mum the movie was ready to go. Maisey pressed play and one of their favourite films burst on to the screen. *Mrs. Doubtfire*. They'd lost count how many times they'd watched it but it just seemed to get funnier each time. They were relaxed and enjoying their evening together. All was well in their world.

With the TV turned up loud and laughter filling the air, they didn't hear the back door open, or the footsteps along the hallway. The first indication of an intrusion wasn't until the lounge door flew open and they were blinded by torchlight.

Maisey screamed.

"Shut the fuck up or we'll shoot," a gruff male voice commanded. He strode with purpose towards the three of them. They could clearly see that he was holding a gun.

"Mum," Maisey gasped.

"It's okay, honey."

"Silence," the man demanded.

"You." He pointed at Jane because she was the strongest. "Stand up and walk to the centre of the room."

There was a short pause before he demanded, "Now!"

Jane looked at her mum, who nodded her head. Jane did as she had been told. A second man walked into the room. He also held a gun and he had rope. The third man brought in a chair from the kitchen and placed it near Jane.

"Sit down," he ordered as he took the rope and bound her hands and legs.

Maisey was next and then Rachel.

"Please. Our mother is pregnant. Please," Jane pleaded.

"It's okay girls. Everything will be okay." Rachel spoke without emotion, as if she had given up.

Time moved slowly. Two men remained in the room and the other left them. They were on edge and paced back and forth. Something seemed to be agitating them and they kept checking their watches. Jane could just see the old carriage clock that used to be her grandfather's on the mantelpiece; although it seemed to have taken forever, fifty minutes had passed.

The third man returned and was angry. He was holding three pieces of cloth.

"He's not coming. Sumink's up. Warwick's missed 'er train. He's still trackin' 'er."

"Wot the 'ell'd we'd do wit' these?"

"Leave 'em like this. Them's the orders."

He handed each man a piece of cloth and each of them placed a gag on one of the women before they turned and left the room.

Footsteps faded along the hallway and out of the house. Somewhere along the street a car engine fired and wheels screamed as a car pulled away. The TV played but no one paid it any attention.

Jane was obviously troubled by what had just happened and wondered if it had something to do with her father's job. His safety was a worry to her right now. Her mother's lack of reaction, however, was way out of character. Her obedience and willingness to comply so easily was off-kilter and of great concern. The baby was due soon and Jane wondered if the shock of the intrusion had brought on labour.

Jane had given some consideration as to who Warwick might be, but her attention had definitely been drawn to whoever 'he' was. One of the men had referred to a man, there had been no mention of a name, but there was a strong hint that he would be coming to visit. It would have been helpful to have been given an indication of how long the three of them had before 'he' would show up.

She tried to speak, but all that came out were muffled sounds because of the gag, it was no use. The binds around her wrists were too tight to work loose and she was sure she'd cut her wrists trying. Although her ankles were bound, they weren't tied to the chair. Her best option was for her to try and stand and to attempt to free her arms from the backrest of the chair. Trying this several times, she failed on every attempt. With each effort, the rope binding her wrists cut deeper into her skin, tears were threatening but she refused to let them form.

Robin Williams's antics were beginning to annoy her and she tried to free her mind so she could think.

Suddenly her mind was taken back to a time when her and her sister had had chair races. Their father had tied them, with woollen scarves, to some old chairs from the shed and they had learned to make them bunny hop. It had been fun. The sunny day had been filled with laughter and pink lemonade. Now she realised, this fun game had been to prepare them in case they were ever kidnapped. In a split second, this fun childhood memory had been shattered as it dawned on her that her father had been preparing her for this moment and her heart ached for his safety.

Bunny-hopping wasn't an option, as the three chairs were tied together. She needed another way. Knowing it wouldn't be easy, she made her decision.

The three chairs had been placed so the backs formed a triangle. This gave plenty of room on either side of each chair. Gradually Jane rocked from side to side: momentum started to build. She hoped the weight of her mother and her sister were enough to keep their chairs stable. Within a few seconds she'd crashed to the floor on to her left side. Unsure if the cracking sound had been wood or bone, she took a moment to compose herself.

From the pain in her shoulder she was sure it was bone.

Taking several steadying, deep breaths before attempting to move, Jane prepared herself for a fight on the floor with her wooden restraint. It was easier than she'd anticipated. The wood had obviously shattered under the pressure, as had her shoulder. The pain was incredible and felt like hot iron rods had been forced beneath her skin.

Now for the next challenge. Somehow, she needs to free herself from her restraints. Again, she took some deep, steadying breaths before attempting to move. She managed to bring herself up to a sitting position but hadn't anticipated the pain that this would cause. A feeling crept through her like she'd never experienced in her life and she didn't know if she would vomit or faint. Neither was practical. Raising her knees and resting her head on them, Jane took yet more steadying breaths until the feeling started to subside. The pain was overwhelming, but she tried to focus her mind on other things. For the first time, she noticed the hastened pace of her heart and the clamminess of her skin.

Conscious that time was passing and unaware of how much she had, Jane knew that every moment was precious. Taking one last steadying breath, she braced herself for more pain. Shifting position, she started to get ready to make a difference.

Wiggling and leaning towards her good side, she began to work her hands under her bottom. Pain shot through her shoulder as she expected it would. What she wasn't expecting was a pain so intense in her left wrist that she vomited. Luckily, she was upright and it wasn't much. With the gag in place, what hadn't come out of her nose, she'd had no choice but to swallow back down. Tears now fell down her cheeks and the back of her throat was burning. Still she fought on.

The pain was too much to handle. Giving up on her idea she comes up with another and moves towards her mother.

Rachel is horrified when she sees her daughter's arm but Jane ignores her the worried look and makes it quite clear what she wants of her. Holding eye contact and then looking down at her wrists: she repeats this process two more times before Rachel nods.

Jane moves again, positioning herself behind her mother's chair and angles herself so that Rachel can start working on the binds. The knots are tight and because of the angle of her own hands it's an almost impossible task, but, gradually the knot begins to loosen.

Finally, Jane feels some give and she wiggles her wrists free. Her bad arm flops and a sudden surge of nausea sweeps through her once again. She turns her head to inspect the damage.

You didn't need an X-ray machine to work out it was broken: the skin remained intact but bone protruded beneath it. It was awful to look at and her eyes didn't linger for long. Plunging her head between her legs, Jane hooked the gag in her good thumb and dislodge it from her mouth. It now hung around her neck and, at long last, she was able to take a decent breath.

"Mum, grunt once if you're okay."

"Uh."

"Maisey?"

"Uh."

"I'm out of the chair, and my hands are free, but my ankles are still tied. I'm working on it. Mum, are you in labour?"

"Uh."

"Thought so. I'm working as quickly as I can. Have your waters broken?"

"Uh-uh."

"That's something."

"Are your contractions still a good distance apart?"

"Uh-uh."

"Shit."

The cracking of wood sounded like an explosion as the front door gave way. Armed men stormed the building and spread out in all directions. Their brief had been to get in, search and to expect the worst.

Rachel was frozen with fear. Jane had tried to escape and that wouldn't go down well. She feared for her young life. Maisey wet herself for a second time. Jane, refusing to give in, fought with more determination than she'd felt in her whole life. Struggling against her bindings, she gave it one last effort to free herself. It was no use, with only one hand she just couldn't manage the knot.

In one swift movement Jane grabbed a piece of jagged wood from her broken chair, leaped to her feet and made for the door.

Darkness overcame her.

Within moments the lounge door burst open and the space was immediately filled with an armed police officer. Rachel faced the door and it took her a moment or two to realise she was safe.

The first officer checked the room and a second one attended to Jane. When she came around she was angry and defensive, and tried to attack. The officer took his time with her, he'd already removed her chair leg weapon and was holding her good hand. Her broken arm was of no use to her. As he talked calmly to her it took her some time to realise he was here to help and not hurt her and her family.

By the time Jane was calm enough to be helped, Rachel and Maisey were already on the sofa, having had their restraints removed. Once Jane was free to move she could not rest. She paced the room.

"Where is my father?" she demanded.

"Jane, dear. He's working late. You know this already," Rachel said.

"How did you know we were in trouble? None of us phoned you, we were all tied up."

"Jane, sweetheart. You need to come and sit down. Your arm!" her mother pleaded with her.

As she turned at the far end of the room, Jane noticed her mother's face for the first time. The baby.

"Mum!"

"It's time, dear," is all Rachel said on the matter.

Jane nodded and instantly knew what was needed of her.

"Maisey, beside the baby's cot is a small suitcase. Will you show this officer where that is please? You also need to show him where we keep the clean towels and bed sheets. When you've done that you need to get yourself cleaned up, okay?"

Maisey looked unsure and it took Jane a minute or so to reassure her that now wasn't the time to be shy, that right now was the time to be a brave young woman, because their mum needed them both to be there for her; the baby was about to be born. She told her how brave she'd been when the horrible men had shown up and that she was very proud of her.

Reluctantly, Maisey disappeared with the officer.

"Paramedics are on their way ladies, but it will be twenty minutes at least. There's a massive incident tonight," one of them said.

"That's fine. We can do this!" Jane reassured her mum.

"Sweetheart, that arm looks so bad. Will you let me take a look?"

"You are the priority right now. Don't you make this about me. Let's get my baby brother delivered and then you can make a fuss if you have the energy, okay?" She gave her mother a playful smile.

Turning to the officer who'd just entered, Jane

informed him that the three men mentioned that a fourth would turn up at some point.

"We've got this covered love. You two get this 'ere baby delivered then we can get you all out of 'ere. Right now, my orders are to secure your property. You have armed protection. No one is getting near you, you have my guarantee on that."

"Do you know who this man is?"

"You do your fing and let me do mine. When it's confirmed it'll be on the news I'm sure, but nowt's been released. If I get the nod, I'll let you know."

"What's the major incident?"

"Train crash. A bad one."

"That's awful."

Jane made her mother as comfortable as possible. All the time police were in and out, asking questions. One of them noticed the wounds on Jane's wrists and ankles, and insisted that she had them covered before she delivered the baby. Jane asserted herself and demanded they were quick about it, telling them the whereabouts of the first aid kit.

"It's in the first cupboard on the right as you walk into the kitchen," she ordered.

Once they returned with their own first aid kit from their car, her wounds were dressed and Jane proceeded with more demands she needed them to meet.

"We need privacy!"

"Rachel, I'm sorry, but this is a crime scene. One of us absolutely has to stay in the room. I know that's far from ideal, under the circumstances, but I promise you, whichever one of us stays, we will give you as much dignity as possible."

"Have you got children?" Rachel asked.

"Two. They're twelve and ten. Both boys," the younger officer stated.

"Then you can stay. What's your name?"

"Chris."

Turning to Jane she added, "And Jane, this is a big ask. Never in a million years did I expect you would have to deliver your brother."

"Well, I like to be different from my friends. None of them could do this Mum, but I can and I will!"

"Even though you've broken your arm and done something horrendous to your shoulder? Darling, please let me take a look."

"It's fine. When the paramedics get here they can deal with it. Right now, we have a baby to deliver."

As Jane arranged cushions behind her mum, Maisey returned with her new friend. She'd already cleaned herself up and was carrying a massive bundle of towels in her arms. Clutched tightly in one hand was a bag with something heavy inside.

"What's in the bag Maisey?" Jane asked.

"Never you mind. It's private."

The officer shrugged his shoulders and carried the suitcase and the bedding across the room. He placed them beside Jane. Unzipping the case for her, he opened it and arranged what he thought she might need on to the lid.

Jane gave him a smile.

"Right Tinker Bell, they're going to need hot water in here too. You can show me where to get a bowl and some hot water. I take it you know how to boss a bloke about in the kitchen too?"

"He's got her sussed out!" Rachel let out a laugh as a contraction took over her body.

"That's Steve. He's got a couple of daughters of his own."

Taking a couple of towels, Jane positioned them under her mum, just in time for a gush of liquid to escape from between her legs. Panic-stricken, Jane looked at her mum.

"That's my waters breaking, honey. That's normal. It won't be long now."

"Have you timed your contractions? I know you can't push until you're ten centimetres dilated and your contractions are a minute apart. I read that in your book."

"They are a minute apart already."

Maisey returned with a glass of water for her mum and Steve followed with a steaming bowl of water, some antibacterial soap and a first aid kit tucked under his arm. Jane and Chris wasted no time washing their hands. Chris saw Jane struggling to put on gloves and helped her. She had no idea how she was going to do this as her left arm and hand were of no use. She could not pick anything up, let alone hold a baby.

Jane looked at Chris and then at her mum.

"Mum, I need to get you undressed but I can't use my left hand. I'm going to cover you with a sheet. Chris won't be able to see, but I need him to be my left hand. Is that okay with you?"

"Sweetheart, this must be just as awful for Chris. Needs must. Chris is this okay with you?"

"Helping to deliver a baby wasn't what I was expecting when I turned up to work this evening, but it's the situation I'm finding myself in. I'd be honoured to help."

Jane and Chris worked as a team, covering Rachel with a bed sheet and working to remove her leggings and underwear. Neither of them could see any part of her body. They didn't seem to need to communicate, each of them knew what was needed and just got on with it. Once they were done, Chris folded the clothes neatly and placed them beside the suitcase. He'd been respectful and Jane was impressed.

"Okay, let's do this. Maisey, don't let go of Mum's hand. Mum, I need to check, don't I?"

"I'm sorry darling."

Taking a deep breath, Jane placed her hand under the sheet expecting to feel for her mum's cervix. She'd read about it in the birthing book, but it was not something she ever expected to have to do when it was her own mother. Closing her eyes and imagining the images from the pages of that book, Jane felt with her fingers.

"Eww that's rank." Maisey was sneering and sticking out her tongue.

"That's enough Maisey. I need to concentrate, so does Mum."

"That's disgusting."

"Steve! Come and get Tinker Bell," Chris called out, as he took her by the hand and escorted her to the door.

"I want my diary! I want my diary!" Maisey demanded.

"Nothing leaves this room until I've cleared it," Chris replied calmly.

"It's private. You can't read it!" she said ,as she kicked his shin, hard.

Chris opened the door and Steve reached in and took Maisey from him.

"I'm so sorry. I've got no idea what's got into her, or what she has in that bag. I know it's been a frightening night but this isn't typical." Rachel was apologising for her daughter's behaviour.

"Mum, you're doing so well. I'd say you're more than ready. You're nearly there. I can feel the baby's head. I'd say you can start pushing if you think you need to."

She nodded her head and smiled. A tear escaped and rolled down her face. Sweat was pouring from her brow. Jane took one of the fresh towels and wiped her face before returning to the business end. She could tell that another contraction was building because the muscles over her mother's stomach were tightening.

"What's my brat sister got in her bag, Chris?"

Chris removed his gloves and replaced them with ones from his back pocket. He opened Maisey's bag wide and took a peep inside the book without removing it. The expression on his face changed as he turned and looked at a few pages. He looked at both women in turn. He closed the book and folded the bag around it.

"Trust me, you are better off not knowing. This does not belong to your daughter and it does not leave this room. Jane, who is your father?"

"What? You haven't been told?"

"No."

"Deputy Commissioner Max Smith."

"And you don't know where he is tonight?"

"Working late. He does that a fair bit."

"If your sister has read what's in that book, it would explain her behaviour. That's all I'm prepared to say right now, and that's for your own benefit."

"Okay, here comes another one. Work with it Mum. You can do this."

A second gush of liquid escaped from between Rachel's legs, closely followed by another contraction. Jane coached her through it and cleaned her up the best she could with her one good hand afterwards.

"It won't be long now. Could I have a sip of water please?"

"Here, let me get that for you," Chris said and held the glass out for her.

Rachel took a few sips and gave the glass back. Chris wiped her face with a towel and gave her hand a squeeze. Jane had busied herself with replacing the wet towels in readiness for the birth, but her mind was on that book and what it might contain. What had her sister got in it?

"Chris, I was hoping the paramedics would be here by now. We've not got anything to clamp the cord with, or some scissors to cut it. All I can think of is one of those cereal clips, but it will need sterilising. Could you get someone on to that please? I don't think we've got long now."

"As good as done."

"Mum, I'm going to take another look. Is that okay?"

Rachel nodded.

Placing her good hand under the sheet, Jane felt for the baby. Smiling at her mum, she announced that she could definitely feel his head sticking out slightly.

"Chris, I need you right now. I won't be able to lift the baby when he arrives and he's making an entrance in the next few minutes."

Chris was by Jane's side immediately and had placed a hand on Rachel's knee.

"Just tell me what you need and when you need it. I won't intervene until I'm asked."

When the next contraction arrived, Rachel managed to push the head out. Chris held the sheet so Jane could ensure the baby was a healthy colour and that his airway was clear. All looked good. Two contractions later, at 21:36, Rachel gave birth to a baby boy. He entered the world into his sister's good arm. Jane had tears rolling down her face.

"Okay, Chris I need you to take him and place him with Mum please."

As Chris lifted the baby, the infant gave a shrill cry and there were cheers from outside the door. After placing him on Rachel's chest, Chris turned to Jane and gave her good arm a squeeze.

"You feeling okay, Jane? You're looking a bit jaded."

Through tears Jane managed a nod.

There was a knock at the door and Chris answered it. It was Steve with the things Jane had asked for. Maisey was keen to return to the room, but Chris turned her away. She could see her mother later, not many children got to witness the birth of their siblings and she had to wait, he was sure Maisey just wanted to get her hand on the diary. That wasn't going to happen. It was evidence.

"We need to arrange a search warrant mate. That book is evidence. Sort it with Nige. Nothing leaves this room except the people. I took a look at the contents of the book – if we were talking about some stupid kid's diary I was just going to let her have it. But were not – it's evidence."

"Okay. I'll get it sorted."

"Right, Mum lets' get him cleaned up a bit and a nappy on him. Some clothes too before he gets cold. Chris, if I put some towels down here, would you lay him on them?"

Jane arranged more towels beside her mum and Chris took the baby from Rachel.

"I'm not looking forward to this bit but it's got to be done. Would you pass me the clip? I might need your help. I'm not exactly feeling at my strongest."

Jane positioned the clip around the umbilical cord and looked at Chris.

"Here. Allow me."

Nodding, she allowed him to take over. Their hands brushed briefly and in that moment, she felt a connection between them. There was a crunch and Chris was holding his hand out for the scissors. Jane passed them to him and he cut the cord.

Suddenly overcome with exhaustion, Jane sensed that Chris knew he needed to take control. Her pain was so intense now that she didn't know how much more she could cope with.

Using wipes from the suitcase, Chris started to clean the baby the best he could.

"Okay, confession time. I don't have kids, I have nephews. I just wanted to make you feel more comfortable Rachel and thought that by saying I'd got kids it would help."

Jane rolled her eyes.

"Come on. You lift his legs and I'll put the nappy under. That's it, now gently lower him. Right, bring the front part through and hold it on his tummy and I'll wrap the sides over. There we go. We're good at this teamwork stuff. Now for the Babygro."

Once the little man was dressed Chris passed him to Rachel and she offered him her breast. It took a little perseverance but, eventually, he started to feed.

"Mum, your placenta hasn't come out yet. How long should that take?"

"Now this young man is feeding, it shouldn't take long."

And she was right. Within ten minutes the placenta was sitting in a bowl.

The ambulance crew arrive moments later and there was a sudden urgency to evacuate the house. Rachel was put on to a stretcher with her baby and taken in the first ambulance. Steve accompanied them as their armed guard. Jane was also put on to a stretcher. She was put into the second ambulance with Maisey. Chris accompanied them as their armed guard.

En route the crew busied themselves with Jane. They inserted a cannula into her right hand and asked many questions about allergies. She assured them she had none. Eventually they administered pain relief and she felt herself drifting into sleep. The last thing she remembered was Chris reaching over and holding her hand.

"You were amazing tonight, Jane."

The remaining officers stayed in the house and kept it secure. They were waiting for Ashbeck. It was the only lead they had on the man and they hoped he hadn't seen the ambulances remove his kidnapped victims.

\*\*\*

The family arrived at hospital moments apart and were quickly placed in a room. They were together with two armed guards outside. Somehow, staff had managed to cram three beds, and a Perspex cot for the baby, into the small space. There was also an en-suite wet room.

Chris was waiting at the nurses' station because Jane needed to be X-rayed and she would need an armed guard to leave the ward: he would escort her. He was seriously considering removing himself from the investigation because he had become too close during the birth. He was emotionally involved now and that could never be good.

Jane was awake, but remained sleepy from her medication. She was refusing to talk to anyone other than her mother: her fear for her father's safety was soaring. Maisey continued with her major sulk over the diary and was moody with everyone, including her mum. She was particularly venomous towards the new baby.

# CHAPTER SEVEN

Carl Ashbeck was feeling energised. His escape from prison had gone to plan. The deputy commissioner had done a good job but he would regret not being with his family tonight. He was now tied up and gagged in the back of the car, heading along the M1 with one of his operatives. Ashbeck would decide what to do with him later.

Right now, he had someone special on his mind. Katie-Anne Warwick. Warwick had been the lead during the investigation on his activities and, ultimately, responsible for his incarceration. He despised her with every cell in his body. Her boss, Phil Andrews, had done his best to protect her over the years but he hadn't cared so much about the other two. He'd given up Jen and Mel much more freely, Ashbeck had soon gained control of their lives. Warwick had proven problematic, however. A tougher cookie to crack. She'd distanced herself from everyone and had simply vanished from sight.

Until now.

Andrews had played his part in the escape too and he wouldn't be able to deny it. Over the years he'd become so greedy for information that Ashbeck had made him his puppet, just like all the other big names he held control over. Andrews was up to his neck in a paper trail that may as well have been a one-way ticket to the inferno guarded by Dante himself. Ashbeck had to smile to himself at how clever he'd been.

Week after week, Andrews had visited him in prison because he was writing a book. It was, apparently, progressing well. The information hadn't come free. An eye for an eye. Ashbeck had been liberal at first but learned quickly that the more he gave, the more Andrews was willing to give in return. In the beginning, it was Andrews who held all the power, but within six months Ashbeck had turned that around. As time progressed the demands grew. Now, each week, Andrews received a bank transfer from Ashbeck's businesses in return for goods he was having made and orders for weapons he was placing with contacts he was supposed to have arrested and allowed to slip the net; orders he was receiving direct from Ashbeck in prison. Although Phil Andrews was unaware of the plans for the prison break he had been involved, from the start, in arranging all the clothing and weapons that the men would use during the operation. Not only that, he had implicated himself in far more heinous crimes too. He just didn't know it yet.

Ashbeck knew this was his time and if he could pull it off, it would be amazing. Everything, in the end, had fallen into place. He'd made the decision that he'd trace Warwick himself, from the outside, when the good news came. One of his operatives had received information that the three women were meeting up.

His long wait was over. He had Warwick and the timing was perfect!

Whatever hoops had to be jumped through, the deputy commissioner had ensured everyone had done just that. Ashbeck had his hold over him too. The well-respected family man had hidden depths that would shock the nation and Ashbeck knew all about it. Bottom line, Ashbeck had been granted a few hours compassionate leave to visit his dying mother.

Obviously, she wasn't actually his mother, but was that of the man's whose identity he'd stolen when he first arrived in London all those years ago. He had never granted her permission to visit him in prison, but when the old lady had started to write to him he, eventually, started to write back. He thought that maybe she might come in handy one day. Today was that day.

Whichever officials had approved his leave, they would lose sleep over their decision, he was sure of that. They had been foolish to allow him out, even with an armed guard.

Ashbeck trusted his operatives to have everything organised and he was confident that everything would be in place. The ambush was so simple and had happened literally two miles from the prison. They'd placed a track in the road that had halted the car instantly. Within seconds the two guards and the driver had been killed, and Ashbeck removed. It was quick, clean and efficient.

Five miles further away, another car was waiting for Ashbeck to use.

His instructions had been clear during his final visit with his right-hand man, Cobalt. A team would be in place to track the women during their meeting and then a second team would intercept each one during their journey home.

Simple.

Everything was in place. He had two of his operatives ready to take care of Jen and Mel. Their instructions were clear. Kill Jen in a car crash and kidnap Mel, taking her to a prearranged, secure location. They could do as they pleased, but they must keep her alive.

Ms Warwick was all his. No one was to touch her. It would be spectacular.

Having placed three operatives in the city, one for each woman, two operatives at Paddington railway station and another close to where he was now, Ashbeck was feeling very much in control. He liked control.

Jen had made good progress but was unaware that she was being followed. Staying a few cars back, the man that would run her off the road had kept her in his sights since leaving the city. His instructions were clear and he'd soon need to get behind her, the junction along the M1 was not too far now and he didn't want to leave things too late.

Mel was on her way home too, where she would be met by her boyfriend of the past two years. She didn't know he was one of Ashbeck's trusted operatives and certainly had a shock coming to her. She wouldn't make it inside her house but would, instead, be bundled into a van that was waiting around the corner and carted off. The boyfriend would already be in the back of the van and Ashbeck would have paid good money to see the look on her face when she realised the man she loved was part of this.

Kate had made her way to the station, as predicted. The call had been placed and Ashbeck set to work. It wouldn't be easy.

Dressed all in black, he silently slid on to the train track, being careful not to step on to the electrified rail. He could see the workmen up ahead. They were working under massive floodlights on another track and wore bright orange overalls. He had to move quickly, because there was so much to do in such a short space of time.

An operative was waiting for him to make the first move. Once he was in range, Ashbeck raised his firearm and took aim. Two men were on the ground before the others had realised anything was wrong. Three remained. Suddenly gunshots could be heard from the other side of the track too. Two more men were down. One remained. Ashbeck made no sound as he approached. As soon as he caught a glimpse of orange he steadied his aim. His shot wounded the man and the operative finished him off.

Moving faster now, the two men disappeared into the shadows. Between them they dragged a heavy trunk on to the track. They were careful not to touch anything they shouldn't. The thing was heavy but they lifted it into place. Opening the trunk, Ashbeck flicked a switch and the two men retreated.

"The car's this way. Thanks for your help tonight."

"You're welcome. Anything else you need, just ask."

Stopping halfway up the bank Ashbeck turned.

"There is one thing," he said.

"Name it."

As he fired his gun into the dark night, he said, "Your silence."

Aware that time must be getting on, Ashbeck returned to the car. Instantly noticing the message light flashing on the mobile phone that had come with the car, he dismissed it and instead decided to put some distance between himself and the scene. The message could wait for now, there would be plenty of time for that later.

\*\*\*

The train had left Paddington station on time. Its passengers were settling down for the journey. It would be a long haul for many of them. Some read books and newspapers, others typed on laptops. One family with young children were starting a board game and another with teenagers were all sitting in silence on their mobile phones. One older lady was just making herself comfortable with the intention of sleeping.

When it happened, the calmness of each carriage turned into frenzied panic. The momentum of the impact sent objects flying and smashed the glass from the windows. Many people were jolted out of their seats and landed with a heavy thud on the floor.

The explosion that followed sent shock waves through the whole train. A ball of fire gained momentum until it engulfed the whole wreckage.

Ashbeck heard the explosion. He pulled to a stop and spun around in his seat. The fire was immense, with black smoke billowing into the darkening sky.

A cruel laugh escaped from him.

"Sleep well, Katie-Anne."

In his elated mood, he pressed the phone into life, dialled voicemail and listen to the message.

"Subject missed train. Repeat. Subject missed train."

Elation immediately turned into anger and Ashbeck let out a growl that could quite easily have come from a wild animal. With the palms of both hands he smacked the steering wheel.

Sitting in stunned silence, he waited for the phone to ring and when it did he snapped into it.

"Hello."

"Mission complete," came the familiar voice of his favourite operative.

"Good man," he said, before ending the call.

One final call had to come soon. Somehow Kate had evaded her fate for a second time. He couldn't let this happen with Jen.

When the phone rang, he took a steadying breath.

This was it.

"Hello."

"Subject in ambulance.  I think she's still breathing."

"Sort it."

# CHAPTER EIGHT

As I slowly began to stir, I rolled over to face Sam. It wasn't until I noticed him missing that I smelt the coffee. Groaning, I emerged from the warmth of the bed and entered the bathroom. Splashing cold water on my face and cleaning my teeth made me slightly more awake.

Returning to the bedroom, I fumbled about looking for the shirt. Although Sam had requested I leave it on, at some point it had been removed and I certainly didn't feel like wandering out into the kitchen naked. All the time I was wondering if I needed to pinch myself to make sure last night wasn't a dream. Parting the curtains, I cracked the window open. Birds were singing and it surprised me just how much greenery I could see from here. London always surprised me like that.

A chill ran through my body and I closed the window. Noticing a robe hanging on the bedroom door, I grabbed it as I walked out. There was no belt and I allowed the robe to fall loosely, exposing the shirt underneath. The news was on quietly and Sam stood motionless and wide-eyed watching it. As I sidled up to him and placed my arm around his waist, he responded by embracing me so tightly I thought I might burst.

"Jesus, Kate. You don't need to see this."

"See what?" He had me confused.

"I'm sure the train you should have taken last night has crashed. No one survived Kate. They have not found any survivors, not one single survivor so far. Oh, Kate!"

As Sam turned to me my muscles went limp. Luckily, he still had hold of me and was able to catch me as I fell, gathering me in his arms. He helped me to the sofa, sat beside me and took both of my hands into his. Falling silent, he gave me time to compose myself. I tried to speak but nothing came out, instead tears rolled down my face.

"You're safe," he said, and was now cupping my head in his hands and kissing my forehead. He allowed his thumbs to caress my cheeks.

"Thank God you're safe."

"Sam, hold me. Please hold me," I asked of him, as my hands found his body under his T-shirt. As I wrapped my arms around him he held me tightly.

"Kate, please don't go home today."

Home needed me but I didn't feel like going. I made a mental note to phone Cathy. I had left her in charge in my absence. She needed the money so I was sure she wouldn't mind if I extended by break. Sam held me for a long time.

\*\*\*

Coffee was probably the last thing I needed right now but it was exactly what Sam handed to me. I wasn't ready to stand so I remained seated. Pointing the remote towards the television, Sam turned up the volume and we listened to the fate of the passengers on the train I had missed by a whisker.

"News just in," the reporter was announcing in her serious voice.

"There has been a collision on the M1 near Luton Airport. A woman has been airlifted to hospital and is believed to be in a critical condition. It is yet to be confirmed which hospital she has been taken to.

"Eyewitness accounts suggest a hooded figure fled the scene immediately after the crash, abandoning the second vehicle. From the description of the clothing, it appears there may be a possible link between this seemingly random motorway crash and the catastrophic train crash.

"More on this story as it breaks.

"Back to the studio."

I could not believe the media had made this link already and suspected they had been told what to say. They were drip-feeding the public in readiness for a press release. I was surprised they hadn't got a leading criminologist at one of the scenes and was sure it was only a matter of time until this was the case.

Across the bottom of the screen there was the normal rolling news: 'A thirty-five-year-old woman is critically ill in hospital after crashing on the M1. Preliminary reports suggest links to last night's fatal train crash'.

"No!" I screamed at the telly.

"What?" he asked.

The details were flimsy at best, but once a detective, always a detective. My gut instincts were kicking in and I didn't like what they were saying. The images I had just watched showed the train I was supposed to have been on and, what looked like, Jen's mint green Mini with the daisy stickers all over it, including the roof. I had immediately recognised it. Grabbing the remote from Sam, I pointed it and hit rewind, then play. We rewatched the footage in silence and I hit pause when the Mini filled the screen.

"That's Jen's car." And I knew how paranoid I was sounding. Wide-eyed, heart pounding and feeling nauseous, a nervousness was spreading over me. Standing, I began to pace the length of the lounge.

"Sam. The train I was supposed to be on yesterday has crashed. There are no reports of anyone having survived. Now this." I swept my hand towards the television while I continued to pace.

"I need to know where Mel is."

"Whoa, whoa, whoa. Let's not get ahead of ourselves. Where's your phone?"

Sam appeared so calm in the mist of my storm and I was finding it as irritating as hell.

"Kitchen, I guess. It'll be in my bag. Help yourself," I snapped and pressed rewind again.

When Sam returned, my phone was in his hand.

"I need your fingerprint, princess," he announced.

Princess?

Presenting him with my finger he swiped my phone with it and scrolled through my contacts. The phone came to life, making us both jump.

"It's Craig. That's Jen's husband, right?"

Sam looked at me for confirmation and I nodded.

Allowing the phone to stop ringing we waited. Within a minute the voicemail alert sounded. Dialling, he placed it on speaker and we listened. The voice announced two messages."Message received yesterday at twenty-three hundred hours."

"Kate, it's Craig. Jen has crashed her car. I really need to speak with you. It's not good news. Er. She's in a coma. Ring me."

"Message received today at eight fifteen."

"Kate, it's Craig again. I hope to God you missed your train last night. Please phone me to let me know you're okay. Jen is still critical. I've tried Mel. No answer. They're connecting this. Phone me."

Tears filled my eyes and Sam began to pace the length of his lounge with me.

"We need to think this through," he said, more to himself than to me. "Okay," he directed to me now.

"This is either a massive coincidence, or this has been planned for quite some time. What was the last case the three of you worked on?"

"Carl Ashbeck."

Sam just looked at me. This wasn't Ashbeck's style and, surely, he couldn't have planned this from prison.

"Before him?"

"Oh, Sam. Where do I start? The three of us worked together for years. It could be any one of them. What I can tell you is that none of them did anything like this. Maybe a good place to start would be to see if any of them have been released lately."

"Come and sit. I need you to close your eyes and tell me about yesterday. Start from when you first left home. Talk me through your day, the people you noticed."

"Let me think a minute."

"No. Don't think. You know how this works, Kate. Close your eyes, relax and talk about what comes to you. Don't think about it. The sooner we do this the more details you will remember."

"I know," I said, before I continued.

Closing my eyes and taking a deep breath, I took a few moments to steady myself. I knew what was needed of me, after all, I had walked many witnesses through this process. I took my time.

"My morning started the usual way. Cathy let herself in and joined me in the kitchen."

"Who's Cathy?"

"She works for me, we've become friends too. We made breakfast for my guests and served them. Once we had cleaned up I took a shower, threw a few things into my bag and waited for my taxi. I knew the driver and sat in the front. We chatted about how busy the summer had been and how good it was that we'd had so much good weather. You know, it had been good for the tourists. He drove me towards Liskeard. The roads weren't busy. I needed to bank some money, so he stopped right outside the bank and waited for me. He took me to the train station and we waited for the train together. He said he'd hang about because he always got a fare when the trains came in."

"Good. Did you wait in the taxi or on the platform?"

"On the platform. The train was on time, we were there about five minutes. I'd pre-booked my tickets because it's much cheaper and you can more or less choose the type of seat you get. The first part of the journey there was no one else in my section of the carriage. The scenery is awesome and I took the time to enjoy it. It's not often I get time alone and I was making the most of it, you know. As the train stopped at various locations it became fuller, but there wasn't much conversation."

"It's a long-haul journey, right? How long ago did you book your seat?"

"I wanted to be near the canteen, the bathroom and I wanted an electricity point so I could charge my phone. I had a table too. I booked it a month ago."

"Did anyone join you at your table during the journey?"

"Yes. A woman with her young daughter. She drew me a picture. I had a notebook in my bag and I drew one for her too."

"What did she draw?"

"Is that relevant?"

"Maybe."

"How? She drew flowers and I drew a seaside scene with boats, cliffs and matchstick people."

"Did they travel all the way to London?"

"No. They got off at Exeter. The woman had said they had been to visit her parents."

"Okay. Did anyone else sit with you?"

"Not for miles. Two men joined me, but I had been dozing. I got the impression they may have been a couple. They didn't make much conversation, just the niceties, you know? They remained in their seats until we reached London."

"They didn't unsettle you?"

"No."

This charade continued until I had exhausted the entire day. Every so often Sam would throw in a random question. I knew what he was doing. He was trying to catch my unconscious mind off guard. But it hadn't worked. To my knowledge, I hadn't upset anyone of late. I hadn't received any threats, nor had I witnessed a crime.

It wasn't until I thought about the three hooded males that I had encountered at the station after I'd missed the train that the hairs on the back of my neck stood to attention. I suddenly felt cold.

He nodded and rubbed his hands together.

"Okay, we're in business. What did you see?"

"It may be nothing, but when I missed the train and turned to walk out of the station I noticed three hooded males walking directly towards me. They were shoulder to shoulder. Their hoods covered their eyes, but there were two yellow eyes printed on the hoods. Like owl eyes. One of them bumped my shoulder and his shrill laughter filled the air. Their trainers were squeaking on the floor as they walked, so when they spun around and started to follow me, I knew what they were up to. I was almost out of the station and went to the first taxi. The taxi brought me straight to you."

"Okay. Did you notice any other hooded people during the day?"

"Loads. Sam, you know I am a bit sensitive around them. I am very aware when one walks towards me. I spent most of the day on edge to be honest."

He took my hand and squeezed it. He made eye contact with me and smiled.

"I know. But think. Did you see any others with these eyes?"

"Maybe, yes. There were a group of them sitting at the bar while we had lunch."

"I'm with you on this. Someone is targeting the three of you."

Dialling Craig from his own phone, Sam waited for an answer.

"Craig, it's Sam Cooper. I'm an old colleague and friend of Jen's. Please tell me that isn't her car on the news." He listened.

"No. I haven't heard from her. Look mate, please send my love to Jen. I hope she pulls through. Anything you need, you get in touch."

The call ended and Sam embraced me.

"I'm so sorry about your friend," he said with warmth.

"You didn't tell him I was okay," I said.

"No. I don't believe in coincidences, Kate. Your well-being is on a need-to-know basis."

Usually calm under pressure, Sam was on edge. In all the years we'd worked together I hadn't seen him act this way. His instincts were usually spot on, so his reaction was doing nothing to calm my paranoia. In fact, it was terrifying me somewhat. I wondered how calm or panicked he'd felt while I laid unconscious on that platform, when my blood was pumping through his fingers. We'd never spoken about these emotions after the incident. Sam had hinted last night when he'd touched my scar. It was a conversation I would hold him to at some point in the near future.

"Who have you guys upset?" he repeated the question and then looked at me.

I just shook my head and shrugged my shoulders. Grief engulfed me and I didn't think I could speak right now without breaking down.

"We'll get to the bottom of this, princess. I promise."

"Princess?" I asked in a whisper and his eyes met mine, his smile broadened into a cheeky grin. Somehow through the grief, my butterflies returned to perform their flips in my tummy. So many emotions were roaring through my body right now and I wasn't sure how it was coping.

"I'm going to phone Phil," he announced and returned to his kitchen.

When Sam had finished on the phone he found me in the shower. He didn't join me. Instead he lingered at the bathroom door, leaning against the frame watching me.

"Pervert," I said as I emerged, water leaving streaks over my body as the droplets complied with gravity.

"Can't help myself," he said, as he wrapped me in a fresh towel and sat me on the end of his bed.

I noticed the serious look he had on his face.

"I need you to trust me Kate." And he raised that eyebrow at me. He wanted a response and he knew I didn't trust easily. We had trust as working partners, but things were different now. For one thing, four years had passed and he had kept secrets from me. And, we had just spent the night together; we had become lovers and my last lover had let me down, twice.

"Since when have you had to ask for my trust?" I gave him what he wanted.

"I've spoken to Phil and I'm heading over to his now. Phil knew you weren't on that train and somehow he knew you'd spent the night here."

"How would he know that?"

"Apparently not a conversation for over the phone. Phil has a plan and he wants to talk to me about it. Do you trust me?" And as his left eyebrow rose again, I felt a sudden comfort at the familiarity and a sudden urge to embrace this man who now called me princess. Flinging my arms around him, I squeezed tightly.

"With my life," I said, into his neck.

Sam gave me a big squeeze, before pulling away and placing a hand on each of my shoulders.

"Don't use your phone. If you need to make any calls use the landline and my ex's name. If it rings, answer it. Don't give your name. If I need to ask you anything I'll phone and will call you princess. Think of a name for me while I'm gone. It will help."

Sam was as serious as I'd ever seen him as he dished out his instructions, but his paranoia had put me on high alert.

"I'll be two hours, tops. Promise me you'll be here when I get back."

I just nodded.

Within moments I heard the front door close and I was alone, wrapped in a towel and sitting on a strange bed. Suddenly feeling incredibly vulnerable, I hurried to dry myself. The thought of putting my dirty clothes on really didn't appeal, so I gingerly opened wardrobe doors and ran my fingers over his clothes; I knew he wouldn't mind. There wasn't much I could use as Sam had immensely wide shoulders. I opted for another shirt and some boxer shorts. Reluctantly, I held my jeans up to the light. They would have to do.

Taking yesterday's underwear and my blouse to the kitchen, I searched cupboards for soap power. I also found the bleach. I washed my clothes in the sink and wrung them out as much as I could. Sam had turned on the heating because he knew I would feel cold. I arranged my underwear over the radiator in the bedroom and hung my blouse on a spare hanger, placing it on to the curtain rail above the heat.

Returning to the kitchen, I filled the sink with hot water and added bleach. I washed every surface I could find, scrubbed door handles and mopped the floor. I could not sit for two hours and wait while time stood still. I needed to keep busy to distract my mind from conjuring up more paranoid thoughts.

Sam had washed the wine glasses and our coffee mugs already, so I dried them and put them away. I wondered where he kept his vacuum cleaner. When I put the bleach away I noticed a duster and polish, so I began busying myself with that task. Returning to the bathroom, I began my cleaning process there.

Finally finished with water, I rummaged in my bag for my hand cream. There wasn't much left but my hands felt grateful for it.

# CHAPTER NINE

Before Sam could knock on Phil Andrews' front door it swung open. Standing beyond the threshold was a silhouette Sam would recognise anywhere. The two men had been friends since childhood; they schooled together, went to university together, joined the army together and joined the police force together. During their undercover operations, they'd lived in each other's pockets and, somehow, they had never fallen out. When Sam had married Lauren, Phil had been an easy choice to be their best man. When their son, Charlie, entered the world, Phil had, again, been an easy choice for godparent. He'd been the only choice for both of them.

Sam had never seen his friend look so stressed.

"You're late," Phil said in way of greeting.

"Something came up."

"More important than this?"

"Linked to this."

"We're in the kitchen."

Sam proceeded through the familiar house towards

the kitchen and the waft of fresh coffee that grew stronger the closer he got.

As Phil poured coffee, Sam stood at the window looking towards the swimming pool.

"He's been in there over an hour already," Phil said of Charlie.

"I think he's addicted to wearing himself out."

"It's been a good distraction."

"How's he doing? I need you to answer that honestly, Phil."

"I don't see much of him these days to be honest. He seems happy though. We've talked about Lauren and her choices, and he's not angry with her because she's gay. He's angry because she had the affair."

"Hmm. Has he spoken to her yet?"

"Not to my knowledge."

"He's not angry any more though Phil. It's about time he picked up the phone or went to visit. What do you think?"

"Works both ways. I've spoken to her a few times, not once has she asked to speak to him or how he's doing"

The two men took a moment to sip at their coffee before continuing with the task at hand.

"I take it you've seen the news this morning?" Sam asked.

"Grim times my friend. Grim times."

"Kate was supposed to be on that train, Phil."

"Thankfully she wasn't. How's she holding up?"

"She's stressed, angry and worried. She recognised

Jen's car on the news. We know Jen survived and is critical because I have spoken to Craig."

"Does Craig know Kate didn't make her train?"

"No. After he told me he couldn't get hold of Mel either, I decided not to share that."

"Good call," Phil said, took a deep breath and continued. "I've viewed the CCTV footage from the station and it appears that Kate was being watched by three men in marked hooded sweatshirts."

"Marked how?"

"Yellow circles on the hoods that look very much like eyes."

"That's new around here. Anything in the system for anywhere else?"

"Nothing historic."

"Recent?"

"Possibly. Tell me about you and Kate. How come she ended up at yours last night?"

"After she missed her train she made her way to the station. I made her a cuppa and told her she could kip on my sofa."

"Yet she was in your bed, you ol' dog you," Phil said, as he gave Sam a playful punch on the arm.

"About that mate. How the hell did you know that?"

"I needed to know she was safe. I knew Kate was at the station and I knew the two of you left together. I borrowed Charlie's keys and snuck in. When I saw the two of you together, I was relieved she was okay and overjoyed the two of you had finally done the deed."

"Why would you think Kate wasn't safe? What the hell is going on that you are keeping to yourself?"

"It's just a hunch and I've made a call. When I know for certain I will let you know. In the meantime, you need to trust me."

"Phil, I've known you almost all of my life and I can tell you are holding something back from me. Every cell in my body is telling me not to trust you right now. Why would you do that to me? To Kate?"

"Sam, I have been up all night working on this. You can trust me. As soon as I get the information I will share it. In the meantime, you need to hope I'm fucking wrong about this."

"Why demand a meeting then not share info?" Sam was getting angry.

"Because if, God forbid, I'm right, I need you two to be prepared. Kate needs to disappear fast. She will need a new identity. We need to set that in motion."

"Jesus Christ, Phil. You can't just demand that of her without giving a reason!"

From behind a closed door, somewhere else in the house, a phone started to ring. Phil didn't excuse himself, but left in haste to answer it. Sam could hear his mumbled voice but couldn't make out any words.

The back door opened and Charlie walked in, a small towel wrapped neatly around his middle. Pool water glistened on his body. He was surprised to see his father standing in the kitchen and took the opportunity to embrace him with his wet body.

"Dad! I didn't know you were popping in."

"You're still wet!" Sam said, through laughter.

"Coffee?"

"No thanks. You know I don't drink it these days," Charlie said, as he refilled the kettle and rummaged around in a tin. "Green tea."

"Seriously?"

"I know. It's rank when you first drink it, but it's started to grow on me."

"You look well, son."

"I feel well, thanks."

Phil returned from his phone call.

"Charlie. Has your father told you about his house guest?"

"Phil!"

"No, he hasn't!" Charlie said to Phil, before turning to Sam. "Who and how long?"

"Charlie, it's early days. You know how you've been nagging me to visit Kate, well she's in London."

Moving over to his father again, Charlie gave him another hug. His smile was so broad.

"That's fantastic. Say hello from me."

"Right young man, your father and I have a work thing to talk about."

"Something I need to run by you, Dad," Charlie whispered into his father's ear. Sam nodded at his only son.

They had just communicated in their own private way. Charlie needed to talk to his father in private and urgently.

"That's my cue. I'll be upstairs."

"Okay. That call was not good news. You know that just before you met Kate, she worked a high-profile case with Jen and Mel."

"Carl Ashbeck."

"That case took its toll on many people. The victims are still in the witness protection programme and most people involved have been moved on. Within a month of that monster being in prison, he managed to get a tattoo. No one knew the significance of it until now."

"Go on."

"Two owl eyes on his forehead."

"Jesus Christ."

"Sam, it appears he has escaped. He was granted leave to visit a dying relative and has gone missing along with Deputy Commissioner Smith."

"And the hooded men Kate saw yesterday, with eye motifs on their heads?"

"Assumed to be his associates."

Phil took a steadying breath before he continued.

"Sam, an eyewitness at the scene of Jen's crash has come forward to say that the man who ran her off the road was wearing one of these hoodies. She specifically described the owl eyes. CCTV footage near the train crash site is being viewed now and I'm waiting the results. I cannot reach Mel, but I know she isn't at home because I have had the local police knock on her door. Right now, I am a worried man."

Sam could tell that Phil was still holding something back. He raised his eyebrows and waited in silence for his friend to continue.

"I have many calls to make this morning and then will come and see you and Kate with instructions. Give me three hours, Sam. That should be plenty of time for you to give her a new look. Hair, clothes, eye colour. Tell her what you know and ask her to brief you on everything she knows about Ashbeck. Give her the code word 'Raven' and she will know that she needs to share it with you. I am putting you personally in charge of Kate's safety. She needs a new identity. Sort it. The two of you need to go away for a while. I would suggest you go to Norfolk in order that you might find out what has happened to Mel."

"Are Norfolk Police not doing that?"

"There are many sightings of these hooded men in Yarmouth. That's where you need to concentrate."

"Why would I change Kate's identity and walk her into an area where you think this gang is operating? If you are right, Phil and they do want Kate, Jen and Mel dead, don't you think that's a suicide mission?"

"There is a slim chance that they think that Kate was on that train. That's not confirmed, but I'm working on a way to get that message across. Actually, you might want to prepare her to hear of her demise on this evening's news."

"You think so? You have just told me that three of them saw her after the train left the station. They won't fall for that."

"Point taken. I'll work on another way to get the message out, but it will go out on tonight's news that she has died. She needs warning. It will be Kate's choice if she goes with you to Norfolk, or into witness protection. She needs to make that choice fast."

"Christ, Phil. Kate isn't even one of us any longer. You're out of your mind. What does Smith have to do with Ashbeck and why is he missing?"

"Three hours, Sam," Phil said, thrusting a credit card into his hand. "The pin is eight, five, six, four. Take Charlie shopping, it'll be faster."

Sam knew that the conversation was over. He headed upstairs, collected Charlie and they went out of the door together. A short cab ride later and they were at the shops. Charlie headed for the men's department and Sam for the ladies. They would meet in twenty minutes. Sam knew the card would be limitless, within reason. Realising he didn't know Kate's shoe size, he rang his own landline and waited for her to pick up.

"Hello."

"Hello, princess. Don't question me, but I need your shoe size."

"Five."

"Thanks. See you shortly."

***

Several outfits later, Sam phoned Charlie and they met up near a 'Pay Here' sign. Charlie was bursting with excitement at having fulfilled his mission. He'd chosen his father some fantastic outfits and was trying to get him to try them on so he could see what he looked like in them, but there just wasn't time.

Instead, Charlie started to tell him what he'd been up to with his covert operation. The screens, cameras and recording equipment, and how he'd converted the summer house. Sam was horrified that he could do such a thing to Phil; his son's obsession was getting out of hand. This situation needed handling, but it would have to wait for now.

# CHAPTER TEN

Frustration was building as I paced the length of Sam's flat. Back and forth, back and forth. What had that call been about? Why would Sam need to know my shoe size?

His return was taking too much time for my liking. Each minute that passed seemed longer than the last. Having exhausted surfaces to bleach, I was now feeling useless and impatient. The news cycle had repeated itself too many times and I had turned the TV off. This strange flat, now plunged into silence, was doing nothing to soothe my nerves. The urge to pick up my phone and dial Craig's number was becoming stronger with each long minute that passed. But I had made a promise to Sam and I wasn't keen to break it. I wouldn't act until we knew what was going on. I didn't even phone Cathy, who would be worried sick at what she was hearing on the news.

Upon hearing a key in the door my heart rate quickened and I froze on the spot. I guess the events of the past few hours had put me on edge and I hadn't calmed down yet. Mustering courage from somewhere deep inside of me, I pulled myself together and forced myself outside of the room. Instinct told me that it was just Sam returning, but my training told me to play it safe. As the door whooshed open, Sam called out.

"Hey princess, it's only me."

Relief enabled me to breathe again and I willed my heart rate to slow down. Moving through the lounge, towards the hallway and the open front door, I was astonished at the sight. Sam was struggling with bags and boxes and I rushed to help him.

"What on earth is going on?"

Sam dumped everything on the floor and used a foot to kick his door shut. Stepping over the many bags, he reached out for me and pulled me in close. As we held each other tightly I could feel his fear. Pulling away slightly, I looked into his eyes and his expression did nothing to alleviate my mood. I had an overwhelming urge to run out of the door, but something stopped me.

Sam broke free and collected some of the bags. I picked up the rest and followed him to his bedroom. Having dumped the bounty on the bed, he took my hand in his and led me to the kitchen. Pulling out a chair, he beckoned me to sit. He chose the chair opposite and studied me for what seemed like forever.

"Carl Ashbeck," he announced into the space between us, as if it was normal practice to talk about such a monster in one's home.

"What about him?"

"He's escaped."

"Jesus. No!" I shook my head from side to side in disbelief. "No Sam. No, that's not possible. No way." I made eye contact with him and when I saw the look on his face I knew he was speaking the truth.

"I need to ask you something. After you missed your train yesterday and you saw the hooded men, did you recognise them? Had you seen them before?"

I thought for a long time. I saw a lot of people but, no, I didn't recognise them. I shook my head. No.

Sam spoke freely because he, of all people, knew the fears I had after I was stabbed by a hooded man on the otherwise empty train platform all those years ago.

"Ashbeck, according to Phil, had owl eyes tattooed on to his forehead in prison."

I could feel the colour drain from my cheeks. Sam stood and I was aware of him moving about in the kitchen but I didn't respond. If he was speaking, I couldn't hear him. Returning to me, he placed a glass of water in my hand.

"Thanks," I said and took sips.

"Phil has made your safety my priority and responsibility. He wants you to have a new identity within two hours. I have scissors, hair dye, coloured contacts and new clothes in the bags. Phil will be over later with new documents and a proposition. Meanwhile, he wants you to tell me about Ashbeck. He told me to say 'Raven' to you and that this code word would prompt you to speak openly to me."

'Raven' had been the code word given to the case at

the time. Only those with access to the code had access to the full details of the case.

"You want me to bring that monster into your home, to talk about what he did to his victims in your kitchen? Trust me, I've worked very hard to reduce the impact he had on my life, you don't want him in yours." I lifted my feet on to the chair and tucked my knees under my chin. I hugged my legs. I was as close to the foetal position as I could possibly get, whilst sat on a kitchen chair.

It didn't go unnoticed.

"No, I don't want monsters in my kitchen and given a choice, I don't want to put you through all that again, but we don't have a choice. Mel's life may well depend on me knowing this information, Kate. I need to know. You need to tell me and right now, this is the only place you are safe."

Moving my hands to my head, I massaged my temples. I had waited seven years for my time with Sam and, finally, our circumstances had allowed us to be together. How was it that Ashbeck chose this very moment to break out of prison and take control? Life could be such a bitch.

"I don't know where to start."

Sam disappeared to rummage through the bags for the scissors and hair dye, and I selected teabags that smelled like berries. They were not usually my thing, but a caffeine overload was the last thing we needed today, so I gave them a try. Sam must like them because he had them in his kitchen, right?

"Here, some sort of fruit tea I found. I thought we'd had enough caffeine."

"Gee, thanks. And here's me thinking you loved me."

"I do love you and I found them in your kitchen, so I assumed you liked them."

"Charlie pretends to like them. I buy them to humour him. I now challenge you to drink what you've made, princess."

"That bad?"

"You can be the judge of that."

It had taken me three years to grow my hair to this length and it was just how I had wanted it. I didn't want to cut it off but 'apparently' I didn't have a choice. Sam didn't waste time. Before I could stop him, strands of long brown hair were falling to the floor.

"I'm not sure where you want me to start. Do you want to know about the investigation that led us to Ashbeck, or do you want to know about him as a person?"

"Give me a brief outline of the investigation – a basic summary. That will give me some background."

"Okay. We'd received a tip from a reliable source, a regular source, that there were people being smuggled into the heart of the city. Straight into St Katharine Docks if you please. So, you could say, right under our noses.

"We were given the name of a boat. Obviously Customs were involved, but it ran far deeper than that. After an in-depth, joint investigation they handled the charges on the people smuggling and we took charge of the murders. I know Customs linked the boat to two others and have since closed in on them too. It was taking time to close down the operation, but they were optimistic of success. We knew we'd only skimmed the surface of our operation but we did catch the top dog – and despite the three of us suspecting there was a great deal more to uncover, our boss pulled us off the case. Personally, I always felt he had a hidden agenda there.

"Ashbeck owned the boat we'd raided, it was the start of his downfall. That's when the cat-and-mouse chase began. We started to investigate him and his businesses. He owned many properties and ran businesses from each. There was this multilayered enterprise from each. The main business was legitimate for each property, with taxes being paid etc. When we looked closer, however, things weren't quite right. The addresses were being used for other purposes. We started to watch a couple of properties and the comings and goings were interesting to say the least. Every six weeks there were four new women of Eastern European origins, various countries, turning up. We kept up with the surveillance, taking photos of everyone entering the building, for weeks. Then the investigation struck lucky. One of the women turned up on the news. It didn't make national news, but one of the surveillance guys happened to see it on the local news while on holiday with his family and phoned me. It was the break we were waiting for."

"Why was she on the news?"

"She had been found dumped on a country road in Norfolk. A dog walker had found her in the early hours of the morning. Our surveillance guy had photographed her entering one of Ashbeck's buildings, a Customs guy had photographed her getting off his boat. Like I say, we co-operated on this one. She was now dead. I rushed to Norfolk and shared enough information with them to obtain the post-mortem results. Her injuries matched those of some women who had come forward claiming to have been abducted, tortured and raped. The DNA obtained from these cases matched that of this poor woman. We had enough to arrest Ashbeck and to serve him a warrant to obtain his DNA. Bingo."

I stopped talking because I didn't want to put into words the atrocities this monster had carried out on these women. I had taken a look into his dark soul and it wasn't a place I revisited with ease – in point of fact, I was not sure there was any place darker I was prepared to go and I wasn't sure that I wanted to pay that place a visit on that morning. It certainly wasn't a place I returned to without mental preparation. It definitely wasn't something I verbalised with ease.

"Why does Phil feel it's important we have this conversation?"

"Where in Norfolk was this woman found?"

"Near a farm close to Great Yarmouth."

"So, he had links there before?"

"It appeared so. We did investigate that, but couldn't find any other link apart from this one woman back then.

He was very apt at covering his tracks."

"Back to Phil. He thinks I need to know for several reasons. I need to keep you safe. Hooded men were seen at Paddington station, following you. They were seen at the scene of Jen's accident and in Mel's village. All of them had these owl eye motifs on their hoods. Ashbeck escaped prison the very day you returned to London and he has owl eye tatts on his forehead. You, Jen and Mel are responsible for his incarceration. He has a grudge."

"Okay, okay. And for the record, Ashbeck was responsible for his own actions and therefore responsible for his incarceration. We were responsible for stopping him in his tracks and yes, I suspect he has a massive grudge about that."

"I stand corrected."

"He's a sadistic bastard Sam." I began my analysis of a man I believed capital punishment should have been brought back for.

"He abducted, bound, gagged, tortured, raped and mutilated his victims until they begged him to kill them. He then released them, naked in the middle of the night, in a rural location. Five died. The lady I already mentioned died of dehydration and another died of septicaemia from infected wounds. Three committed suicide after their release."

Tears filled my eyes and I took a steadying deep breath. Sam took hold of my shoulders and squeezed.

"What happened to the women that survived?"

"They received medical treatment, therapy and were given new identities. They entered the witness protection programme for their own protection. Some gave evidence in court. I hope they are safe, Sam and that Ashbeck does not find them."

Sam did not pass comment because we both knew there were no guarantees in life.

"Were his victims all women?"

"Only women came forward. Sam, I'll admit to you that the case bothered me more than I ever let on. I don't know if Phil would let you see the evidence, I certainly don't want to have to view it again. But the photos can't convey what he did to those women, you know? Psychologically."

"You didn't tell Phil that at the time?"

"No, but I think he knew. How could he not? He moved the three of us – that's how you and I ended up as partners."

"You came with a health warning, Kate. I was told you had worked that case – but not the details – and that you had started to take risks. I was trusted to babysit you."

"But I didn't stop taking risks, Sam."

"Not to begin with. But you did in the end. You resigned and opted for the quiet life in Cornwall, didn't you?"

Neither of us had touched our fruit teas, so Sam collected them and reboiled the kettle. He had many more questions about Ashbeck that I answered, while he applied the hair dye. While the stuff began to work its magic, Sam made normal tea and produced hair clippers from a drawer, passing them to me.

"Here. To complete our new image, I need a shaved head."

"You don't need to do that."

"Oh, I do. You'll see why later."

Plugging them into a socket, Sam moved a chair closer and sat. It didn't take me long to complete the job at hand. I moved in front of him and took his face in my free hand, lifting his chin upwards so I could take a better look.

"Still sexy," I said smiling.

Sam was clock-watching and when the time was up he rinsed what remained of my hair in the kitchen sink. I felt itchy where hair had become trapped between my clothes and skin, so I took the conditioner into the shower and finished the process there. Sam followed and watched me through the steam, he jumped in once I was finished. Two can play at the watching game and I admired his muscular body through the steam and condensation. When he'd finished I hid his towel behind my back: a moment of fun amidst the serious situation we found ourselves in.

I was about to come face to face with the new look me and, I had to admit, I was feeling slightly nervous. Let's face it, Sam wasn't a hairdresser and I'd never had anything other than dark brown hair in my life. The thought of anything different wasn't appealing.

"Get dressed first, so you get to see the whole new look."

I had no idea what clothes Sam had chosen, but I guessed they would be in line with my new look. Rummaging, he selected trousers and a top, and passed them to me.

"Here, try these. There's a belt somewhere too and some boots."

I retrieved my underwear that I'd washed earlier, from the radiator. Dry enough. Slipping into the clothes, I had to admit I liked the feel of the black trousers. They were some sort of shiny, stretchable material, as thick as denim. They were a slender fit but not skinny. Red was certainly not my colour, but I put the blouse on none the less. Perhaps my new blonde hair would make a difference. Tucking the blouse into the trousers, I threaded the belt through the loops and tightened it. Sam looked the happiest I'd seen him all day. He walked around the bed, to where I was getting dressed, with high-heeled boots in his hand. They were a little high and a bit chunky, but I put them on. Sam was not finished with me yet. In his other hand was a small red silky bag. I knew what it would contain and it was not something I would usually bother with. Make-up. Rolling my eyes, I took it from him and had a look. Lipsticks and nail varnishes in reds and purples. Eyeliner and mascara in black. Contact lenses in green. I truly was evolved.

Sam took my hand and led me around the bed to his full-length mirror. He was still naked because he had been helping me, rather than concentrating on himself. He unveiled the new me and I was blown away. I didn't recognise my own reflection. Not even slightly. My hair was far shorter than I could have imagined, perhaps just an inch or so long, and very blonde. I wondered where Sam had learned his hairdressing skill but didn't ask. I'm not sure I even wanted to know. The clothes he had selected showed off my figure far more than I was used to doing: I'd developed good high cheek bones from somewhere, I'd not noticed them before.

"You are one sexy chick. People are going to turn their heads for you, princess."

"My own mother wouldn't recognise me."

"In my book that is a good thing." And I'm reminded that there's not much he doesn't know about me.

"I feel rebellious," I said, laughing.

"The pair of us look hard and cold. People will notice us. They will stare and whisper."

I turned to face him. His shaved head and day-old stubble, when accompanied by his cool stare, did make his look cold and hard. He was giving me that look now as he dressed. He had chosen a black shirt and a slim-fitted suit. Rather than shoes, he opted for boots with a slight heel. He finished the look with a selection of gold rings he picked out from a box in the bottom of his wardrobe and a thick chain he put around his wrist. I couldn't help but wonder where they were from.

"Where on earth did you get these?" I asked.

"Here. See if any fit you," he said, passing me the box. "Had them years. Just old family stuff I collected."

I rummaged about and found an obnoxious-looking diamond ring that I thought might suit my new image. I studied the inside and noted that it was hallmarked. I couldn't make out the tiny marks, but the ring looked gold and it felt heavy. To my untrained eye it was a quality piece and deserved better than to be thrown in a box and discarded at the bottom of a wardrobe. I was suddenly unsure about the family connection. It was a bit of a squeeze to get it over my knuckle, but fitted okay once on. I couldn't help but conjure stories in my mind about the truth behind this box of wonders and shook off the thought that the true owners lost their jewels through crime.

"What does Phil want me to do?"

"That's for him to ask. My advice is don't be bullied into anything. What he's asking is dangerous and you don't work for him any more. You have other options and you don't have to do them alone."

"He wants me to go undercover. That's what this is all about."

"Whatever you decide, you needed to change your appearance."

The doorbell sounded and Sam rushed to the door and picked up the receiver.

"Hello."

"It's Phil."

"Come up."

I joined Sam in the hallway, briefly. I had applied the red lipstick.

"I would," he said cheekily.

"You already did!" I said, through a giggle.

Disappearing back into the bedroom to take the plunge with the green contacts, I expected them to make my eyes water. They were surprisingly comfortable. I applied mascara.

Following the sound of the familiar voices, I joined the men in the kitchen. Phil was making coffee, obviously comfortable and familiar in Sam's kitchen. When he turned to face me, he did a double take. Mission accomplished.

"Kate, good God. I would have passed you on the street. How you doin'?"

"I'm not sure. Tell me, Phil. How am I doing?"

"Excuse me?"

"You seem to know more about what I'm up to, or need to do, than me, so, I thought you might know how I'm doing."

"Hmm. Any family Kate?"

"No," I lied.

"Then I need to send someone to run your B & B while you are gone."

"You can leave that well alone. My friend can manage." I did not make eye contact with him.

"I need photos of you both for your new IDs. I've got my camera. I also need to bring you both up to speed. I am in contact with Craig Jennings. He is giving me four-hourly updates on Jen's condition. She is critical but stable and in an induced coma. She has sustained a head injury and will have scans later today. As yet, I have been unable to make contact with Mel. She hasn't shown up for work and, as you know, that is not her form."

"Why do you think Ashbeck has something to do with all of this?"

"We'll get to that in a minute. Kate, it is vital that you are kept out of harm's way. You have two options. You were seen by Ashbeck's associates leaving Paddington station last night, having missed the train that you were supposed to have died on."

Nothing like being direct.

"We have footage of you being followed out of the train station and also leaving the police station with Sam after his shift. CCTV cameras picked you up outside this building just before you entered. They also picked up three hooded men. Ashbeck knows where you are. We are going to get you out of here, but we haven't come up with a plan yet. It will be going out on tonight's news that you are dead, so get your head around that. Kate, I know you have family, so please let me inform them first. Don't let them hear about this on the news. There will also be a press release, about Ashbeck's escape, going out on the national news this evening. I have people tracing his previous victims to give them fair warning first, but that's proving more difficult than you might imagine. Kate, we need to keep you safe. We get you out of here, then you have a choice. You go into the witness protection programme, or undercover. My preference is that you go undercover with Sam, in order to find Mel, but it's your call. We have good intelligence that she might be in Great Yarmouth, Norfolk."

Phil paused and looked at me to ensure he had my full attention.

"Whatever you decide you must make one promise. You must not visit Jen in hospital or, God forbid, attend her funeral if she doesn't make it. Is that clear?"

"That's not fair and you will not contact my mother."

"No, it's not fair, but I do not need to remind you of how cruel Ashbeck was to the women who were strangers to him. I don't even want to imagine what he'd have in store for you three if he abducted any of you."

Phil realised, too late, he'd voiced what Sam and I had dared not mention until then. What Ashbeck might have planned had been buried deep within my psyche and now it hovered in the air between us, like some sort of sick prophesy. Until that moment, I hadn't dared think that what he might have in store for any one of us, might be far worse than what he had already inflicted on previous victims. Please don't let him have Mel. She knew more than Jen and me about what his victim went through, because she'd not only seen the physical wounds, but had helped them psychologically too. He would have no mercy for Mel. He'd had years to plan whatever he'd got in store for her.

So, there it was, hanging in the air between the three of us, like an unpleasant stench that none of us was willing to inhale.

"We need to face that reality and work this as a worst-case scenario, Kate.   As yet, there has been no message of a ransom."

"That's not his style!"

"Nor is causing car accidents and train crashes!  But yet he's done that!"  Phil's voice was raised and his fist crashed on the table for impact.

"Sam said earlier that you'd linked the two crashes. What evidence do you have, Phil?"

"Ashbeck himself showed up on CCTV footage at the site of the train crash.  He was seen firing a gun several times and scrambling up the embankment. Minutes later the train crashed.  Preliminary tests are suggesting he planted a bomb.  A hooded man with the eye motifs was seen running Jen off the road and then fleeing the scene, abandoning his car.  A witness has come forward and has given a detailed description." He paused before continuing.  "It also appears that two further hooded men showed up at the accident site before the ambulance arrived."

"Okay.  How did he escape?"

"That's under investigation, but it appears he was granted leave to visit his mother who is dying.  That is unusual for a prisoner of his calibre, the prison officer placed his objection during the application process and, obviously, this is being looked into.  The officer's also suggested there was pressure from the deputy commissioner during the application.  Like I told you earlier, DC Smith is also missing."

"Jesus Christ. Has anyone checked on his family?" Sam asked.

"Being done now."

I had a few thoughts and without thinking, voiced them.

"Phil, for Ashbeck to escape and pull this off he must have had vast contacts on the outside, as well as on the inside. How did he know Jen would be on that road, what train I was supposed to catch and where to abduct Mel? Is the force still watching his businesses? How has he been operating from inside?"

Phil's body language changed. He picked up a pen and clicked it on and off, shifted in his chair and fiddled with his tie.

Clearing his throat, he began to speak, "I, er, hmm, I'm not sure. I guess he must have people on the outside still. Er…"

"And the inside?" Sam interrupted.

Sam and I exchanged glances.

"I'm not going into witness protection," I announced out of nowhere.

"Then you'll be heading to Great Yarmouth. I'll make all the arrangements. You guys need to get organised. Sam, I will make sure that Charlie knows that what he will be hearing on the news is false. That boy's been through enough."

"Cheers."

Phil's phone sounded and he took the call in the hallway. Sam and I remained in the kitchen and awaited his return. I could tell by his expression that Sam mistrusted Phil right now and from his little performance earlier, I totally understood. He was holding back on something. We did not speak but I had something on my mind that I needed to share and I wondered if Sam felt the same.

When Phil returned, his facial expression was glum.

"The deputy commissioner is still missing. His family are safe, now. They were at home, but had been bound and gagged, tied to chairs and abandoned. The eldest daughter broke free and delivered her mother's baby. They have been moved to a private room in hospital.

"The armed response team found some evidence that has led to a search warrant being issued. The family remain under armed protection."

"I'm not telling you how to do your job, mate, but don't you think it's time you got the commissioner involved?"

"Sam, you know better than to tell me how to do my job. You need to trust me. Three of my best detectives have been placed in danger and I take that extremely personally. I am relieved that you missed your train. I am sickened to the pit of my stomach about Jen and am sure as hell worried sick about Mel. You need to find her."

Phil produced a camera from his bag and we moved into the lounge. Sam's curtains were pale and he used them as a background. He took two images of each of us and was gone, with the promise of returning within two hours.

# CHAPTER ELEVEN

Jen lay motionless in her hospital bed. The machines surrounding her bleeped, buzzed and pinged, reassuring everyone that her body was still going through the motions of living with their help. Craig Jennings, her husband of ten years, hadn't left her side since arriving late last night, despite assurances that someone would contact him if there were any changes. Her parents had been contacted but told to stay away for now. They wouldn't be allowed in to see her yet. Jen's motionless body hadn't undergone a forensic examination. No one, except the gloved medical professionals saving her life, could touch her, not even Craig, and it was the hardest thing he had ever had to do, to fight the urge to embrace the only woman he had held close to his heart.

Two police officers stood at the foot of Jen's bed, facing the entrance to the ward. For reasons Craig hadn't been made aware of, they were armed. They would remain there until their relief showed.

Medical staff were being attentive and were talking to Jen as they worked with her. She did not respond.

Craig feared for his wife. What worried him more than anything was just how much of her would be left if she ever awoke. What long-term damage might there be? What would her quality of life be? His for that matter? Could he cope with caring for her if it came to that?

The obvious head trauma looked severe. What they hadn't established yet, was the extent of the internal damage. Scans would be forthcoming: meanwhile, all they could do was to keep Jen sedated, her heart pumping and her lungs breathing. Her induced coma was essential, the medical staff had explained, so that her body didn't go into shock. With such severe injuries, the shock alone would probably kill her, was what they had said to him.

Craig was putting his faith in their medical knowledge, for he was out of his depth.

"Show me a sign sweetheart," he said aloud.

The only response was the sound of the monitors and machines. *Bleep, blip. Bleep, blip. Bleep, blip.*

"She can't respond Mr Jennings," the gentle nurse reminded him.

Eventually, those attending to Jen's every need, convinced Craig to take a break. The café would be open by now and he needed to keep himself strong. Jen needed him to stay strong. They had told him that he needed to eat, drink and freshen up. They had given him their complete assurance that they would phone him on his mobile the instant there was any news, but they were not likely to hear from consultant for at least two more hours.

Having agreed to the terms, he leaned towards his wife and told her he loved her. He wanted to take her hand in his and to press his lips against it. He wasn't allowed to touch her. With tears in his eyes, he turned and walked away. His heart felt like it might shatter into a thousand pieces.

Wrenching himself away had been one of the most difficult things he'd ever been asked to do. Numbness now seemed to be taking over his body and his emotions. He had dried his eyes and somehow, without thinking about things, was putting one foot in front of the other and walking out of the intensive care unit. Now that he couldn't see Jen, the predicament that they found themselves in didn't feel so real. Walking, without any real purpose along the corridor, Craig did not notice the man heading his way or what he was wearing.

\*\*\*

The man in the corridor had a special mission. He had received it as a direct order from the top. Operation Hoot had begun last night and he had never been so excited. His keenness to impress his superiors had earned him this special task. Right now, Operative Four was a proud man.

Patience had served him well. He had waited seven hours before the husband had emerged from the ward. Stopping at the intercom outside the intensive care unit, he pressed the buzzer and waited for the reply.

"Hello," the female voice eventually said.

"It's Craig Jennings, I've changed my mind," Operative Four replied.

The door buzzed, indicating that the lock had been released. Taking a steadying breath, Operative Four, hiding his face as much as possible, entered and busied himself washing his hands as he had been told to do by his superior.

Confidence seemed to ooze through his muscles and Operative Four started walking towards the first bed. He knew it wasn't the one he needed because he'd been told that two police officers were standing guard. Upon reaching the first bed, he had to make a fast decision. There were two ways he could turn. Glancing left, he couldn't see any uniformed officers, so he glanced right. There they were. Turning to face them, he raised his left hand and pretended to massage his forehead – blocking the majority of his face from view. As he reached the woman's bed, he turned to face her. There was a nurse sat at a computer station and she spoke.

"Mr Jennings, please come and put an apron on."

Ignoring this irritating woman, the man proceeded towards Jen. He felt two more pairs of eyes on him, as he sensed that the two officers were now watching him. He needed to move fast. Operative Four reached towards his back pocket with his right hand and felt the coldness of the loaded gun against his fingers. The safety had been disengaged already. Within a moment he'd removed the gun and had started to draw it around his body. The two officers were fast to react and were on him before he had pulled the trigger. As the three of them hit the ground the gun exploded, echoing around the whole ward. Screams filled the air.

Craig had not reached the end of the corridor, when he heard the explosion. Instinctively he knew Jen was in danger. Time seemed to stop. Spinning around, he broke into a sprint and skidded to a halt outside the ward in time for the doors to open. Through them, the two officers were escorting another man who had been cuffed. One of the officers, the taller one, was carrying a bag in which he had placed a gun.

As Craig looked at the cuffed man, he could envisage Jen lying in her hospital bed, blood gradually seeping into the pillow on which her head rested. Rage overcame him and without a thought on the matter, he landed a punch on the cuffed man's nose.

Blood poured from both nostrils and dripped on to the floor.

"Bloody hell! Now we have to get him seen in A & E before we can take him in. That'll delay things. Fuck's sake, mate!"

"Nice one mate!" the second officer said to Craig.

Craig had never hurt anyone in his entire life and had no idea what had come over him. His knuckles hurt and when he tried to flex his fingers he was unable to. Great.

Despite the commotion in the corridor, other visitors were now being evacuated from the ward with panicked looks on their faces. Hospital security guards were arriving and were securing the area. An armed response team had been deployed. Security had just gone up a notch.

No non-essential people were permitted to enter until further notice, including the consultants, unless it was deemed urgent. The nurses on duty made that call. Each patient was allocated a team and they were the only people allowed access for now. No family. No other visitors. The hospital's own security team were out of their depth and unarmed. They didn't stand a chance against gunmen. As far as they were concerned, the faster the armed response team turned up the better.

It was the longest hour of their working lives, waiting for their replacements. When, finally, a team of six hard-looking men were escorted through the corridors of the hospital and into the area of the intensive care unit, the relief on their faces was visible. Four men remained guarding the external door to the unit and two men disappeared into the ward and stood at the foot of Jen's bed, their guns on show for all to see.

An officer was also on the way to interview Craig too, because he had just committed an assault. One of the hospital security guards took Craig's arm and led him to a room just along the corridor. Shortly after, a nurse that he recognised entered. The expression on her face grim.

The security guard gestured for Craig to sit. He, himself, remained standing. The nurse, without a word, came over and sat beside Craig. Taking a deep breath, Craig steadied his nerves. He was about to receive the news that Jen had just been shot. Numbness overcame him as he waited. Each second that passed dragged into an eternity of misery.

"Jen's condition is unchanged, Mr Jennings. Whoever that man was, he did not have time to fire his gun in her direction. By all accounts, the weapon fired because the safety was not engaged. No one was hit."

Craig heard the words, but they were not what he had been expecting. He looked blankly at the nurse and she repeated what she had just said.

"But the gunshot?" Craig asked.

"He missed," the nurse replied, in a kind voice.

Taking more deep breaths, Craig began to comprehend what the nurse was saying to him.

"I need to see her," he said with urgency.

The security guard moved to block the door.

"No one is allowed in or out until further notice," he said.

"I want to see my wife," Craig demanded in a raised voice.

"Soon," the kind-hearted nurse replied. "Just as soon as forensics have done what they need to do."

"Forensics?" Craig enquired.

"Mr Jennings, we are already waiting for forensics to run their tests on your wife. The tests they need to run just got longer. Your wife has just been threatened by a gunman. Mr Jennings, I am going to be frank with you. I have never had to work under such conditions in my life. Your wife has come to us with extreme injuries because someone tried to run her off the road. The reports are all over the news. Her accident is being linked to that horrific train crash that happened last night. Something is going on. Something big. My team are having to work under the protection of an armed guard. Would you please shed some light on what the hell is going on?"

"I have no idea. Honestly, I don't. All I can tell you is that my wife met up with two friends in London yesterday. One of them was on that train last night and the other is missing. You know about Jen. That's all I know."

Carl Ashbeck's 'Operation Hoot' was causing chaos. Soon it would inflict unimaginable fear.

# CHAPTER TWELVE

Needing some time alone to get my head together, I quietly disappeared off into Sam's room. So much had happened in the past few hours, my system was feeling overwhelmed and in need of a reboot. Missing my train and bolting to my old place of work had saved my life and I had also happened to fall into the arms of the man that had held my romantic interest for quite some years.

As I sat on the end of the bed, I lost myself in my thoughts. What was it about this man that gently removed me from the grasp of death and why had I given myself to him so easily? I knew we had danced around our feelings for years, but even so. Was romance so out of reach at our age? Maybe I should have been stronger, played harder to get? We could have been slightly more old-school about this: I should have insisted on being wined and dined, perhaps a trip to the theatre even. Maybe romance would happen now. I hoped so, because sex wouldn't be enough to get us through the mess we were now faced with. Going off together and working undercover wouldn't be easy – I was certain of that.

Don't get me wrong, we had worked well together. But, I think that had more to do with the chemical forces between us than our compatibility as colleagues. If it hadn't been for what went unspoken between us, the working relationship wouldn't have been teamwork but a competition of who could outsmart the other. We would have been a dangerous duo, to say the least. Phil took a massive risk putting us together. And, in my opinion, it was a massive risk us working a case together now, our personal circumstances had made the shift from colleagues to intimate partners.

Without any doubt in my mind, Phil would place Sam in charge of the investigation and I was not sure how I felt about that. Let's face it, I didn't even work for the department any longer. I was unfamiliar with any new procedures and I certainly hadn't worked undercover ever in my life. It made good sense to place Sam in charge, but it didn't mean I liked it! Ashbeck had been my case back then and no one knew the case better than me. Plus, Jen and Mel were my colleagues on that case and they were my friends too. That made them my responsibility, right?

None of that would count and I knew it.

All that aside, at the end of the new case, when I returned to Cornwall, what would become of Sam and me? How would we cope with a long-distance relationship? London and my remote part of Cornwall weren't exactly easily connected. We would spend more time travelling than we would together on days off. The logistics were not in our favour. I didn't want to think about that now, yet it kept popping into my head.

My eyes were starting to feel irritated. A combination of lack of sleep and contact lenses I suspected. Gently removing the lenses, I cleaned them, the solution I'd discovered in the bags, and stored them in the little case I'd taken them from. Hopefully they wouldn't be needed for long. I didn't think I was going to get used to them in a hurry.

Allowing my mind to drift to Jen's predicament, I wondered if there had been any progress in her recovery and hoped Phil had more information when he returned. Thinking of her generated a new drive to pick up my phone and speak to Craig. I also needed to know that Mel was fit and well, and that her life wasn't in the balance in another hospital, or some hellhole I didn't want to comprehend. I needed to know she was not dead. Closing my eyes, I said a silent prayer for my two friends. I could not remember the last time I'd prayed.

Eyes remaining closed, I reached up towards my head with both hands. Allowing my fingers to pass through my now short hair, I didn't feel that I belonged inside my own body. Nothing seemed real right now.

"You hungry, princess?" Sam interrupted my quiet time.

"Not really," I replied. I still hadn't thought of a name for him, I really needed to work on that.

"Tough, you need to eat. Come on," he insisted with excitement.

Gathering myself, I stood and caught a glimpse of the new me in the mirror and was momentarily taken aback. Walking into the kitchen, Sam seemed to have sensed my mood. On his table sat a massive plate of chips for each of us and in front of mine he'd placed a bottle of tomato sauce beside a bottle of salad cream. Suddenly I felt overwhelmed that he knew me so very well. This simple gesture ran far deeper than it might have appeared on the surface; he was feeding my soul. When we'd worked together we'd spent many hours solving issues, personal and work, over this very meal.

"Thanks pumpkin," I said with a massive grin. I had no idea where that had come from, but I was sticking with it!

"Pumpkin. Really?" And his eyebrow rose.

"Yup. For as long as you call me Princess, you are my Pumpkin," I said, as I selected the tomato sauce and smothered my chips.

Shaking his head and laughing, Sam stabbed a chip with his fork and started to eat, he would have already soaked his chips in vinegar. I wasn't finished, selecting the salad cream I took my time squeezing the creamy-coloured sauce over the already smothered chips. I loved this messy snack and I hadn't eaten it in four years.

Sam hadn't given me a fork. He knew me better than that. For this meal, there was no other way but to use my fingers. Always. It didn't matter where I was. Fingers. As the first chip entered my mouth, it tasted amazing. He had won me over. My bad mood was finally lifting and I loved that he knew how I ticked. Taking our time with our food, we stole moments of eye contact. Our legs had found one another's under the table and were entwined. When I had cleared the final chip, I gave Sam my full attention and smiled.

"Not hungry then, princess?"

"Not any more. Thanks, pumpkin."

Phil had been due at midday. He was late. The three of us had a lot of planning to do before Sam and I walked out of this flat, but we couldn't do that without our documents. We had about eight hours left to get everything in order.

# CHAPTER THIRTEEN

Phil Andrews had walked himself straight into trouble. He had been taken in by Carl Ashbeck and now found himself at his mercy. Rightfully speaking, he should report what he'd done, but perhaps there was a chance he could redeem himself first. A very slim chance, but a chance none the less. Despite how careful he had been during his visits to keep personal information to himself, Ashbeck had been clever. He now held power over Phil like a puppetmaster. There was no doubt in Phil's mind that Ashbeck was well and truly in charge.

During the past four years Phil had been conducting interviews. Research that had provided invaluable information for his book. He was due to retire in a few months from now and when he did so, this project would keep him occupied. It would, hopefully, make a generous contribution to his retirement fund too. It had been Phil's team of detectives that had worked so hard on the Ashbeck case. Ultimately, it had been Phil that had led them all to believe that this case had taken its toll on them all and that they all needed a fresh start, to be around new people and that the case shouldn't be spoken about. He'd made everyone involved sign a document that restricted what they repeated. Thus far, no one else had released a book on this monster so, it appeared, he'd got away with it. He had ensured that he had the monopoly on the story. A clever tactic on his part, he thought.

Unbeknown to Phil, Ashbeck was tailing him from prison. Well, one of his soldiers was. Phil couldn't take a piss without Ashbeck knowing about it. He was someone Ashbeck knew and trusted, and had proven himself of unimaginable value to the cause. Thankfully, he was also someone that Phil trusted enough to share his every move with too. Topping it all was the ease of the flow of information this man was sharing with Ashbeck. He had proven indispensable. Ashbeck was paying well for this service, so owed nothing in favours. The soldier had no idea how a prisoner had access to such high-value amounts of money, but that wasn't his concern. The young man he was relying on was impressionable, trusting and was playing straight into his hands. The young fool.

Locating two of the detectives that Ashbeck was looking for had been easy. Phil had led him direct to the front doors of Jen Jennings and Mel Sage. But, Warwick had proven far more problematic. Andrews had yielded nothing on her over the years. Not once had he mentioned her name, her location, or even if she still worked for him. Even the young lad he had trailing Andrews hadn't heard him speaking to, or about, Warwick and this frustrated Ashbeck considerably.

The more he thought about her, the more he wanted to smell her fear and taste her blood on his tongue. He had dreams about the moment he took her life. It had to be him that took her life. In the beginning, he needed it to be up close and personal, but now the urge was too strong. As time passed, it didn't matter how it happened – but it must happen – and he must be in control.

Of course, Andrews' time was up now, there would be no more visits. He would kick himself when the truth came out about Ashbeck's former American life; when the full story emerged and someone else got to write that book. Ashbeck was ready for that story to emerge now. Andrews had been a pawn in his little game, running errands from prison in order that he could arrange to kill the detective team that had put him inside. The same team that Andrews had headed in the first place. Poetic justice, Ashbeck called that. There was a plan in place that would see Ashbeck go so deep underground that no one would find him, of that he was sure.

He trusted only one man. Despite his young age, he had every faith that he would pull this off.

Ms Warwick couldn't hide forever though and, despite seeming to have dropped into oblivion, even she had to emerge at some point. And the timing couldn't have been better when she did. Mel had shared her plans to meet with Jen and Kate with her boyfriend. Fantastic. What Mel wasn't aware of was that her boyfriend would turn straight to Ashbeck: he would be highly rewarded for this information – possibly even promoted. The three detectives were very much in danger.

\*\*\*

The three operatives that had received their orders on the morning of the meet had met up early and were already in place when the three ladies had arrived at the bar in Covent Garden. They wore their hoodies but, as directed, removed the hoods so they blended in. They ordered alcohol-free lager and sat on stools at the bar the entire afternoon. Kate, Jen and Mel had opted for a table nearby. Their conversation was easily overheard and despite having been told that Warwick was a cold-hearted bitch, the young man couldn't help but disagree. Although she fitted Ashbeck's physical description, there was a massive difference: he had described her as a cold-hearted bitch that only cared about herself. The young man found her to be the complete opposite. She seemed to show warmth and compassion towards her two friends, and to anyone else she was interacting with.

Ashbeck was wrong about her. It had been easy to watch this woman, to be captivated by her and he wished she didn't have to die this night. She was soft and gentle, and despite her being at least twenty years his senior, if circumstances were different, he could imagine approaching her and offering to buy her a drink. But today, he would not dare approach this woman. He could not risk being seen talking to her. It was bad enough he was in the same bar. Later, he would also be in the same railway station. If someone noticed, it could lead to implications down the line and that was something he wanted to avoid if possible.

Her downfall had been to meet up with her friends and he wished there was a way he could tell her, to warn her of her fate without implicating himself in some horrific end. But that wasn't possible, he would have to follow orders. He'd seen with his own eyes what happened to operatives that didn't follow orders and it was nothing short of torture. Newcomers to the business had been forced to watch what happened to those who didn't obey orders, to keep them from straying out of line. It certainly worked. Once you'd seen the suffering you were keen to please.

When he'd applied for the job four years ago, the job description had sounded too good to be true. And to begin with he'd been happy. As time progressed, however, the demands on him intensified and with these demands came fear. The pay rewards were good though, there were no grumbles there. If things went well tonight, he knew he was in for a handsome reward.

He didn't want to contemplate what was in store if things didn't go to plan.

Waiting in a nearby car park was another operative, who would follow Jen's car. His briefing had also been clear. Mel would travel home by train and the operative who would meet her would give her the shock of her life.

# CHAPTER FOURTEEN

As Phil re-entered Sam's building he was on the phone, speaking as loudly as possible. He wanted to be heard. There was a man across the street, watching, and he suspected he'd been there all night. He wanted him to hear what he had to say. This needed to be a performance worthy of an award if his plan was to work.

"Sam, I'm entering your building. Keep her talking. Jesus Christ! Get the door open!"

Rather than taking the lift, Phil ran, three steps at a time, up the stairwell. He continued yelling into the phone. Constantly, he listened for the front door of the building and he wasn't disappointed. He didn't hear the lift, so suspected that at least one hooded figure had entered the building and was following him up the stairs. His plan was working so far. Good.

When he reached Sam's door, it was already open. Entering, he slammed it shut behind him. As soon as he had done so, he drew his handgun. He moved along the hallway and into the lounge with his left index finger pressed against his lips. He needed the silence of his two friends.

"Kate. Listen to me," Phil said in a calm, but authoritative voice. "Kate, please put down the gun," Phil said in a softer, gentler voice.

"It doesn't have to be like this. We can protect you. Both of you."

*Bang! Bang!* The gun exploded and the sound reverberated around Sam's flat. Still Phil held his finger to his lips. Phil had fired the gun twice, there were no bullets in the chamber.

Pulling a face like he'd just sucked on a sour lemon, Phil walked over to us.

"There is at least one hoodie in the building, he followed me in. Everything's in place. I need to make a call to my team and you're out of here. I need silence from both of you until further notice."

Phil dialled a number on his mobile phone.

"It's Phil Andrews. I was too late. Two bodies. Gunshots. Sam's flat. Do you know the address?"

He listened.

"That's right, yes. Okay. I'll wait here and secure the scene."

Within five minutes, sirens were sounding outside the building. Four police officers swarmed the building. I didn't recognise any of them. One was a woman. The team were making a noise near the front door, enabling Phil to speak with us.

"There is a suitcase for each of you. They are in the vehicle that will take you from here. I'm sure I've covered it all, but if you think you need anything else I can forward it on.

Nitty-gritty," he continued.

"No real names. You guys need a pet name and when we talk, I don't need to remind you, I am Boss. I cannot convey how important that part is," he said, looking each of us in the eye in turn.

"Your safety is compromised, Kate." He didn't add that his own reputation and career were compromised also.

"What do you think is going on?" I asked of my old guv. "Why now? What is his next move?"

"We're not sure yet. I have made some quiet enquiries and there are a couple of possibilities. One of them scares me, to be honest, but I think I need to get a little more information before I share it."

"Hang on a minute, mate." Sam's voice was low and angry.

"If we're in this, we need to know what we're up against. Kate should be dead." He turned to me. "Sorry princess." Then back to Phil. "But the bottom line is, he's made attempts on Kate and Jen, and we have no idea what state Mel is in."

"It's more than a possibility he has Mel. He has escaped from prison and has somehow disappeared from our radar. We always knew he had a network on the outside. There is a nationwide manhunt for this monster, Kate, but we know him better."

Turning to Sam, he added, "Do not let him get his filthy hands on Kate. That is an order."Kate, I expect you to bring Sam up to speed on the case. Do not spare any details because they are all vital. You are under direct orders to share information, despite any previous agreement you might have signed. However painful it might be for you to revisit the case, you need to put that to one side and discuss it. Be warned, the images are in both of your suitcases. Is that clear?"

I nodded before Phil's attention was directed at Sam.

"Sam, once you are fully informed, I need you to create a profile of Ashbeck based on your training and your knowledge. If Ashbeck is responsible for recent events this means his MO has shifted. Your input, both of you, could be make or break for this case. He is responsible for breaking out of prison and I will get those details to you as soon as I know the circumstances. Assume that he is responsible for the train crash, car crash and abduction. That way we have a worst-case scenario and, if we are correct, it will hopefully get us a step ahead. I knew I'd kept you up to date on your undercover training for a reason." As Phil finished speaking, he turned to face the kitchen window before continuing.

"I wish you both all the very best of luck. Whatever you uncover, trust your instincts. You are both good people and you need to remember that during tough times. My advice is this – do not lose who you really are."

Turning and facing me, he added.

"Kate, you have had no training to work undercover and you are not even employed by us any more. If you want to back out you can. I can arrange some emergency protection for you. In the event you join Sam, you do so as his partner and not as an officer. Is that clear?"

I nodded.

"Okay. From now on I am Boss, Kate you are Princess – and Sam?"

"He's Pumpkin," I added.

"Pumpkin. Jesus Kate, you expect me to call him Pumpkin?"

"Like I said to Sam, for as long as I'm Princess, he's my Pumpkin."

Shaking his head, Phil turned to leave us to brief one another and to finalise our plans.

"Whoa," Sam said. "You can't walk out of here. We need some answers."

"I've watched two hours of continuous news today, Phil. There's been no mention of an escaped prisoner," I added.

"It will be reported later. There are a few lines of enquiry to follow first," he said.

"How long has he been out?" Sam asked.

"That's just it. I can't get a definitive answer," Phil said, as he edged towards the door. He was going to turn and leave at any moment.

"What I want to know, Boss," and Sam had a mean tone to his voice, "is how do you personally know that these events are linked to Ashbeck?"

"I just do and I need you both to trust my instincts."

"You don't work on instinct. You work on evidence and facts. So, what evidence and facts do you have, mate?"

Sam was furious with his friend, he continued to hold eye contact.

"You expect us to walk into an area in which you believe this gang operates. Quite frankly, I'd rather get Kate on a plane to Australia, rather than take her some place that contains people who want her dead. We are prepared to put ourselves at risk and all three of us know that you are holding back vital information. That is out of order."

"It's on a need-to-know basis, Robert." Phil used Sam's middle name because he had no intention of calling him Pumpkin.

"As information becomes vital, I will share it. I promise. In the meantime, I am asking for your trust." Phil turned and exited.

Passing him in the hallway were two more men, each with a trolley. Phil suspected Kate wasn't going to like this bit and he wasn't going to hang about to witness it.

They entered the flat and unzipped the body bags.

I took one look at the two trolleys entering the lounge area and froze. No way was I going to get into one of those! Turning my head towards Sam, he was refusing to make eye contact with me. Great. He was on Phil's side on this one. Edging towards me, he rested his face against my ear.

"They're not like conventional body bags, princess. No one can see in but you will be able to see out and you will be able to breathe. I know it looks daunting, but trust me. Phil would have made these himself, you know." He finally made eye contact, they had the kindest look about them and his left eyebrow rose slightly in request of my trust.

Although I remained unconvinced that I should get into one of these bags, I did trust Sam and I softened my lips into a slight smile. That's all he was getting from me right now and, apparently, that was all he needed. Squeezing my hand before he climbed into the first bag, he then proceeded to gain my trust further.

"Okay. Zip me in please.

Right, pull any face at me," Sam requested.

I stick out my tongue and touch my nose.

"I forgot you could do that. You know, I still can't, however much I try."

I changed my expression to a sneer.

"You look so attractive when you snarl up your face like that."

Okay, he could see. But no one needed to think for one second that I was happy with this and they would be hearing my views.

# CHAPTER FIFTEEN

Charlie Cooper had made the most of his long summer. His A-level exams had ended months ago and, despite the pull of university study, he had decided that he needed a year away from education. He had applied for several jobs and had been lucky enough to be able to take his pick of the offers. In just over a month, he was embarking on a job that trained and paid for him to become a personal trainer. Sport was a passion. He would get this qualification under his belt first, so he could work and pay for his sports degree. Life was improving for Charlie and things had never been so good between his father and himself. As much as he wanted to move into his dad's new flat, he didn't dare leave Phil's just yet. There were secrets to uncover and he was almost there.

Many months ago, he'd come across a random key and found that it had fitted the lock into Phil's office. Right now, he was staring at a box of black, hooded sweatshirts. Using a pen, he lifted one to reveal owl eyes embossed on the hood. Frowning, he set it back neatly. Further investigation (well, a good old-fashioned snoop about) revealed a black book of phone numbers. There were random names he didn't recognise and what appeared to be mobile numbers beside them. Carefully, he used his phone camera to capture every page. Nothing else seemed new or out of character, so he exited, locked the door and returned the key.

He'd needed to speak with his father and couldn't believe his luck when he'd popped in earlier then dragged him out shopping. Not that he liked shopping mind, but this had been different. An undercover mission would be exciting and he wanted in. The information he'd shared with his father this morning had made Sam so angry, but not with Phil. He'd warned Charlie to keep out of it and to keep his obsession under control. He'd cut their time together short and hadn't given him time to explain what he'd found out. Patience, Charlie, he thought inwardly. All in good time.

Returning to the summer house, he ensured the door was secured and the curtains were closed. Opening a cabinet, that he had installed himself, exposed six small monitors. Each gave live coverage of different parts of the house. Uncle Phil was being monitored. His every move and every visitor were logged in and out. Phil couldn't take a piss without Charlie knowing. It was an interest that, by all accounts, had got out of hand. He'd been interested in surveillance since a young age. It had all started when his father had given him a spy pen one Christmas. Gradually, over the years, Charlie spent his money on various pieces of equipment and it was now paying off. Uncle Phil was up to no good.

With no activity in the house, Charlie knew it was safe to try the phone numbers he had found in Phil's home office. Selecting a new burner phone, he thumbed through the images on his normal mobile. Some of the names and numbers he recognised, Kate, Mel and Jen. He knew Kate personally. She was his father's work partner, before she'd got stabbed and moved away. After his mother had moved on, he had wished she was his dad's partner in his private life too. There had been no one since his mother had left for another woman and he knew his dad held a torch for her. Now it looked like they had finally taken the plunge and he couldn't be happier for them. The other six numbers belonged to Jane, Heidi, Melissa, Paula, Rachel and Naomi. Who were these women? Something told him not to phone them. To hold back.

When he'd moved into Phil's a year ago, Charlie had had the utmost respect for his godfather. Phil had given him the key to the summer house and exclusive use of the swimming pool, and Charlie had made both areas into his own private space. He'd changed the locks to the summer house and installed a cabinet, which Phil knew nothing about. He'd be horrified at its contents.

The first monitor had been installed when Charlie noticed Phil had a frequent visitor he hadn't liked the look of and he'd wanted to keep an eye on the situation. The visits had been monthly, initially, but had gradually become more frequent. They were weekly now and money was changing hands for boxes of goods.

Phil's body language had changed over time too. In the beginning, it was obvious he'd been in charge, but as the visits became more frequent, it was evident to Charlie that the other man was making Phil anxious. Charlie was sensing danger. Phil had got himself into trouble.

It hadn't been until the past three weeks, however, that Charlie had lost all respect for Phil. Not only had his personality changed, but Charlie felt he was constantly on edge. He'd overheard several names being mentioned too and when he'd googled them, he'd realised that Phil was involved with some extremely sinister individuals. He'd wished his father had given him more time to explain this morning: he was sure what he had to share was important.

Charlie's ears were alerted to the sound of the front door and he turned to face the monitors. Phil was home. He headed straight towards the kitchen, collected the pot of coffee that had finished percolating and a mug. He carried them to his office and unlocked the door. Quite literally bolting himself inside, he set the mug down on his desk and poured himself some coffee.

Phil's office was once the dining room, before he was widowed. Remnants of its past use were still visible. The bone china dinner service was still displayed in the glass cabinet and the table that could have sat ten people now served as a massive desk. Some of the chairs remained in corners of the room and were used to store piles of work. Phil had built bookshelves that complemented the furniture and had filled them with his lifetime collection of books. Some were first editions and quite rare, and the reason, apparently, why he kept the room locked. There were the trophies from his extensive travels too. Some odd bits that, frankly, showed a darker side to this man. Another reason to keep the door locked, in Charlie's view.

Phil, hidden away in what he thought was his private space, picked up the telephone and dialled. Charlie adjusted a camera and zoomed in. He recognised the number immediately, it was the prison where Ashbeck was being held.

Charlie sat wide-eyed, as he learned of Ashbeck's escape and the involvement that Deputy Commissioner Smith had had in instigating it.

His fingers flew over his keyboard as he commenced a search. The newspaper articles that flashed up on his monitor, all displayed the same name associated with Ashbeck. Katie-Anne Warwick had been the arresting officer and the lead detective on the case.

Kate was back in town and Ashbeck had escaped from prison and had tried to kill her. Charlie didn't believe in coincidences. He was under no illusion that Kate and his father were in danger and his need to contact them had just hit the top of his priority list.

Returning his focus to Phi, who was now dialling another number, Charlie turned up the volume control. When the two men connected, Charlie recognised the voice immediately. It was the commissioner. The top man in London's Metropolitan Police. Phil had just learned one thing from the prison and was now having a completely different conversation. Politics.

Something was poking out of the top of Phil's jacket pocket. Zooming in, it looked like a new mobile phone. Something told him he needed to get his hands on it.

Another phone rang and Phil reached for an inside pocket.

"Andrews."

After a short pause, he continued with an outburst. He was clearly angry with the person on the other end.

"Where the hell are you? You've caused enough trauma. You need to walk into the nearest police station and give yourself up. You don't want to think you're going to get your filthy hands on anyone, you horrible little man."

Charlie, as paranoid as it made him feel, was convinced that Phil had just spoken to Ashbeck.

He seriously needed to speak with his father, but knew he'd gone undercover and wouldn't have his old mobile. A plan started to form and he was convinced he needed to get his hands on the mobile in Phil's jacket. He sent his godfather a text.

*Phil, you seemed stressed earlier. Takeout from your fav restaurant tonight, my treat. What do you say?* The response was immediate.

*I'll take you up on that, but it's my treat.* Perfect.

# CHAPTER SIXTEEN

Riding into the heart of the city, zipped into a mock body bag, pretty much felt like I'd landed in hell. Phil would pay for this. The view wasn't worth seeing – the roof of the van we were riding in held no interest and wasn't a distraction enough from the discomfort of the metal stretcher under my body. Our driver had navigated through the streets without, it seemed, a thought that Sam and I might be getting bruised in the process. When, finally, he started to slow and I sensed our journey was ending, we were suddenly plunged into darkness as the van descended a slope. Underground.

Jolting to a halt, the stretchers we were on continued to rattle for a few moments. Voices were gaining volume outside the doors. I could hear my heartbeat and I felt nauseous. Sam was being uncharacteristically quiet and I read this as a sign to stay silent. We weren't done yet; our journey wasn't over.

The van doors opened and Sam was first out. Someone grabbed his stretcher and yanked it free. He was wheeled away. I wasn't far behind. As the woman pulled me free from the grips of the van, she spoke to our driver.

"Follow me, please. You need to sign them over in the office. Not seen you in here before."

"Yeah, first time. You been here long?"

"Ten years."

"Lucky you."

"Tell me about it. I'm Jade, by the way."

"Jamie."

"Let's get these two signed in, then you can be on your way."

With that the woman must have started to walk, because my stretcher was now in motion. I could feel every minute bump in the concrete floor vibrate through my body. I wanted to scream; it took every little bit of reserve remaining to stay silent.

It wasn't long before the woman was unzipping the bag and the rush of fresh air was the most pleasant feeling. Taking deep breaths and sitting up, she took my arm and helped me to my feet. Sam was already sitting in a lounge area and he nodded at me in a form of greeting. He was being cold in his greeting. We were undercover now, amongst strangers. I nodded back, just as coldly.

"Please, let's make introductions." The woman was motioning me to join Sam.

Having moved into the lounge area, I noticed the pot of coffee and cups all perfectly set upon a tray. I paused at the sight of the two suitcases. Inhaling deeply and allowing my breath to escape slowly, I willed my mind to relax as

I could feel tension building. The last thing I needed was a migraine and the early signs were definitely emerging.

Sitting opposite the man I pretended was a stranger, I felt a strange mixture of emotions. I was rather apprehensive that I was about to embark on an undercover identity. Yet, somehow excitement at this prospect was also bubbling to the surface. Looking over at Sam, I noted that his mood had become elated at this very prospect. I knew how much he'd loved his undercover work. I also knew it had almost got him killed. Sitting to my right were two suitcases and two briefcases. Within them, I was sure, were two new identities.

"Good morning," the woman began.

"Sir, we have been here before. You know what to expect. Madam, I know this is new to you. Trust me when I tell you that you are in good and very experienced hands. I have been informed that you are a fast learner and that your instincts can be trusted. I have created both of your new identities, am proud of who you are to become. The information that you provide will come directly to Boss or to me, either way, I will be the one that filters it through to the correct people, press etc. I will be the one who creates the stories, controls the media and keeps departments talking to each other. Any questions?"

Silence.

"Good."

The woman, who had not shared her name, walked over to the two briefcases, took one in each hand and gave Sam his first.

"It's good to be working with you again, sir."

"Cheers. It's good to be back."

Turning to me, she gave me a reassuring smile and handed me my identity.

"Welcome. I'm very much looking forward to seeing what you're made of. You look like you can handle pretty much anything. If Boss put me in one of those body bags, I think I'd shoot him."

"Thank you," I replied, as I took hold of the briefcase. I passed no comment on my feelings about 'Boss' right now. I did not give this woman any indication of my feelings. I gave her nothing of the real me.

Giving me direct eye contact, she levelled with me.

"Part of my job is to not get personally invested. And I'm okay with that. The guy over there and I go back years, and until yesterday, I had no idea what his real name was. Until he was in the room moments before you today, I still hadn't made that connection."

She had Sam's full attention now.

"I know exactly who you are, your involvement with Ashbeck and your personal investment in this. I know everything about both of you on record. You are a brave woman. I know how you would react if Boss walked through that door right now."

Okay, so she thought she had me sussed. I still said nothing. I didn't even smile. Quite frankly, she hadn't said anything personal to suggest she knew anything.

"Samuel; wasn't what I'd imagined to be honest." She had started on Sam.

He didn't respond either and I wondered if his insolence towards the woman differed because of my presence. I hoped not.

"Let's just quit this little performance thing you two seem to have going on that you don't know one another. I know you spent the night together. Boss really has fully briefed me. I want to talk to you both about the dangers of going into the field with," she paused for effect, "can I use the expression, baggage? I hope that doesn't sound too crude."

The woman, who had yet to give her name, sat in a chair positioned between us. If either of us wanted to look at her we had to turn our heads or move our bodies. Neither of us bothered. Instead we fussed over pouring coffee. We didn't offer her any. I sat my briefcase on the floor, beside my feet. Sam gave me a playful wink and I fought back a smile. His sign to me I was doing okay, playing my part well.

"How many field operations have you worked?" It was Sam who broke the silence.

"That's not my area of expertise, Sam. As well you know."

"Then you are not to judge what constitutes as baggage. You and I have worked together in the past. Have I ever compromised a case?"

"Not to my knowledge."

"Have I ever provided negative results?"

"Never."

"So, what's your problem?"

"Katie-Anne has had no formal training in undercover work. She's emotionally invested in you, in Jen Jennings and Mel Sage. She was Ashbeck's arresting officer. He sure as hell's going to be invested in her. I've read through what can only be described as an impressive file, on a woman who has shown great resilience, perseverance and risk-taking. And that is a major concern."

"My brief to Katie-Anne was to act cold-hearted and emotionless towards whatever situation she found herself in and whoever she met. This was her first undercover task. How do you think she's done?"

"Remarkably well, given the circumstances."

"Okay, Kate show the woman the real you. Let her see just how much you transformed for this little performance."

Taking a steadying breath, I relaxed my facial muscles and turned to face her. My expression had softened. I smiled.

"Would you like some coffee?"

"No, thank you. I can't stand the stuff. But I know Sam here can't get enough of it."

Well, she had that right.

"For the record," I said, smiling, "Boss won't be joining us if he knows what's good for him, not after putting me in a body bag. I wouldn't need to shoot him – he'd fall to the floor just from the look I'd give him."

"Come on ladies, you have to admit, it's a good way to disappear."

"Even so Sam, you knew what to expect. Kate didn't and that's not fair."

Smooth move lady.

"So, what do we call you?"

"Despite the circumstances being different this time, and I know exactly who you guys are, I am still not allowed to give you my real name. Sam has always called me Jade."

"Oh, you pushed my stretcher from the van?"

"That's right, I did. Do you recall the driver's name?"

"Jamie."

"Impressive."

"Hardly."

"Okay guys, it's time. You need to discover who you are. I'll give you twenty minutes to go over your new papers, then I'll be back to answer any questions."

Jade stood and walked away.

Sam and I looked at one another before reaching for our briefcases. Flipping the top of my case over to expose my new identity felt strange. Many thoughts raced through my mind and the one that kept returning was how would I manage to submerge my real identity in favour of a character I would play. Could I simply file Kate away in a box while I pretended to be someone else? More importantly, would it be possible to get her back out again? I silently wished I'd paid more attention in drama when we were analysing characters. Back then I couldn't imagine why I would want to put myself in the shoes of the characters to understand their feelings. Right now, I wished I had that skill.

Rummaging through the top layer, which was all paperwork, a sadness darkened my mood. Sam and I had only just found one another and already we were changing who we were. Doubt that we could survive this so early on in our relationship stirred in the pit of my stomach and spread through me like a virus. The throbbing in my head returned, as did the tightness in my shoulders and neck.

Resting on the top was a passport, driving licence, bank cards, library card and a set of certificates presented in a folder. Flipping through my new qualifications, I had a degree in journalism and various smaller qualifications showing interest in crime, society and forensics. I wondered what Sam's contained. Finding my passport and opening it at the photograph page, I did not recognise the person looking back at me. My short, blonde hair had changed my whole look. Beneath the new documents were clothes, including underwear.

"I'm not sure I'm comfortable with Phil choosing what I wear."

"He didn't, princess. I chose for you and Charlie chose for me."

That made me feel a lot better.

"This is going to take some getting used to." I stated the obvious.

"I've done this before and you're a fast learner. You'll be surprised at how quickly you adapt. Always remember, the only people we can trust right now is each other."

"And Jade?" I replied.

"Nope. I'll explain later. Something stinks."

"Great start."

"Just you and me now," and he looked up. "Here, you need to see this," he said, handing me a document.

I took it and was astonished to see that it was a marriage certificate; we were going undercover as a married couple. James and Lorraine Peterson. We were both investigative journalists.

"Journalists," I said aloud.

"I think you're missing the point. Married," he said.

"Well, hmm. That too," I said.

Coffee had hit my system and I needed to move. Standing, I started to stretch my muscles.

"Sit down, now," Sam said very quietly, but with a firmness I was not about to argue with. "Study your papers."

I stretched out a couple of muscles, but did not pace like I normally would. Instead, I returned to my seat and continued to leaf through my paperwork.

"Are they watching us?" I whispered.

"Hmm," he replied.

"Oh."

Within twenty minutes, Jade returned. She commented on my restless moment and thanked Sam for making me return to my seat. She assured me that no harm was done and that it was just the three of us in the area now, if I wanted to stretch my legs.

"Who else was here?" Sam asked.

"That doesn't concern you right now. Just know they were happy to proceed. Kate, I have had a contract drawn up for you to sign. This needs to be done before you leave the building. You both leave in one hour. Do either of you have any questions?"

I had many, many questions. None of them for Jade. I started to read through the contract and motioned for Sam to join me, two sets of eyes were better than one. He seemed pleased that I'd requested his input, but kept a professional distance between us and that pleased me. Everything seemed in order and when I had Sam's nod of approval, I placed my signature at the bottom of the document and handed it back to Jade.

"Thank you, Kate. Now, I need to ask what you know about Ashbeck," she chirped overenthusiastically.

"Nothing I'm willing to share with you."

"Excuse me?"

"That contract doesn't give you the right to my knowledge, or to any privileges to what I might know on any cases I might, or might not, have worked on, Jade. It gives you insurance cover if things go wrong."

"If we are going to pull this thing off, don't you think we need to share information?"

"What I might, or might not, know is on a need-to-know basis. If you need to know, trust me, you'd already have been briefed."

Sam locked eyes with me and had the broadest smile on his face. I had just read the situation perfectly. Jade was fishing for information. Information, after all, was power.

# CHAPTER SEVENTEEN

Having been told to take the lift to the ground floor we were doing just that, our new identities gripped firmly in one hand and each other's hand in the other. Our suitcases stood at our feet. Sam and I were looking deeply into one another's eyes.

"We'll remember who we are, I promise."

I wanted to believe him.

"But it won't be easy."

"Are we able to talk openly in here?"

"Definitely not."

"Okay. Then what I have to say will have to wait until we're outside."

We rode the remainder of the way in silence. It didn't take long. When the doors opened, we simultaneously reached for the suitcases and stepped on to the street. Darkness had fallen, which surprised me. As did the fact that we'd stepped directly on to the street.

"Okay, princess. You are free to speak your mind. But do so quietly."

"As much as I want to get to the bottom of what's

going on, I feel that we are being pushed in a direction that we're perhaps not ready for yet. I'm going to be frank with you, Sam, I'm sceptical about going undercover. We've not been fully briefed: I do not appreciate having information withheld from us one little bit."

"Life is never easy. If they're not going to give us what we need, then we'll just have to go and find things out for ourselves. Have faith in yourself, Kate."

Deciding I needed to stay silent, I let Sam lead the way and I allowed his words to drift in my mind. After all, he had been here before and knew what he was doing. In reality, I actually had no idea where we were and wasn't sure how I felt about that. Within a few minutes, we had merged into a busy area filled with bars and restaurants packed with people. The buzz of excited voices sounded far more inviting than what awaited us and momentarily, I was tempted. It wasn't my place to fight crime any longer, right? But Jen. And Mel. They were my friends and they were in so much trouble. They needed me. They would put themselves on the line for me. I owed it to them to do this. In that very moment, I felt the transformation. I felt the muscles in my face tighten and the look in my eyes harden. I'd proven to myself and to Sam I was capable of being hard cop earlier; he'd made this transformation, so now we both had to live with it.

We made our way through the streets. Sam seemed to know where we were heading. I was glad one of us did. Apparently, it wasn't time for small talk, so I kept my thoughts to myself. I wondered what Sam might be thinking and had no doubt that his priority was Ashbeck. He'd listened intently as I'd explained the crimes he'd committed; yet he'd asked no questions. I was sure he'd have many, but maybe he was processing what I'd given him and biding his time. None of what I'd had to say was pleasant. Perhaps he was making a start on his profile. Either way, I left him to his thoughts.

"Okay sweetheart, our car will pick us up from here in three minutes."

"Seriously?"

"Do not lose your cool, under any circumstance," he said, and he was as serious as I'd ever seen him.

Instantly, I knew Phil would be in that car and that I could not say a word to him. I nodded my agreement but said nothing. Instead, I channelled my anger at Phil into my new character. Phil would see me in action too. He would not be greeted with the sweet Kate that he knew so well. He would, instead, be met face on with the hard-faced bitch that has been forced into this situation. He would get nothing from me unless his attitude changed.

Adrenaline surged through my veins and anxiety pricked at my consciousness as the car pulled up beside us. I silently hoped that I looked calmer than I felt right now. The last twenty-four hours had been a rollercoaster ride of emotions for both of us and I wasn't looking forward to the crash when, finally, Sam and I reached our destination. Sam opened the boot and lifted his suitcase inside, before doing the same with mine. Walking back to the passenger side of the car, I opened the rear door and motioned Sam to enter first. He could sit next to Phil. It would have been very rude for him to have refused and he rolled his eyes as he passed me. The two men shook hands. Once inside the car, I reached over Sam's lap and extended my hand towards Phil. We, too, shook hands and it was a crushing gesture on my part.

As we passed the train station where I was stabbed I felt a hand on my knee, squeezing. Placing mine on top of his, we held on to one another as if our lives depended upon it. The silence between us didn't matter because we didn't need words to communicate. This gesture meant everything on a day that had been rotten and I was reminded that in moments like this we would remember who we really were, we had to. Our survival depended on it. My heart melted a little, but externally, I remained like stone.

The journey seemed to take an eternity, but when we finally arrived at Paddington station Phil headed off to purchase tickets. Sam and I collected our luggage. When Phil returned, he had some final words of advice.

"I used cash," he said, as he handed me both tickets.

"Be careful. You don't fool me with this new hard as stone exterior thing you have got going on. The higher you climb, the harder you'll fall."

"Thank you for your concern, but I'm just doing my job."

"You have until noon tomorrow for full disclosure, or I'll be going over your head on this," Sam said.

With that Phil span on his heels and was gone.

"I'm intrigued to learn what you've found out," I said. "Come on, let's get on this train."

When we were settled in our seats and on the move, I finally felt my body begin to relax.

"You okay, princess?"

"I'm shattered. You okay?"

"Fairly tired too. A beautiful lady kept me awake most of the night."

"I think she might let you sleep tonight."

"That's a shame," he said, smiling.

When I woke up, my head was resting against Sam's shoulder and he was watching me.

"Welcome back, princess," he announced.

"Gee. Sorry. How long have I been sleeping?"

"Most of the journey. We're arriving in five."

"You should have woken me."

"You needed to sleep and it's given me time to run with some ideas."

Suddenly alert, Sam had my full attention. I needed to hear his ideas. I raised my eyebrows in anticipation of some answers. I smiled to myself as I realised I had just raised my eyebrows. Just over twenty-four hours in the company of this man and I had already picked up one of his quirky traits.

"Not here. We'll talk as we walk."

As the train pulled to a stop at Reedham station, Sam organised our suitcases. He carried them both and I carried the two briefcases. I wondered if I looked as tired as I still felt and I suspected that I might. The chill morning air caught me by surprise as I stepped on to the platform and for the second time this week, I wished I was wearing a jacket. Nervousness kicked in almost instantly and I found myself looking about for youths in hoodies. Would I ever be able to feel comfortable at a train station, or was I on high alert due to more recent events? A combination of the two, I guessed. There were no hooded persons around, which relieved me. Feeling thankful, I quickened my pace to keep up. Falling in beside Sam, I offered to carry my case but he was having none of it. Chivalry was still very much alive in his world. Noticing the lack of a coffee kiosk, my heart sank.

"Shit, they not heard of coffee here?" Sam seemed to read my mind and added a curse under his breath that wasn't supposed to be for my ears.

As we exited the small station, I remembered something that Mel had shared with me. She lived just around the corner from the station.

"There must be a café or something somewhere. Even one of those machines at a supermarket would do right now."

"Whoa, wait a minute," I said and stopped in my tracks to turn and face the road sign we had just passed. 'Station Drive'. I was right.

"This is her road." I was almost whispering.

"What number?"

"Not sure, but she sent me a photo so hopefully I'll recognise it."

Turning into Mel's road felt strange. Despite having been invited to stay, I'd always found an excuse not to; and here I was when I suspected she wasn't in. Walking past a parked car, I had to do a double take at my reflection in its darkened windows.

There was a lady approaching with a dog on a lead. A Border collie that was bouncing and very excited. Its tail wagged enthusiastically as it got closer to us and it started to bark in a non-threatening way.

"What a beautiful dog," I said to the lady.

"Thank you," she replied and stopped to chat. "You can fuss him if you like, he's very friendly," she added.

"Hello boy," I said, as I squatted at his level and allowed him to sniff my hand, before embarking on a full-blown fuss.

"Who are you staying with?" the lady asked.

"Oh, I think we're a little lost actually," Sam said.

"We're looking for a hotel, but I think we got off the train a stop too early."

"Oh, you're in the wrong place if you're looking for a hotel. Sorry, but you won't find one around here."

Glancing over at the house beside us, I detected signs of a struggle. Sam noticed too.

"Best we get back to the station and wait for the next train. I think you're right; we got off too early, sweetheart. I should have listened to you." Sam was play-acting.

"We'll find something, somewhere. How frequent are the trains? Perhaps it would be better to find a taxi?"

Sam and I could not take our attention away from

the track marks over an otherwise well-kept lawn. Noting our interest, it was this woman's chance to share her views on the matter.

"Such a shame. Mel takes such good care of her garden and some creep drove over it in his van. Backed right up to her front door and churned it all up."

"That's awful. When was this?" I said.

"Night before last. I don't sleep that well and I heard the van and a scream. By the time I looked out, it was driving away."

A scream. Mel. Oh no!

"Your friend, is she okay?"

"Well, that's just it. I know she went to London to meet up with a couple of old friends. I think the three of them used to work together. I saw her come home, because I was walking the pooch. But she's not there now."

"Did your friend mention she was going anywhere else once she'd got back from London?"

No. Before she went to London we had arranged to have a coffee the morning after she'd got back."

"But she didn't turn up?"

"I'm really worried."

"Have you reported this to the police?"

"Yes. But I don't think they were that interested, to be honest."

"I think you have every right to be worried. Maybe you should speak to them again, especially if she's not back yet."

"Here, take these," Sam said, as he handed the lady two business cards. "If you don't get any help from them give us a ring, or text one of us, and we'll see if we can get you some news coverage. Too many people go missing and nothing is done about it these days. Let's get something put in motion."

"Oh, that would be fantastic. I'll ring them when we get in. I'm glad someone cares. Now, where are you two heading?"

"Great Yarmouth."

"Oh, you have got off too early. If you head back to the station there should be another train along shortly. If you don't want to wait that long the taxi firms leave their cards on the noticeboards. Either way, your best bet's to head back to the station."

"Thanks."

"Listen, let us know how you get on later. We'd be relieved to know your friend is safe, or may be able to help in some way if she is missing.

Lori, would you please phone our boss, just to check if he'd be up for running the story?" This wasn't a request. It was an order. An urgent one at that.

"Just one thing. Would you be prepared to give us your name please?"

"Mandy. Mandy Wiseman. I live over there," the lady replied and pointed to her house.

We had found a possible witness and a possible crime scene. Both situations required urgent attention. I excused myself and made the call in private.

Boss picked up on the third ring. I explained the situation and he said he'd send forensics along immediately; apparently, he had already dispatched a team into the area and they were close. I wasn't sure where his resources were coming from and wasn't sure I wanted to know. Something was telling me he was using a private forensics company.

Progress.

"I hope your friend is okay, Mandy. Our boss is happy to run the story if need be," I assured her.

"Oh, wait a minute. I have a photo. Hang on." Mandy fumbled with her jacket pocket.

"Here."

Staring back from the image on Mandy's phone was a selfie Mel took with Jen and me. Sadness pricked at my heart as I was drawn back into the memory of that moment. Consciously pulling myself together and finding composure I didn't feel, I forced myself back to the here and now. Mandy was speaking.

"This one," Mandy was saying, "died in that train crash. This one was in that car crash that made the news and now Mel is missing." Tears filled her eyes.

"Mel never did mention much about her London life, but I recognised their pictures. I sure hope she's not mixed up in something bad."

"If you could send your photo to my number that would be really kind. It would add a very personal touch to my story and I would ensure you were thanked for providing it."

Eager to get away, Sam started to take control of the conversation.

"Mandy, you have been very informative. Thank you for your time. Please phone one of us if you get more information, won't you? Doesn't matter what time."

Mandy nodded.

"We need to get going for now, but if it's okay with you, we would like to pop back and see you in a couple of days or so?" Sam's eyebrow rose in anticipation of an answer.

"Yes. I'd like that. Perhaps next time you would like to join me for a coffee at the house?"

"That would be lovely. Thank you," I said.

"Mandy, don't take no from the police. They should be taking this seriously."After a brief farewell, we left Mandy to the rest of her day, whatever that might be. I suspected there would be a lot of chatting over coffee and speculating what Mel was into and what had happened to her. Perhaps Mandy would glean some information from her neighbours. Then again, perhaps not.

Sam and I walked in silence until we were sure we were out of Mandy's earshot. Turning back briefly, I made sure that she hadn't followed us.

"Jesus, she's just shown us an image with me in it. She physically pointed at my face and said I was dead. Not a single sign of recognition that that image was of me. So weird," I announced.

"She believes you're dead," Sam said, looking at me. "Belief is a powerful thing," he added.

"I'm done with this place for the day. Can we go to our hotel now? I'm cranky, thirsty, hungry and in need of a shower."

"And in what order would Madame like those things resolved?"

# CHAPTER EIGHTEEN

Luck had been on our side when we returned to the station. With just ten minutes until the next train to Great Yarmouth, we sat and read information about the swing bridge that had originally been commissioned in the 1840s. The current bridge was built in about 1902 because of the need for two tracks. It was still in operation today. An amazing feat of engineering.

Despite having slept on the train, fatigue was setting in. Sam seemed to still have plenty of energy and I was reminded of how apt he was at hiding how he was feeling. When we arrived in Great Yarmouth he ordered a taxi, as I was wearing my heart on my sleeve; I'd made it more than plain I was too tired to walk. Our early arrival at the hotel, we'd been assured, wouldn't be an issue; our room would be ready. While Sam sorted through the paperwork with the pretty receptionist at the desk, I emptied change into a vending machine like I was some sort of Vegas hotshot. Fully stocked with varying soda drinks and chocolate bars, I had a renewed smile on my face.

Climbing the stairs to our room, Sam could not contain his excitement, apparently loving the seaside nostalgia. He was full of childhood stories and family memories of similar places, and I wasn't sure how much of it was an act. It was a big show in a loud voice to make people notice us.

Opening the door, he stood back and let me enter our room first. Had he not put the idea of 'seaside nostalgia' into my head, I would have hated it immediately. Spacious, old-fashioned, yet warm and cosy. Lovely, large bed. It was all a bit over the top, but we had to make this home for the next two weeks.

"You take the first shower, princess. I've ordered food, so will wait for room service."

"You sure, pumpkin?"

"Go on, before I change my mind," he said, giving me a cheeky wink.

I didn't need telling again because I was done with feeling dirty. Tension had built across my shoulders and I already had a headache. Standing under a hot shower was just what I needed.

\*\*\*

Wrapped in a complimentary towelling robe, I emerged from our en-suite feeling much better. Sam took his turn and I waited for the food. Standing at the window, I allowed my mind to drift back to the interviews with the man that had haunted my sleep for so many years.

He was the poorest example of our species that could walk this earth and I had looked him in the eye and held his gaze. Never did I think I would meet a soul as dark as his, let alone attempt to understand it. Silently I prayed, to whoever might listen, for Mel's safety and Jen's recovery. I was miles away, because I didn't hear the bathroom door or Sam walk up behind me. His gentle touch was enough to startle me and I jumped.

"Hey, princess. Come here." He turned me around and held me until someone was knocking on our door.

"Room service," a voice beamed from the other side.

I let Sam deal with the welcome intrusion and began to shift furniture about. Placing a tall vase of fake flowers on the floor, I moved the circular table away from the corner and positioned a chair and the dressing table stool around it. I would not eat from my lap. This charade made Sam laugh, but I did not care. He wheeled our meals over and I busied myself with setting the small table. It was only just big enough to accommodate the two of us, but I made it work.

We started with the plates of fried breakfast. Despite feeling that hunger might well consume me, I didn't think I could possibly finish such a large plate of food but I would give it my best shot. There was no doubt that Sam would do it justice; never had I known someone eat like him and still look so trim.

We ate in silence and that was somehow comforting. Feeling full, I stood and poured two cups of coffee. Placing them on our small table, I took the opportunity to brush

Sam's shoulder with my hand and leaning in, I placed my cheek on his head and rested there for a moment. The warmth of the moment touched my heart in a way I didn't expect and tears formed. Fighting them back, I composed myself and returned to my seat. It hadn't gone unnoticed. Sam reached across the little table for my hand and I placed mine into his. He was also searching for my eyes, but I wouldn't make eye contact with him right now. I could feel the burn of his on my face, but I knew the tears would come if our eyes locked.

"Princess, look at me."

I looked everywhere but where he wanted me to look.

Standing, but not letting go of my hand, Sam moved around the little table and squatted beside me. With his free hand, he cupped my face and turned it to face him. He was not going to give me a choice. I made eye contact with him and the tears fell. There was no holding them back. They were tears for Mel, tears for Jen, tears for all the other women that Ashbeck had mutilated, but they were also tears because I felt so overwhelmed. The elation of being in love, the happiness, excitement, the newness; the anger that someone you locked up had escaped and tried to kill you and your friends, the uncertainty, the anger, the danger, the fear.

I looked away for the slightest of moments.

"Don't you turn away from me, princess. You need to do this and it needs to be with me. You know what you have to do, don't you?"

I nodded. Sam needed me to tell him why I was upset. He needed me to 'open up' about my 'inner feelings' because I might share something important.

"I need to blow my nose first though, please?"

Without breaking eye contact, Sam reached for a napkin and handed it to me.

"Here, use this. No blowing, just wipe it for now.

Okay. You poured us the coffee and put the mugs on the table. You then touched my shoulder. Why did you do that?"

"What, touch your shoulder? Suddenly, I'm not allowed to touch you?" I was defensive.

"Don't get defensive. I love that you touched my shoulder and you can do it at any time. That's not what I'm asking. Let me ask you another way. Er. We have been touching each other and hugging one another practically non-stop since you walked into the station two nights ago. What was different about that time? You touched my shoulder, touched your cheek on my head and it did something to you emotionally. That's what we need to talk about, princess."

"I know," I said and gave him a smile.

The silence between us was a long one. Sam was done talking and was waiting patiently for me to open up to him. His eyes were kind and my heart was aching for him to hold me close. I knew he would, but not until this part was over.

"While we sat eating our food in silence, it was like there was this invisible comfort blanket wrapped around me, Sam. I felt warm, protected, loved. There wasn't one little bit of awkwardness, despite the silence and that was so lovely. When I had poured the coffee and put the mugs on the table, I touched your shoulder as a silent thank you. At that very moment, I felt the need to place my cheek on your head. I don't know why. But the moment I felt your warmth on my cool face, I had a rush of emotion that was rather overwhelming. The emotion wasn't just to do with you and I, it was fear for Mel, Jen and Ashbeck's other victims. It was anger that he'd escaped from prison and an overwhelming sickening feeling that I'd not told you something important. The trouble is I have no idea what that might be. It's just something I'm sensing."

"Okay, we need to try and work out what that might be. We'll work on it later. I have a copy of the file and we will need to go over it together, maybe that will prompt your memory. Maybe it wont. What I do know is the file isn't complete. What I'd be interested in knowing is what you think is missing."

I just sneered. I really didn't want to go through that file, to see the images I knew would be there. To revisit.

"Can I please blow my nose now?"

Sam nodded, stood and kissed the top of my head.

"It's an overwhelming situation; it's going to be a tough two weeks."

With hunger pangs finally beginning to subside, my mind drifted to Jen. Her critical condition was of great concern and I really wanted to visit her, despite having been told I couldn't. Making a mental note to question that boundary if she woke up, I turned my attention to Mel. Missing and possibly at the mercy of Ashbeck. That thought was too much to bear; I so desperately wanted to find her. It was for Mel that I would put myself through viewing that file. At some point that morning I suspected that Sam would share his thoughts too and he needed as much information as possible to get the full picture. I had my own idea of what we were in the middle of and it reeked of revenge.

Watching Sam clean his plate and picking at my leftovers, my mind drifted to how I had cheated death for the second time in four years. Selfishly, I wished that we could have had a better start to our relationship. As soon as I'd thought it, I hated myself for even thinking that way. We were together, weren't we? Shouldn't I be grateful for that? Wasn't that more than my friends had right now?

"Walls have ears. Let's take a walk on the beach. It'll clear our heads and give us privacy to talk."

\*\*\*

Stepping out from the hotel, it wasn't many minutes until we had the privacy we craved and felt that we could speak openly.

"From everything you have told me, I think it is fair to begin with Ashbeck having a narcissistic personality disorder. By all accounts, he has the ability to communicate well enough to manipulate a whole team of people into supporting him and getting involved in his crimes. He will do whatever it takes to get that support, because it is a means to his endgame. He has, therefore, the capability to present himself within society as sociable, approachable and friendly. Despite the atrocious crime that placed him in prison, he was the model prisoner.

"His crimes were traumatic, both physically and psychologically. He achieved sexual gratification through mutilation of his victims and didn't worry about leaving his DNA evidence. What I can't pinpoint right now is what causes the need to act out his routines. What happened in Ashbeck's past to trigger his behaviour? What drives him? What turned him evil? What is his endgame now?"

Listening to Sam, I realised what I had missed telling him and it was something important. Very important. I had tried so hard to forget Ashbeck's final act with each of his victims that, when it became so important to remember it, I hadn't.

"Sam, I've remembered what I need to tell you. And I'm so sorry I left this out. I have purposefully put it to the back of my mind all these years, but I think it might be important."

"Go on."

"I looked into this at the time, but didn't come up with anything that linked to anything beyond tarot cards. Ashbeck certainly never hinted at what it meant to him."

Sam stopped walking, grabbed my arm and turned me to face him. He has a stern look that unsettled me.

"What card and where does he place it?"

"Does the ace of spades mean anything to you?"

"It speaks volumes to me. I wish you had told me that yesterday, princess."

"I'm sorry. Like I say, I've spent years trying to forget this case."

Feeling foolish that I had forgotten about the card, I knew I now needed to find the courage to verbalise what Ashbeck did with it. Perhaps my withholding of this information had been my way of distancing myself from what might be happening to Mel.

"The ace of spades was his calling card. The final part of his modus operandi." Finally making tear-filled eye contact with Sam, I continued. "He placed it in the mutilated genitalia of his victims."

"Jesus!"

"Mel dealt with the psychological impact he had on his victims. She held each of their hands through the examinations. She sat with them before their operations and was there when they came around from the anaesthetic. Mel saw their wounds, witnessed their pain and was there every time one of them wanted to end their life. If Mel knows Ashbeck is behind her abduction, she knows what's coming. She knows he will mutilate her in the same way."

"Did he ever mention Vietnam?"

After thinking about the question, I shook my head. "Not to my knowledge. Why do you ask?"

"Some American platoons left the ace of spades with the bodies of women and children after murdering them and displaying the bodies. Ashbeck is the right age and I wonder if, somehow, he may have been there? We certainly need to look into that possibility."Okay, we are dealing with a manipulative individual, who appears to have employed a team, despite being incarcerated. This shows he has an influential charm that gets him results. On the surface, we can expect him to be well dressed, clean, tidy and organised. He will have surrounded himself with people who feel obliged to protect him, while he despises each and every one of them. This won't be evident to them, or to others watching. He will favour one in particular and this will definitely be evident by the time he spends with him and through responsibilities given. At the first failure, this person will be eliminated and a new person promoted. This will be done early, by Ashbeck himself, in front of others, because in his eyes, it will create fear that he will read as respect. Ashbeck will control the movements of his people and give them tasks and a timescale in which they should be completed, there will be consequences if deadlines are not met. We should look for signs of these consequences. It appears that several operations are running simultaneously and that takes military precision, you know? Planning. This suggests that someone high up in his gang has military experience in covert operations. We know who we are dealing with and know who he has abducted, so have a heads-up with what his next moves may be. The location of his next act is unknown and that's what we need to focus on. We'll discuss that later."

"I saw Ashbeck a couple of times after the trial. He alluded to having a military past but Boss dismissed it."

Sam turned to me and his eyebrows were turned inwards in a frown.

"Full disclosure means you tell me all this in the beginning. Jesus, Kate! He's American?"

"If he is, I am unaware of that fact."

Looking down at my feet I mumbled a thought aloud.

"Perhaps you should ask Boss if he did look into the military claim. I was reassigned and it was made very clear that I should never speak of the case again."

"God damn that man. I know he knows more than he's letting on!" Sam growled. More softly, he added, "Princess, there is nothing in this world that you and I cannot talk about."

"I realise that. Sam, I've never told you I had therapy to help me process what that man did. Part of that process was to help me file away the memory in order that I could move on with my life. Every time I closed my eyes back then, I saw what that man had done to his victims and, right now, I'm struggling to get the images out of my head again. The more I talk about it the worse it's getting. Do you want to know what I learned about the card?"

Sam nodded his response and I continued.

"What I learned is there are fifty-two weeks in a year represented by fifty-two cards in a pack. The year is made up of thirteen lunar months and they are represented by the thirteen cards in a suit and that our four seasons are represented by four suits. Red is feminine and black masculine. The feminine suits represent warmth, positivity, growth. The masculine ones, cold, regressive and negativity. The ace of spades specifically relates to the week of Yule – the first week of winter – and reflects famine or a time of the wolf. It is a time when offerings were made to the dead and associated with the ace of spades, as it represents the death of the year. Death comes to us all at some point, which is why it is the trump card. Within the world of tarot reading this card is known as the sword, which translates to a symbol of war and represents many emblems of death. Of all the cards he could have chosen, he places this card in the vaginas of his victims. He lets them live, but every one of them that we know survived had begged him to kill them. Sam, if you are right about this Vietnam connection, he wouldn't have had access to tarot cards: but he would have had access to playing cards. Am I correct?"

I allowed him a few moments to digest the last part of my statement and started to regulate my breathing because I needed to steady my nerves. He was reassessing his profile and had I been honest in the beginning, he wouldn't have needed to do that.

"I have two scenarios running through my mind right now. The first is that it will be quick, in order to make a statement. The second is not and that he will hold Mel until 21$^{st}$ December. If he's become obsessed with cards to a greater extent than before, the ace of spades is directly associated with that date."

"What scenario scares you the most?" I asked.

"Neither are great. We need her out of there."

Sam reached inside his pocket, retrieved his phone and dialled Phil. He did not answer and Sam ended the call. Less than a minute passed before his phone jumped into life, he answered on the second ring.

"Why did you send us to Yarmouth?" he listened.

"No, Boss! Why Yarmouth? What are you not telling me? You must have a bloody good reason to believe we are needed in a specific place. I know you are withholding something and you need to share that with me now!"

Sam was greeted with the dial tone.

"I have known him almost all my life. I no longer trust him."

Heading up the beach towards the hotel, Sam and I spotted a lone man looking directly at us. We began walking in zigzags across the beach and the man's stare followed us. He was wearing a black hoodie, but rather than having the hood up he was wearing a baseball hat.

"Do you think he has owl eyes on his hood?"

"From his behaviour, I would suggest he has."

"Then I guess we're in the right place."

Not wanting to return to the hotel just yet, we headed towards a café that we'd spotted earlier. Sam ordered another coffee, but I decided on a Coke. I was done with coffee for the day.

We both positioned ourselves so that we could see the entrance to the cafe. It was busy in here and despite most couples choosing to sit facing one another, we sat side by side, neither of us wishing to have our back to the door, for we were both on high alert.

Glancing over to the next table, I noticed this morning's papers stacked for customers to read. The byline immediately gained my attention. Standing, I selected a couple of papers and returned to the table. I pushed one under Sam's nose.

"Take a look at the top story." I looked up at him. "How surreal is that?" I wasn't sure how I should feel about reporting on my own death.

"Did you know about this?" I asked.

Sam shook his head and continued to read. When he looked up at me he paused for a long moment, before returning to the paper without speaking. He turned the pages until he found the story containing his name. The story was connected to mine, but instead of focussing on the newsworthy aspect of the crash, it covered the impact such events had on the families left behind. The fabricated story featured interviews from previous disasters and speculated on how the train crash victims' families might cope, or not cope, as a result of this event. It was a strong, powerful article.

"Drink up," he said. "We need to take a stroll on a deserted beach."

We both finished our drinks. I stood.

"Just popping to the ladies."

"Me too," he said. "Well, the gents," he added with a broad smile.

\*\*\*

A sea breeze kissed our faces as we returned to the beach.

"It's so weird. I don't actually feel in control of my life right now."

"You'll adapt. It takes a little time. Don't forget, we have moments like this to be us," he said as he held out his hand for me. As I took his hand in mine our finger entwined and in that very moment I felt like me. The butterflies in my stomach were back and they were fluttering once more. It took this moment for me to realise that I needed to feel our love, rather than to expect it to happen, because things were so different now. It was not just about our looks, but about the situation, the location and our emotions. Every once in a while, I'd decided, I should close my eyes and imagine, rather than rely on visual prompts. I longed to run my fingers through his hair rather than feel the bare skin of his scalp and wondered if he felt the same about my short hair.

Spontaneity is a wonderful thing and I felt the urge to do something silly. Rather than walking along the beach, I started to push against his side, gradually edging him towards the lapping waves. Allowing me to have my fun, he played along and, to give him his due, he almost let me push him into the water. Instead, he lifted me up and threatened to throw me in. Slightly startled by his strength and the ease in which he lifted me into the air, I pleaded with him not to do it.

"No. No. I'm sorry!" I laughed.

"You're going in," he replied in mock anger, stifling laughter.

Our eyes locked and he placed me down in front of him. Our chemistry pulled us closer to one another and we embraced. Sam slid his hand beneath my top and found my scar. With his other hand, he placed my hand under his shirt and on to the scar where he was shot, and instantly my mind was taken back in time to that awful day and the blood pumping through my fingers as I attempted to stem his bleeding.

"Our scars can play a part in keeping us grounded. When we need to remember who we really are we have them and the memories they hold. You and I have this amazing bond. We have saved each other's life. Not many couples can say that."

I hadn't lingered when my fingers had found his scar when we had made love. I remember touching it and moving on quickly to explore other areas of his body, because I didn't want to think about his blood pumping through my fingers during the struggle to save his life. Standing on this beach now, listening to the sound of the waves, the seagulls squawking and feeling his warm breath on my face, we took our time to allow this moment of connection. Powerful moments like this were to become our way of coping; I just didn't know it yet.

Sam turned to face the parade of hotels on the seafront. "Seaside nostalgia. I love it."

Smiling at him, I began to run up the beach towards the road.

"Race you," I called back.

Despite having a good head start Sam was soon chasing my tail and pretending to trip me up, grabbing at my waist and laughing. Another stolen moment of fun in a very serious world. Reaching the pathway first and extremely out of breath, I turned to face him. He span me around and placed his arm around my shoulders. Placing mine around his waist, I leaned my head against him. He planted a kiss on the top of my head. Briefly, nothing was wrong within my world.

# CHAPTER NINETEEN

Hearing my fake name spoken aloud by a stranger took me a moment to register that I was being spoken to. Turning, I smiled at the hotel receptionist.

"I'm sorry. I was miles away. You were saying?"

"I knew I recognised you the moment I set eyes on you," she said, waving a newspaper in the air. "Why didn't you say you were journalists? I might have something that'll interest you."

Wondering if she'd seen through my disguise from the image Boss had given the papers, I hoped that the relief I felt wasn't evident.

"Might you?" I said, glancing at my watch. "You have two minutes to convince me."

With a broad smile now spreading over the woman's face, she became instantly nervous.

"Really. Oh. Er. Well. You see, there's been this bloke hanging about. Probably nothing. But he's acting all weird."

"And you think that's newsworthy?"

"Not in itself. No. But I've noticed lots of different

men about. Watching. They are all wearing the same clothes. Kinda like they belong to a club or something."

"Go on," I encouraged.

"There's something about them. I can't put my finger on it what it is, but they are unsettling me."

"You say they wear the same clothes. Explain that part to me."

"These black hoodies with two yellow eyes," with two fingers on her right hand she stabbed at her forehead, "right here."

She had my attention and, making an effort to learn her name, I looked at her badge. Vanessa was written in bold across a gold background. Could this woman be our second key witness? Just how much might she know?

Making eye contact with Vanessa, I responded carefully. I did not want to startle her.

"Okay, Vanessa. This is what we'll do. At the end of your shift come and knock on our door. You and I can go for a walk. We can have a chat then."

Vanessa's excitement couldn't be contained. She reminded me of a child on Christmas morning and I wondered why a woman in her late forties would react in this way. For some reason, this intrigued me. With the other guests there was a level of professionalism, but she appeared to be bursting through those boundaries for my sake. Why did she think I would be interested in her story? Did she know more than she was making out? Was I being set up? Making a mental note to stay vigilant, I bade her goodbye and returned to Sam.

Heading to our room, I noted the frown on his face. I knew he'd heard the entire conversation despite appearing busy with something else. I also knew he wouldn't let me meet with Vanessa without him tailing us. We could trust no one, especially when they threw themselves at us with the very information we were seeking.

Suddenly feeling a craving for chocolate, I hoped we had some in our room. I had something else planned for starters though and as soon as we reached our door and were inside the room, I pounced on Sam. Responding how I wanted and needed him to, we made frantic love. There was no time for romance, sensual touch, or lingering in favourite parts, just an urgent need to feel alive and wanted. One more stolen moment in this messed-up world in which we found ourselves immersed.

"I know you will follow me later, when I talk to Vanessa. So, thank you, pumpkin."

"When we get back I'll run us a bath. You can raid the minibar again and we can sit in bubbles and steam. How does that sound?"

"Perfect," I said and planted a kiss on his forehead.

Our mobiles sounded simultaneously.

"Boss," Sam announced.

"Anonymous," I responded.

"You first," he said as I hit answer.

"Hello. Lori Peterson."

I listened intently as the woman on the other end gave me a low-down on how her day had evolved. Agreeing and disagreeing in what I hoped were all the correct places, I gave her my full attention and promised that Sam and I would visit her soon. I thanked her for her time and for letting me know so promptly.

Turning to Sam, I was not sure if I was pleased that something had finally started to happen, or if my anger at Phil had peaked even higher.

"Mandy Wiseman. She has given her statement, quite literally five minutes after we left her. From her description, to Phil in person. Two other officers were also present, from her description one was Jade. He seems to have his own private army going on, Sam. What's that all about?"

"I'm going to seriously lose it with the man – what, he's following us now? And what the hell is Jade doing tagging along? Since when was she part of all this?"

"Do you trust her?"

"All she's done in the past is create the fake identities that have allowed us to go undercover. To my knowledge, she's not an investigator – but what do I know? In all honesty, I know nothing about her. She was sceptical of you though, princess. Right now, I don't trust my own shadow."

"Something's shifted between your last undercover job and this one." I was pointing my finger at him. "Phil revealed your identity to Jade this time and he'd never done that before. She took great pleasure in letting you know she knew every little detail about you and about us. Some of it displeased her too."

"And that has been bothering me. Whatever Phil is up to, I think she knows a little about it, or they are both knee-deep."

"Do you think they are involved in whatever is going on? Do you think it is that bad?"

"I can't quite put my finger on what's going on, princess, but I know it's not good. If he's involved then I hope he ends up dead."

"You don't mean that!"

"Don't I," he said and it wasn't a question, more a statement. The cold look in his eyes conveyed to me that he was quite serious and I found myself wondering if he would pull the trigger himself. I shook this thought from my consciousness, there were enough dark images emerging from this case as it was; I didn't need to start imagining others.

"What else did Mandy say?"

"There's been door-to-door enquiries, but not everyone was in. She took it upon herself to visit them after they'd got home from work. It turns out that one of them has CCTV footage of the kidnapping. They copied the file and Mandy has a copy for us. Mandy mentioned hoodies with yellow eyes! The originals are being collected by the rest of our team later. She is holding us to that coffee and has invited us for ten tomorrow. Apparently, she is also baking us a lemon drizzle cake. She asked me if we were really journalists or working undercover and she said she'd though of something that might interest us, but didn't want to tell us over the phone."

"Jesus! She said all that? She has us sussed out. I bet she's the sort of neighbour that keeps a book with everyone's comings and goings in it. Lemon drizzle. Lovely. Text her 10:30," he replied.

"One more thing. She said that Mel gave her an envelope a few months back in case anything happened to her. She'd just remembered about it. She didn't want to open it but didn't trust the police officer. Would we open it with her tomorrow?"

"Figures."

"And that Mel was wearing one of these awful hoodies too."

Suddenly I had Sam's full attention and his eyebrows were alternating between frowning and being raised. This revelation unsettled me too. Was Mel somehow involved in all of this? She was so passionate about helping Ashbeck's victims I couldn't see how she would be.

"Okay, pumpkin. You need to phone Boss back."

Sam took a deep and steadying breath, dialled and waited.

"Hi Boss. Yes... Yes... Nope... Okay. Now tell me how you knew to send us to Great Yarmouth. I know you have info you've not shared."

It was no use asking. Sam had no control over when Boss would end the call and he had done so abruptly. It was my turn to raise my eyebrows in anticipation of hearing what Boss had had to say.

"He's holding out on something, princess. I know he is. He has confirmed that Mel is in the CCTV footage and that everyone was wearing one of those bloody hoodies. What does that mean? Why owl eyes?"

"They might not be owl eyes. That's what they look like to us, but they may well be another animal. Maybe time will tell."

Both our phones alerted us to new messages. They were identical. Boss had sent a report through for us to read.

"Read, digest, discuss," Sam advised. "That way we are more likely to have different suggestions, opinions and, therefore, avenues for further discussions and detective work."

"Okay," I agreed and actually thought it a good idea.

Going to press tomorrow was the story of Sam's demise. Lori Peterson would report on how he was killed in the line of duty during a drug raid in the city. Three bullets had entered his body and he had died in hospital during the night. His devastated son had no comment at this time, other than to request that his family were left alone to grieve in peace. James Peterson would report, using historic police fatalities, on how this affected the family and community.

After reading the articles in the paper that morning about myself, I had been expecting something along these lines for Sam. There was an actual drug raid and shooting reported on the national news, so Phil had tapped into this resource for the benefit of our investigations.

More than anything I wanted to find Mel and to receive news that Jen was awake and responsive. Normality could then resume: I so longed for normality.

Two weeks Boss had given us. Was that enough time? What happened if we ran out of time? I couldn't think about that.

As I opened the second document, an uneasiness started to creep into my consciousness. It had been reported that a hooded youth had managed to get on to Jen's ward and had brandished a gun to her head. He had been arrested. His jumper had had eyes on the hood. It was bold to have snuck into a secured ward and I was sure that he was now involved in a good cop, bad cop interview – I hoped this routine was leaning more towards bad cop, for he had threatened my friend, an officer – and he was in a whole heap of trouble. I was also sure that an investigation was heading straight for the hospital too.

Fear for my two friends was intensifying each hour that passed. I needed to read on.

Phil had contacted Yarmouth police, in connection with Mel. He conveyed the details he'd shared with them and that they were taking this matter seriously. He had informed them that James and Lori Peterson were working for him directly as undercover agents and that all press releases were authorised through him personally. As I continued to read, it was evident Phil had done some name-dropping and had asked that any leads were shared with Sam and I, and that this was a direct order from the commissioner himself. If confirmation was required, then Phil suggested they ring the commissioner personally. We were to be kept informed of all progress on the case from their end and our phone numbers had been provided. This was a two-way deal. If we had a major breakthrough in the case we were to contact Andy Preston on the provided number.

Wow. Glancing over at Sam with an array of questions for him, I was relieved to see that he was waiting for me to finish reading.

"What do you make to that?" I asked.

"We are only getting fragmented information," and his comments surprised me. "For Boss to be this thorough and to share that we are working for him is massive. He has had to trust someone in order that we get info and he doesn't trust easily."

"I'm scared for my two friends," I said, holding back tears.

"I know. There's nothing I can say that would make that go away right now. Maybe we can use that to our advantage. This is a very personal situation for you and you want a good resolution. We both do. There's something we need to think about later and that's who you three have upset. There's a couple of things I want to try because they've worked for me in the past."

"Okay. Like what?"

"You'll see.

Something doesn't sit right with me, princess, but I can't put my finger on it." He looked at me a long moment. "Right now, you are the only person I trust in all of this."

I was startled by this comment because it was so out of character for him to be judgemental, especially about his colleagues.

"You have known Boss for so many years. For you to not trust him is massive. Is it a gut feeling you have or is it based on more than that?"

"He keeps saying how big a deal all this is. How does he know it's big? He knows something he's not sharing and I don't like that." Getting up, he moved to the window and cracked open the curtain just enough to spy through the gap.

"Talk to me, pumpkin. Come and sit because together we need to analyse."

Disheartened at the prospect, Sam came over. Placing two chairs so that they faced each other, we sat close enough so that our knees were touching.

"Why the lack of trust?"

The silence in the room was speaking volumes to me and I began to feel spooked. Sam was starting to scare me.

"I've not done this work for years and here we are, plunged into a situation with no real briefing, or expectations, or information. We are both being forced to live a lie. Our deaths have been faked, so who would know if something happened to us both?" Finally, he made eye contact. "That's a dangerous position we're in, princess."

"We need a burner phone. Do you know Charlie's number? I think you should phone him just in case Phil has told him you are dead."

"I know his number. That's actually a good point. He wanted to speak with me about a private matter anyhow. This shit about the commissioner," he continued, "if that's true then I am convinced we are in deeper than we could ever have imagined."

"Maybe it's his way of putting the pressure on to get co-operation?" As the words escaped my mouth I doubted them.

"In that case, why tell us he's involved? We don't need to know about political agendas to get co-operation, we just need the contacts. He's messing with my head because he knows how I think and react." Looking up at me, he added, "We worked together back in the day and that information would have blown our minds, and he knows it."

Nodding, I stood and walked to the minibar. Selecting two miniature Scotch bottles and glasses, I poured drinks and left Sam to his thoughts for a few moments.

"Here, drink this. I think we need to be careful how much we drink because we need to stay responsive and alert – but one isn't going to hurt."

"Cheers!" he said, and he downed it in one gulp.

Sipping mine, I allowed the warmth to spread down my throat and into my stomach.

"I have an idea, but not here," and I was quietly pleased with the thought that had just popped into my head. I rummaged in his pocket and removed his phone, placing it with mine under a pillow. Frowning, he complied and followed me out of the door.

Passing through reception, I let Vanessa know we'd be back within the hour.

As we headed back towards the café, I used the cash machine and withdrew some money. Taking the money and squirreling it away, I turned to Sam and took his hand. There were a few people milling about, so I kept my thoughts to myself for now.

"We shouldn't be out without our phones, princess," he whispered in my left ear.

"I know. Why is that exactly?"

"Protocol."

"You're being paranoid about Boss and I'm just taking it a step further, that's all. He knows our every move. I think we're being bugged," I whispered with a hint of anger.

Sam's hand tightened its grip around mine as he pulled me past the café. He quickened his pace and, so I could keep up, I was almost jogging.

"Let's not have this conversation now."

We moved in silence, crossed the road and found a quiet spot on the grass along South Beach Parade. Sitting, huddled together, we began to talk openly and frankly, but our voices remained a whisper.

"This shit is freaking me out. I don't know how you did this for so many years. We've been sent to this place," I paused and gestured with a sweep of my arm, before continuing. "Where on earth do we start with locating my friend?"

"That's simple, princess. The bloke that was watching

us earlier is still watching us. He knows exactly who we are. We play him at his own game. We follow him."

"How does he know we are here? That's what I can't work out. We're dead, remember."

"Me either. We have changed everything to be undetected. Something stinks. Come on," Sam said and got up.

Offering me his hand, he made a public display of pretending to struggle to get me to my feet. Laughing, we headed straight towards the man that had been watching us since our arrival.

Sam had made a decision. He was done with the lack of information. By the time we reached the road the man had gone. We headed straight for the nearest phone shop, which wasn't far. There were three other customers, so we browsed until the assistant was free. We ordered two pay-as-you-go phones and ensured they were both loaded with plenty of credit. With a new determined look in his eyes, the Sam I knew and loved was emerging through his changed identity, and I couldn't have been happier to see him. Feeling reassured, I felt there was a new spring my step and that I was ready for whatever the day had to offer. This was settling for me and I began to feel more confident. Perhaps it was just us getting used to our new situation. But I felt that there was more to it than that. We'd worked together for three years, our every move could be predicted by one another, our moods instantly recognised. Just a look, or a simple gesture, had become a private language between us. It was all falling back into place. The familiarity between us was emerging through the mess we had been dumped in. The trust.

Once out of the shop, the first thing Sam did was to send a cryptic text to Charlie. *BYAM BBMFIC 121 PCM TSTB AWC.* When he showed me, it blew my mind.

"And he'll know what that means?"

"Yep. Just you wait and see."

"And what does it say?"

"Between you and me. Big bad motherfu\*\*er in charge. One to one. Please call me. The sooner the better. After while, crocodile."

Shaking my head and smiling to myself at the fact that Sam would know that text language existed, let alone use it, I felt slightly ashamed of myself at being left behind with the times. I'd not a clue what that message was about.

"The first and last set of letters is how we know a message is from each other. The middle bit tells Charlie not to trust Phil and that he needs to phone me in private as soon as possible. We used it to leave notes that his mother wouldn't understand."

"Amazing," I said, as Sam's new phone buzzed into life.

Charlie and Sam talked at length, filling each other in on what was occurring. I considered walking away to give them some privacy, but Sam grabbed my arm and mouthed 'stay' at me. Their call had lasted ten minutes already and they didn't sound as if they were anywhere near finished talking. I signed to him that I was popping into the shop to buy a drink and he indicated he'd like one too.

The store was empty apart from those who worked there, so it didn't take me long to get back to him. He was just finishing his call with Charlie. After he'd hung up, he turned to me and was momentarily lost for words. Never would I have imagined that he couldn't find words to express himself. There was a first time for everything.

Grabbing my hand and marching me towards our hotel, Sam was taking charge.

"Ask nothing," was all he had said to me.

Arriving in our room, he grabbed a couple of changes of clothes for each of us and shoved them into a rucksack. He entered the bathroom and returned with our washbags. Silence was heavy between us, the moment that had passed between us earlier, which had given me a little reassurance, was long gone. He made no attempt to hide his paranoia.

"Meet with Vanessa now. Find out what she knows. You are not going anywhere with her, so she needs to talk to you out in the open at her desk."

"Come on then. Let's do this."

We headed towards the reception in silence. The desk appeared unmanned, so I rang the bell. No one came and I wondered if we'd missed her because we had popped out. Sam, being taller than me, elevated his height by standing up on the balls of his feet and lent over the desk.

"Jesus!" he shrieked and ran around to the other side of the desk.

Following, I was stopped in my tracks at the sight. Lying motionless on her back, Vanessa's dead eyes stared up at us. Sam was feeling for a pulse, but we both knew it was too late. There was a hole in her forehead and carved into both cheeks was a pentagram, a five pointed star that the modern world associates with black magic. Reaching into my pocket I dialled and requested the police. We waited in silence until they arrived.

I wondered if Vanessa's conversation with me earlier had been overheard and that her knowledge had got her killed. I had failed to protect a possible witness and I had to live with that.

Sam was processing the scene with his eyes and taking images with his phone. He had already photographed everything that he though relevant by the time the police had arrived. There didn't seem to be any signs of a struggle and whoever was involved had made a reasonable job at cleaning up after themselves. There was a small trace of, what looked like, brain matter on the wall. Sam had captured that also.

Each moment that passed felt like an eternity until, finally, we heard the sirens getting louder as they approached. I met the two officers at the door. They were very young and I prepared them for what they were about to see. I suggested that they didn't touch anything until forensics had processed the scene. For a moment, I had forgotten I was undercover and Sam came to my rescue. He introduced himself as James Peterson, a retired officer. He explained that he had kept up his first aid and that he had checked for signs of life and there were none.

Upon seeing Vanessa's mutilated face, one of the young officers ran outside and vomited. At least he'd made it outside. I knew from experience that this moment would never leave him. It was his first murder scene. I was sure it wouldn't be his last.

After giving them our details we were allowed to leave. We had been asked to attend the station tomorrow to give our statements. We didn't have any details of the attack, but it was us who had discovered the body.

Picking up the bag he'd packed, Sam took my hand and we walk out of the hotel. I had no idea where we were going, but I knew better than to ask. I gave his hand a tight squeeze and he reciprocated.

# CHAPTER TWENTY

Fighting every instinct to sob, Mel focussed on the positives of her situation. Positives were hard to find but she'd had plenty of time to think of what they could be. She'd found two and was hanging on to them. She was alive and if she didn't sob, she could breathe. The situation which she found herself in, however, was a drastic one. It was making demands on her body that she never expected to experience. Unaware she had been missed and reported missing, she was praying that her friend and neighbour sensed an issue. They had been due to meet for coffee, after all. Mandy Wiseman would notice, she knew she would. She noticed everything. Please God, let Mandy notice me missing.

A searing pain made her head feel like it needed to explode. Stress, dehydration, the tightness of the blindfold or, perhaps, a combination of all these things, were to blame. Despite the cloth gag dripping with spit, her mouth felt so dry. The mattress beneath her had seen better days and she wondered how many women before her had been in this place and what had become of them. She knew what had become of some of the victims because she had been there to piece them back together, psychologically.

The cold, damp air and the soiled mattress were reminders that she had survived this ordeal so far. Her pride was damaged, of course it was, but she was physically unharmed. Despite this, Mel could not help but wonder if she might die in this wretched place.

Hours had passed since her last visit from one of them. So far, she had received four different visitors: each of them mocked and intimidated her before threatening to rape her. Mel said a silent prayer that she would avoid this fate. Fear engulfed her, however, because she was very much aware of who her captor was. Her first visitor had made that quite clear. 'He' hadn't visited yet and she dreaded the moment that he did. His revenge on her would be unbearable, she was sure of that. Her previous visitor had been the most violent so far. He had lit a torch and stood it on the floor so that she could see. Producing a knife, he had slit her blouse open to reveal her bra. Holding the knife to her throat, he had run his tongue along her stomach, from the waistband of her jeans up to her breasts, laughing at her. Fear gripped every cell in her body as she'd anticipated his next move.

The relief was almost overwhelming when he'd produced a bottle of water from behind him and untied her gag in order that she could drink. She had gulped the entire bottle and thanked him for his kindness. There was no food. She had learned not to speak again because it resulted in a slap around the face. She'd tasted blood because she had bitten her tongue as a result of the force. Producing fabric from his waistband, this excuse of a man replaced her gag and blindfold. Suddenly plunged into darkness, Mel felt her heart rate quicken. She listened acutely in an attempt to predict his next move.

"Later. Who knows, I might have something for you when I return," he'd said to Mel, as he'd walked towards the exit.

Within a short time, Mel needed to urinate. She had an ache in her back that she hoped wasn't the start of a kidney infection. Fever was beginning to make an appearance too and this wasn't a good sign for her. Kidney infections were a regular issue for her at times of far less stress than she was now enduring. Drifting in and out of sleep, she was aware that she felt damp and, at some point, her bladder must have given way. She was now soaked in urine that was starting to smell. Her sodden clothes were sticking to her clammy skin. There was no way of moving because she was bound at the ankles and her hands were bound behind her back. She was tethered to the wall behind her. In the beginning, when she'd had more energy, she'd managed to shift her position so she was leaning on the wall – only to discover it to be cold and damp. She'd then struggled to move away from it.

Minutes felt like hours in this silent, damp, cold, dark place. She felt a shiver run through her body.

With every breath exhaustion grew until it engulfed her. Allowing herself to drift closer to sleep, she wondered if it would be better to just give up and die. Surely it was better than the fate that awaited her. She had given his victims a reason to live and she knew he would make her beg to die. She didn't want to give him that satisfaction, that power over her.

Hours must have passed because when a sound woke her the air felt warmer. Mel's senses were on high alert, especially her hearing. The slightest noise usually meant a visitor. Feeling her heart rate pick up pace, she took a steadying breath. Then another.

A burst of light entered as the door swung open. Although Mel couldn't see, something felt different.

Rushing to her, Eddie SandersEddie began removing her binds. First the blindfold. As her eyes adjusted, the familiar sight of her boyfriend was overwhelming. The relief must have been evident on her face. She was safe. He had found her. Her hero.

Silently, Eddie set to work. From his bag, he produced a crude looking tool and some ink. Mel's eyes widened and she shook her head at him. He was part of all this. How? Why? She had trusted him. She thought he was different.

With the tool, Eddie cut into Mel's stomach. Not too deep. Just enough. He carved a thirteen-step, unfinished pyramid that was now gleaming with blood. It covered the majority of her stomach. Pouring the ink into the wounds and rubbing it in stung her, but she didn't flinch. She refused to give him that satisfaction. If he removed her gag she would spit in his face.

The master himself would finish the artwork. They were his orders.

"You stink, you dirty bitch," Eddie scowled.

Mel refused to make eye contact. They were done.

"Okay lads. She's all yours. I'm done here."

Thirteen hooded men entered. The first used a knife to remove her ankle binds and jeans. Somehow, she knew what was about to happen and she willed her mind to leave her body. She would not be mentally present while she was being attacked. Each of the animals took their turn. When they were done, Eddie returned and retied the ropes that bound her ankles and wrists. Without a word, he walked back through the door, closed it and turned the lock.

# CHAPTER TWENTY-ONE

Jen remained motionless in her hospital bed, the machines continuing to beep and buzz. Craig, sitting dutifully beside her, was now allowed to hold her hand. Not that she could feel him doing it. But, somehow, it made him feel a little better.

It didn't matter how hard he tried, whatever he did, there was just no response from her. He'd tried talking to her and stroking her hand. He'd even tried singing. When he though no one was looking, he even stroked her face. He wasn't supposed to do that and within moments a nurse had come along and had asked him to stop.

There was no indication that she knew he was there. She showed him no sign that things were going to be okay.

He couldn't stop looking at her battered face either and was dreading the scan results. How could there not be any brain damage with all the bruising and swelling she had?

Punching the gunman had resulted in fracturing a couple of knuckles in his right hand, but it had been worth it. He'd certainly no regrets there, even if he did get into a little bit of trouble. He was now sporting a plaster cast, but he knew his pain was nothing to the pain his wife was going through.

"Please pull through this, my lovely," he whispered.

***

Jen knew Craig was there, she could feel his presence, but somehow could not reach him. Why can't I talk? Move? What's wrong with me? Why can't I even open my eyes? I keep trying but they don't seem to work. My ears work, why nothing else? I can hear voices. Oh, maybe that's not a good thing. No Jen, pull yourself together, they're not that kind of voices. Think lady, think. What is the last thing you can remember before this? Before what seems like a hospital. Am I in hospital? Yes, I think I'm in hospital. Oh. Oh no. I was driving home from seeing Kate and Mel. The car behind me. The driver with the hood. The man who pulled me from the car. The man with no face.

The heart rate monitor suddenly soared and the nurse assigned to Jen was suddenly attentive. Jen's eyes opened momentarily.

"Jen! I'm just going to move your left arm and place a pillow under it. I think it'll make you more comfortable."

Jen heard the rustling of bedding but couldn't feel the woman, she assumed was a nurse, move her arm. Suddenly frightened and confused, she concentrated very hard on opening her eyes again.

"Welcome back, Jennifer," the elated voice sounded.

"Craig is here, right by your side," she assured her.

Within moments, a whole team of specialists were at her side. It had taken every effort for her to open her eyes and they were tightly closed once again.

"We need to reduce her sedation gradually," a male voice said.

"Her reactions are not going to improve much until then," he continued.

Various people tested her reflexes and shone torches into her eyes. They informed her of their every move. Jen couldn't feel anything. But she could hear the whole lot.

What if I'm paralysed? Jen thought, before drifting back to sleep.

# CHAPTER TWENTY-TWO

Stepping out of the building on to the street, Sam and I head towards the pier, thinking that it would be quiet at this time of the day; but we were very wrong. People buzzed about with excitement. Some tucked into ice cream or burgers – one lad was screaming at his mother for both.

"See, there's a reason right over there why I never wanted kids, Sam," I said laughing.

"See, you bring it up, but I bet you won't actually have a proper conversation about it."

"I'm glad I didn't have them with my ex, though. Just imagine trying to explain that Daddy ran off with their grandmother. How damaging would that have been, hey?"

"I agree, but back when you made that decision you didn't know they would be doing what they did. I think you made that decision many years before you even got married."

"What I like about us is that there are still some things we have left to discover about one another," I said, because he was right, I was not ready to have this conversation and I was already regretting my flippant comment.

Despite the time of year, the town remained busy and I guessed that was good for the area. I used this to my advantage to change the subject.

"We need to find somewhere quiet," I announced, as we walked hand in hand.

"You're not wrong," he agreed.

The final rays of sun were getting lower in the sky and would soon disappear altogether. Neither of us had eaten since breakfast and despite the vulgar scene we'd just witnessed, we were getting hungry. It did seem to become a cop reaction, to be honest, to crave food after seeing such sights.

It was time to reassess our next move, so we bought fish and chips and returned to the beach. The sound of pebbles beneath our feet was fast becoming the sound of privacy for us. Our place of retreat. Of safety. The tide was reasonably high but, without much light remaining, most people were heading away. Selecting our place, we sat and ate. With no sauces to add to my chips I'd had to settle for vinegar.

"We can't go and see Mandy tomorrow," I announced.

"I was thinking the same. There's too much risk. We know we're being followed and we can't lose another witness."

"I think it better if you phone and cancel, you're stronger than me." Leaning in close, I whispered into his ear, "You can play bad cop."

"Perhaps. Perhaps not. We risk losing her trust as well you know."

Picking up his burner phone, Sam dialled her number.

"Mandy, it's James Peterson. Do you remember meeting me with Lori?"

He listened.

"There's been a major development at our end, but that means it's not going to be possible for us to visit you tomorrow. Would it please be possible for us to reschedule?"

Again, he listened.

"Mandy wants to talk with you," he said, handing me the phone.

"Mandy, hello. How are you today?"

I listened to the voice on the other end of the line.

"I have seen through your disguise. It's your eyes dear, despite your coloured contacts and your cheekbones, they are just the same as on my photo. But don't worry, I can keep such a dangerous secret. For, you see, I have my own secret too. Maybe I will tell you about it someday. Now dear, don't underestimate how much help I could be to you two. If you prefer, I can come and meet with you, rather than you heading over here. I am not frightened of whatever ghosts you are chasing."

"Mandy, I don't know what to say."

"Just find our friend dear."

"We have every intention of doing that."

The line went dead.

Turning towards Sam, tears started to trickle down my cheeks.

"Whatever did she say to you, princess?"

"She knows who I am. She says she can keep such a dangerous secret and that she has secrets of her own she'd like to share with me one day."

"How does she know?"

"My eyes and my cheekbones. What if she's involved?" I added.

"She's not. I got this vibe that we could trust her, princess."

"I'm all out of trust right now. Except for you. I trust you."

"Well that brings me to my conversation with Charlie. We need to talk about him."

I raised my eyebrows.

"He is our eyes on the ground. We don't have enough time for the full story, but cutting it short, he's been spying on Phil for a while. In his home office, the bastard has a box full of black hoodies. Guess what they have on the hoods?"

"No way!"

"Yes way. He has also found a manuscript. He has photographed some pages and will send them to us later. All this time he has been visiting Ashbeck, month after month, and writing a book about the monster. Ashbeck literally has the man eating out of his hands."

"Sam, Charlie is not safe there!"

I am angry with Phil but, moreover, I am scared for Charlie.

"I know. I've told him he has no choice but to go to his mother's until we return. He wasn't impressed with that and had his answer ready for me."

"Will you let her know what's going on?"

"No way, she's the biggest gossip out there, you know that. What Charlie said next blew my mind," he looked up at me before continuing, "so he's joining us here."

Alarmed at this news, my eyes widened and jaw dropped open.

"What could Charlie possibly know to have convinced you that here is safer than anywhere else?"

"He recorded a phone conversation this morning between Phil and Ashbeck. They are in direct contact. He is up to his neck in this."

I nodded, knowing how difficult it was going to be for him. I hoped we could keep him safe here.

"So, the bag you are carrying about. Am I to assume we are staying somewhere other than the hotel tonight?"

"You assume correctly. If you're right about being bugged, it could be the mobiles, the suitcases, or anything that Phil provided. This bag is my own so I know it's clean. How paranoid am I?"

"How paranoid are the both of us? But, hey, we obviously can't trust Phil. We were right about that."

"I am wondering about Mandy's secrets. What do you think they might be, princess?"

"No idea. Once all this is over I might pay her a visit

and find out."

"We have no legitimate leads on Mel's whereabouts. That worries me no end. I think we need to buy ourselves some black hoodies and blend in. Maybe follow some of them about town and see where that leads us. What do you think?"

"I'm not sure I want to go as far as wearing a black hoodie, but yes, we could follow some about. But we do it together."

"Blending in is one of the things we can use to try to get information. It does work, you'll see. You know, I'm proud of you, princess."

His last statement surprised me.

"Well, thanks. And me of you."

And I was glad we had that cleared up.

"Yeah, but I've don't this before. It's a slow process. I'm impressed with how you're holding up. I thought you were going to be as impatient as hell."

"That's so not me, being patient, pumpkin. It's me having complete trust in you. Beneath this hard exterior, I'm as frustrated as hell with this situation."

"Okay. This is what we do. You've maxed out your card at the cashpoint today already. I'm about to do the same. That will be the only trail Phil will have on us. We are going completely off the grid. We'll stay close to here, I spotted some bed and breakfasts up the road we can try. Pay for everything with cash. When it runs out, we go out of the area to get more and head straight back. Once we've found a room, we'll head out and scan the streets for evidence of these men. Vanessa told you she'd seen several 'hanging about', so let's find them."

Sam's phone alerted him to a text. He showed me, but I had no idea what it meant, although I did know it was Charlie. Sam explained that Charlie was packed and ready to leave. His train was in half an hour, so he'd catch up with us when he arrived.

"How come you guys text in code?"

"It's not code. It's just text talk. We started it because the ex was always looking at his phone. She can't get her head around the language, so it gave us privacy."

"And now it's just your thing you do?"

"I guess."

"Sweet."

"Do you wish you'd ever had kids, princess?"

"I decided a long time ago not to. As you know, my adoptive parents weren't great role models to me. I've got no idea about my biological parents, so have no idea what genes I'd be passing on."

"You'd have been a great mum."

"Maybe. But I was never in the right relationship to want to start a family, so that's that. Right. Come on. Let's gather this mess up, find a new place to stay and start scanning streets."

"You just don't want to talk about kids."

"That's the trouble when you start dating someone you know so well. They know you too well," I said, holding out my hand and smiling.

\*\*\*

Walking, hand in hand, with our arms bumping every so often, we exited the beach and started walking some of the backstreets. It wasn't long until we caught up with a hooded figure. Standing in the shadows against a building, we allowed a healthy distance to grow before resuming our trail. We silently hoped we were not being followed and that we were walking straight into a trap. As we twisted and turned through the town, I noted the street names. When the individual disappeared through a door, Sam noted the house number. This was our agreed plan of action. Walking past, we did not detect any activity within because all the curtains were pulled across the windows. Sam wrote the address down in his notebook. Within five minutes, we were following another hooded figure. This one was broader than the first. I wondered if he was carrying a gun and wondered why I didn't get this feeling with the first.

Suddenly, Sam reached out and grabbed my arm, pulling me into the shadows. My heart soared and he placed a finger over his lips to silence me. I could not see what was happening but could tell Sam had visual contact. I took this opportunity to check behind us for any movement in the shadows that might indicate we were being followed. Nothing. I could hear my heart beating and, although I knew it was psychological, my knife scar started to ache.

"Okay. There are two now, so we need to give them space," he whispered.

We stepped back out on to the street and continued. I kept a mental note of the street address and Sam glanced at the house where the two men met. He wrote the number in his book, before passing it to me to write the street name.

We continued this process for two hours. I had no idea how far we'd walked in those two hours, but we had gathered five addresses.

When we returned to our new accommodation we were shown to our room. Sam produced a remarkable quantity of things from his bag, including his personal laptop. Firing it up, he fished out the notebook from his pocket. This would be far easier with the search facilities of a police station, but we were off grid. We could not afford to blow our cover when there were other ways of getting the information needed.

Typing the first address into the system didn't produce the name of the owner of the house. Instead it said that a company entitled Monarch Properties had owned the place for three years. The second address was the same. Looking at one another and entering the third, we were not surprised to learn that it was too. Once the fifth address was entered, we were expecting the same result and we were not disappointed.

Further research would cost money and we had decided to stop using our cards. We needed the information though.

"I'm going to do something I probably shouldn't, princess."

I watched in silence as he typed his ex-wife's card details into the computer. I didn't comment, I didn't judge and moreover I didn't stop him. We needed the information.

The search on the properties took just a few moments. Monarch Properties was the trading name of the owner. The owner was a name so familiar to us both that we were stunned into silence. It couldn't be. We really were in this deeper than we thought. Phil had been right. This was big. Clicking the website link that was provided with the report took us to a page of butterflies that fluttered about. There was no information, just butterflies. A simple search told us they were monarch butterflies.

"We are in danger, princess."

"I know, pumpkin. What now?"

"We need to think."

"Any one of those places could be where they are holding Mel."

"I know, but we can't raid them on our own."

Grabbing a notebook, I drew a grid of boxes. There was a column for everyone involved in this case. I placed each person's name in the top row and started adding information. Sam started this process on his own piece of paper. Two brains were better than one and one of us might come up with something the other hadn't thought about. We were building an information sheet, in the absence of an incident board, because we were not working from a station.

From our stash of belongings Sam passed me a can of cola. I cracked it open and took the first drink, before passing it to him. Just like old times we were brainstorming, sharing and there was an unspoken understanding between us. This comforted me no end and I knew it comforted him too.

With my pen poised over the paper, I could not think of anything else to write. Glancing at Sam, he was still busy making notes. I stood and stretched, and decided I needed to freshen up. Finding my washbag, I entered the bathroom and stripped. The shower was basic, but the water felt fantastic on my tired muscles. Before too long the shower door opened and Sam joined me. He didn't say anything but held me for a long time. We allowed the water to cascade over our bodies before we broke away and washed ourselves. It was a tight squeeze, but we managed.

Sam put the news on while we dried and dressed. There had been a blaze in Cornwall, but we only caught the end of the story. I was suddenly on high alert, the relaxing shower already forgotten. Looking on Sam's laptop, I found the story and was faced with the reality that my home and business was ruined. Devastation swept through me. I had lost everything. I pray, once more, that no one had been hurt, or worse. Then I paced like I'd never paced before. Anger rose from the pit of my stomach and I fought back tears. I would not cry because I would use this emotion against this monster. He would not win, but I was left wondering if this was his work or a coincidence.

I did not believe in coincidences.

Sam remained composed and wrote the information on both sheets of paper.

"The best way to get to the bottom of this mess is to work on it, princess."

"I know," I said.

"Okay. Come and join me, and we can compare our thoughts. Who should we talk about first?"

"Vanessa. She's the one that lost her life."

"So, what do we know about pentagrams?"

"Black magic. Witchcraft. Devil worship. Just a thought, why don't you run a search for the keywords?"

Sam grabbed his laptop and activated his search engine. He types 'black magic'.

"No," I said. "Call it what it is. Type pentagram."

Deleting his original text, he replaced it.

"Also try 'fire', 'owl' and 'eye'."

Sam typed and pressed enter.

"Jesus, we're on to something, princess."

Glancing over his shoulder, he clicked on the first link and we read, in silence, about the top ten Illuminati symbols.

"If Ashbeck is behind all of this his MO has changed somewhat."

"He's had plenty of time on his hands to plan this. Isn't the New World Order about being enlightened? He thinks he's been reborn!"

"What he did before wasn't his introduction to killing. If you're right about him being in the army, I think he may have murdered and I made that my views clear before. His techniques were too perfected. Did you bring his file?"

"Of course!" Rummaging through his rucksack Sam produced what had now become a dog-eared looking file and opened it. Passing it to me, I reluctantly began leafing through it; I knew exactly what I was looking for. When my eyes fell on the memo, I recognised it instantly.

*Phil. Having spent a considerable amount of time with Ashbeck and having studied his psychological reports, I am drawn to the conclusion that his seven victims that make up our case against him cannot possibly be the only ones. There has been no gradual build up to these frenzied attacks. You should seriously consider contacting Interpol to discuss the possibility of international interest in this man. Please give this matter your urgent attention. Regards, Katie-Anne Warwick*

"Here, read this memo I sent to Phil," I said, sliding it over to him. "Needless to say, it wasn't acted upon."

"I agree with you. He should have. Do you think he moved you on because he intended to get involved, or because he was already involved?"

"I can't answer that, to do so would be speculative. Makes me wonder though."

My mind was drifting. There was something we hadn't thought of, but I couldn't place it. I allowed myself to retrace the day in my mind and it dawned on me.

"Pass me the laptop."

In the property search I typed the name of the hotel and pressed enter. Monarch Properties owned that too.

"No way!"

Next, I typed the address of this bed and breakfast, and it came up with the owner's name, the lady who had checked us in earlier. Relief was evident on both our faces.

"Phil booked us into a hotel owned by the very gang we are chasing," I said with disbelief. "Check on Charlie again."

Paranoia began to sweep through both of us.

"I think it's time you phoned Craig, princess. I don't trust that Jen is being protected by the right people."

"I don't have his number."

"I do. Pass me the laptop."

Hidden beneath layers of files, he opened one called 'Coms' and I instantly knew it stood for communication. He punched Craig's number into his burner phone and passed it to me.

"Craig, it's Kate. I am working undercover so I know you've assumed me to be dead. How is Jen doing? I know about the accident and her condition."

"Oh God. Oh God. Kate?"

"Yes Craig. It's me. How is my friend?"

"She's awake. She is getting stronger, but it's taking time. Oh Kate, she might be paralysed," Craig said, struggling to compose himself.

"Oh God. I'm so sorry."

"She'd love to see you."

"I know. I'll be there as soon as I can. But it won't be for a couple of days at least."

"How's Mel? I can't get hold of her."

"Nor can I," was all I said on the matter of Mel.

"Craig, I need to go. Take good care of my friend. Craig, listen to me. You can only trust yourself on the matter of Jen's personal safety. Only you can protect her. Do you understand me? You cannot trust Phil. Do you understand me?"

"The number went through as withheld. Craig does not have our number."

I nodded because I knew it was probably for the best.

Jen was waking up and I wondered if she knew that she would be paralysed. I couldn't imagine how that might feel. I silently told myself I needed to stay positive and that the paralysis was a temporary stage of Jen's recovery. Let's hope I wasn't kidding myself. I hadn't given Craig any time to give detailed explanations and now I wish I had.

"Okay, I have a thought I need to voice," I announced.

Sam raised his eyebrows. He wanted to hear my view.

"What if Jen holds the key to solving this case and Phil is purposely keeping us away? Let's face it, we have lost our trust in him."

"You, my beautiful princess, have a wonderful mind. It's taken us what? Two days, to re-establish a fantastic working relationship and I absolutely love that we can just pick up where we left off all those years ago, despite the fact we now know precisely where we stand in the bedroom department."

"Are you saying you want to visit Jen sooner rather than later?"

"I just think if we leave it too long it will be too late for Mel. If Jen knows something it could make all the difference,

but she's not communicating yet."

"Not yet," I said with a heavy heart. "But Craig said she's getting stronger each time she wakes."

"We'll phone Craig tonight for an update. As soon as there's a channel of communication, however small, we will visit."

Cupping his face in my hands, I placed a big kiss on his forehead.

"Thank you," I said, for I knew our visit would lift Jen's spirits and that would help with her recovery. Her knowing that Sam and I were working together on this and that we were together, would give her hope that she would be safe again.

*** 

"Okay, princess. You can phone Craig while I pop out. I'm in need of a run and I will scan some streets while I do it. I'll be back in an hour."

"We should do that together. Don't leave me here alone. Please."

"You will be fine," he assured me. "No arguments. I'm feeling controlled and I need to let off some steam. Don't take this personally, I just need to have a run on my own."

"Whatever." I opened the door, he exited and I made sure it slammed so he would know my mood. I instantly felt childish and regretted it, but he was already gone.

From the window, I watched him run with ease along the street and out of sight. An uneasiness spread through me and I was unable to settle. Instead I paced the around the room. I didn't want to be on my own right now but I understood his need to escape. I resented that he had done so. Tension was building between us, despite those moments when we felt we were on track. Something wasn't right with us and why would it be when we had been immediately faced with this situation? I decided to take a long, hot shower. Not only would it pass the time but it would relax me. Perhaps I would be in a better frame of mind for his return. Let's face it, he hadn't deserved my outburst.

The hot water felt amazing as it pelted my skin. I had twisted the shower head so that a strong jet of water blasted out. It was having a massage effect on my shoulders that felt very good. When I had taken as much as I could handle, I turned the water off and wrapped myself in a towel.

Emerging from the bathroom, swathed in my towel, I froze. It took me a moment to realise who was sitting on the end of the bed. It certainly wasn't Sam.

Phil held my gaze for a long moment.

"You two thought you'd outsmarted me, but you were wrong," he said. Instantly, I knew that Sam's instinct not to trust him had been correct.

"I don't know how mixed up you are in all of this Phil, but you need to put things right."

"I have absolutely no idea what you're talking about, Kate. I have had no choice but to risk this operation because you and Robert have gone AWOL. What the hell were you thinking?" He was shouting.

Grabbing some clothes together, I returned to the bathroom because I would not have this conversation in a towel. As I closed the door Phil's foot prevented it from shutting. I was horrified at his brashness. He stood in the doorway.

"Fine," I said with attitude. "If this is how you want things you can fucking well watch me."

Releasing my towel from my hands, it cascaded on to the floor. My naked body, still damp, glistened under the ceiling lights. My anger spiked.

"Have you seen enough, Phil? Should I get dressed now? I would very much like to get dressed, but you obviously think I need your permission. Do I have your permission, or are you still perving at me?"

Taking a step towards me, Phil bent and picked up my towel, handing it to me.

"Cover up and calm down."

"Calm down? You have a nerve." I almost spat my words and I could not stop them any longer because I was so angry. "You barge your way in here, corner me when I am naked and have the nerve to tell me to calm down."

Phil held both hands up in front of him, his palms facing me. His signal to me that he didn't want any trouble but was prepared to defend himself if I caused some.

"Get out!" I demanded.

Phil reached for the door and closed it. I had pushed him too far and I cursed myself for losing control. I was cornered and very much in trouble. Phil took three steps towards me. When he was close enough, I struck his face with my right fist. I felt my fist connect with his left temple. As I raised my left hand he caught it and within a fraction of a moment I was restrained. I was a good bit shorter than this man and a whole lot weaker, but I had no intention of giving up. Struggling against his grip, I attempted to break free. He held me close, my arms were locked in an impossible hold behind my back. I was completely under his control. As his body pressed up against my naked form, I could feel that he was turned on and I was repulsed. I wanted to scream but couldn't find my voice. Tears filled my eyes and escaped down both cheeks. Nausea rose from the pit of my stomach and burnt the back of my throat.

"I could fuck you right now if I wanted to."

I held my breath for a long time. Moments felt like an eternity. I tried to struggle again, but he responded by pressing me against the wall even harder. My fate was very firmly in the hands of this man and I thought I knew where it was heading.

"Get dressed," he said, as he let me go and stormed out of the bathroom.

Sliding down the wall I crouched, holding my knees against my chest. Fighting the urge to sob, I took some deep breaths to compose myself. I grabbed at my clothes and fumbled to get dressed. My hands were shaking; uncontrollably. I could feel shock taking over my body and my senses. Walking to the sink, I ran cold water and splashed it on my face. I wanted to lock myself away but there was no lock on the door. Instead, I mustered all the strength I could find and entered the bedroom to face the monster I had once considered my friend and who I'd have entrusted my life to.

Phil was sat on the end of the bed as if nothing had happened, smiling at me.

"How long will Robert be and where has he gone?"

"He's gone for a run and is due back any moment." My voice was trembling.

"Okay, princess."

\*\*\*

Sam's pace was faster than he was used to. He wanted to cover as many streets as possible within the hour. He also wanted to suppress how he was feeling because he hated that Kate and he had just argued. Cursing, he reminded himself that two of her friends were in mortal danger. As he turned a corner, he narrowly avoided bumping into a man. A hooded man with owl eyes. Gradually slowing and stopping in a doorway, he turned and looked back. The man had gone. Edging back towards the corner, he glanced round just in time to see the man disappear into a cellar. Standing in the shadows, he waited for the man to emerge. After fifteen minutes he did; and Sam saw his face. Progress!

When he was sure the coast was clear, Sam approached the cellar door. Trying the handle, he wasn't shocked to find it was locked. He sensed something was very wrong: he immediately felt a tightening in his gut – danger lurked beyond this door. Making a mental note of his bearings, he headed back to Kate to share his news.

# CHAPTER TWENTY-THREE

Sam was more than surprised at the sight that awaited him when he returned to their room. Kate looked distressed at the unwelcome intrusion that now sat on the end of their bed. Phil did not even stand to greet his lifelong friend.

Kate was pacing and her arms were wrapped around her body. Sam instantly knew something was very wrong, that something had happened between them in his absence.

Turning towards Sam, Kate exposed her bare arms, one at a time. Extending them towards him and turning her arms over, she showed him the red marks that were appearing, then tilted her head towards their guest.

\*\*\*

Our eyes locked and I tilted my head towards Phil. Our silent communication was enough for Sam to understand that Phil had been rough with me. I dared not tell him to what extent right now, or I believed with all my heart that Sam would lose it with Phil. I would of course tell him, but not until Phil had left.

"What's going on?" he demanded.

"Our little friend has paid us a visit," I taunted. "But he thought he'd wait until you went out so he could intimidate me. I don't know why he would do that really, so I am assuming we're getting too close to the truth and it's his way of making us back down."

My voice was no longer timid or shaky. Sam's presence had given me strength I did not feel.

"We were right," I continued, "not to trust him. He's so out of his depth in all of this that he's drowning. Look how stressed he is. Don't forget Phil, Sam and I are trained to spot the signs."

"How long after I left did he show up?" Sam asked me.

"I don't know. I was in here for a few minutes then went for a shower. When I emerged, he was there, just sitting on our bed," I said, jabbing my finger at our bed.

"But he didn't remain sitting there, because he's hurt your arms."

"Hopefully his headache will make him think about what he's done."

"Has he hurt you anywhere else?"

"Nope."

"Get off our bed," Sam said and reached for a chair. "Sit here."

Sam positioned me the pillow end of the bed and sat beside me, placing himself in the middle. He sensed something more had happened but was trusting me.

"Kate, are you okay?" He was looking at me. He could tell that I was shaken to the core. He smiled, reassuringly. He was letting me know that he was in control now and that he would not let Phil hurt me again. He had positioned himself so Phil couldn't even look at me.

"I have news, Phil. Can I trust you with it?"

"I am your boss. You had better," he said.

"You said that some information was on a need-to-know basis. I need to know right now, so you had better start talking." Sam raised his eyebrow.

"If you have questions I will answer them." Phil was being cautious.

"Who owns Monarch Properties?"

"Holy crap, how do you know about that?"

"It's called investigating, Phil. You sent us here to get a result. Right? That's what we intend to do."

"The hotel you booked us into is owned by them. Why would you do that?"

Phil just shook his head.

"Look at me, Phil. We are supposed to be mates. What the fuck is going on? What the hell have you got yourself mixed up in?"

Phil raised both hands and buried his face into them. It was time to come clean.

"Monarch Properties is owned by Ashbeck."

"You sent us to a hotel owned by the man we are chasing?"

"I'm sorry. I didn't have a choice."

"Oh, you had a choice, mate. You made the wrong one. When Vanessa was murdered we knew something was very wrong. We already had our suspicions, as you well know. Tell me Phil, what are you getting out of all this?"

"I was writing a book about Ashbeck. I have been visiting him regularly in prison. He has played me."

Sam sensed my body language and held his hand out to ask me not to talk. He was right. Phil was engaging with him and my interruption could stop that.

"Tell me how Ashbeck ran Monarch Properties from prison. How has he managed that?"

"When Kate and her team caught Ashbeck they couldn't link anyone else to the crime. This business was so deeply hidden that it wasn't linked to him. He has a right-hand man that has kept things ticking along. This has given him all the money he needs now he's escaped. I had no idea any of this was planned. Please believe me."

"Are you in contact with him?"

"No."

"Don't fucking lie to me, Phil. I know you are. I'll ask again. Have you spoken to Ashbeck since he escaped?"

"Yes!"

"Why has his MO changed?"

"He's been bored and he's been doing lots of research."

"What research?"

"You have found Monarch Properties. What else have you found?"

"I'm the one asking questions!" Sam said. "A simple Internet search for owl, monarch and pentagram revealed an interesting find. What can you tell me about Ashbeck's links to the Illuminati?"

"To my knowledge he has no link other than in his head."

"Are the recent murders ordered by him?"

"Yes."

"Why did you not think we needed to know all of this, Phil?"

"I knew you would ask when you were ready to know."

"That's not good enough. You were hoping that we wouldn't find out to cover your own arse. Where is he holding Mel?"

"I have no idea. I promise, I do not know!" Turning to me, he added. "Kate, please believe me when I say I wouldn't want anything to happen to you, Mel or Jen."

Anger rose inside me and it took everything I had left not to react. He wanted me to react because he wanted Sam to lose it with him. I wasn't about to make that happen. Instead I stayed silent, I focussed on Cathy, prayed she was safe and that no one was hurt in the fire.

"You are no longer a part of this investigation Phil, I am going to make sure of that. I have already gone over your head with the help of a contact. Kate, you don't know this yet and I'm sorry you're hearing this at the same time as this scum. You may have been watching us over the past few days, but rest assured, I have had someone tracking you too. I just didn't know about it. Right about now your home is being raided and they are recovering CCTV monitors and recordings dating back months. Apparently, so far, they have found a box of black hoodies, contact numbers, manuscripts, phone recordings and lots more incriminating evidence, all stashed away inside your office, linking you to Ashbeck's escape, to his recent murders and to Mel's kidnapping."

Obviously, I knew what Charlie had discovered, but the rest was news to me and I could not help but wonder if he was bluffing and if it was just his anger talking. He certainly sounded genuine. I hadn't known Sam during his undercover days and was unaware of his capabilities. What I did know was how much distrust he had for Phil right now and, despite them having been friends for so many years, I could not help but contemplate when that trust had started to fade.

"Are you going to arrest me?" Phil asked.

"Nope, you are free to leave at any time. Keep watching your back though, because someone will be coming for you. You will be held responsible for your part in all of this."

# CHAPTER TWENTY-FOUR

Once Phil had left, Sam turned his attention to me. I knew I had to be completely honest with him, but I wasn't sure if I was ready to have that conversation. I had allowed my anger to prevail and had placed myself in danger. It was a stupid thing to have done. Despite the threat, and the intimidation, he hadn't harmed me beyond bruising my arms during the restraint. What he had done was to leave me a lasting memory that would take me a while to move on from.

"Like I already said, when I came out of the shower he was sitting on the end of the bed."

"What were you wearing?"

"Just a towel. I was still wet. He started a conversation, but I wasn't at all comfortable. I wanted to know why he was in the room. I gathered some clothes and went to the bathroom because I didn't feel comfortable being in a towel, in fact I felt vulnerable. I wanted to get dressed. When I tried to shut the door behind me, his foot blocked the way. I lost it with him."

"I wouldn't expect anything less from you, Kate. He had no right to break into the room, or to follow you to the bathroom."

"I got so angry. I'm sorry."

"None of this is your fault. What did you say to him?"

I repeated the events as best I could remember and didn't skimp on the finer details. When I was finished, tears were freely flowing down my face. Sam moved closer to me and held me for a long time. I held him back so tightly I thought I might crush him.

Taking both my hands in his, Sam looked at my bruised arms. They were starting to turn purple.

"Have you washed them?"

"No, of course not."

From inside his pocket he produced two large evidence bags and tape.

"I took these out with me just in case I found something." I allowed him to bag both my hands and lower arms and taped them in place. I knew I was about to be taken to the police station, that DNA swabs would be taken and that I needed to make a statement against my old boss, who I had once considered a dear friend.

"I have some news to share, princess. I might have found a significant location."

My eyes widened and l leaned towards him with hope and anticipation.

"Where?"

He told me about the street he'd found, the man he'd seen and the cellar. Were we ready to raid this gang?

Please let Mel be safe. Please let Ashbeck be many miles from this place.

Despite the police station not being too far away, Sam still ordered a taxi. He had a look of concern on his face that dug deep furrows between his brows. A sadness had come over him that I knew would take him a while to emerge from. He didn't want me on the street right now because he sensed I was more shaken than I was letting on. He was right of course, but I was trying to stay strong for my two friends. They needed me right now. I could crumble when all this was over.

I thought I would be feeling nervous having to repeat my story, but a calmness had come over me. I think by telling Sam the hardest part was over. Once the taxi driver had dropped us off and was driving away, Sam turned to me.

"Princess. You need to know something. I have hidden cameras all over our room. Now you have a choice. You can say that you knew about them, or I can destroy the evidence. It's your call. If you tell the police, you had better make sure that your statement is spot on."

I had forgotten that he'd brought cameras.

"What if they think I encouraged him?"

"They won't. If it goes to court that would be the defence's argument though. Your call, but I need to know now."

"Hand them over," I said. "He had no right to threaten me like that."

"Okay. You make your statement and I'll get the search warrant arranged."

# CHAPTER TWENTY-FIVE

The raid would take place at two in the morning. Although the station had been on high alert for the event, they wanted time to brief everyone involved. Backup was arriving from other locations and they had already been briefed outside the area. They were arriving in unmarked cars, by bus and by train over the next few hours. After all, we didn't want this gang to become suspicious of extra police activity.

As is tradition for such events, food had been ordered. Everyone would eat and bond during the build-up. Adrenaline would be high tonight, as anticipation and excitement built.

Andy Preston was in charge. He assured us of his team's experience, vigilance and expertise. He had been honest with us in regards to how different their experience was compared to those working in London stations, but had promised, on his reputation, that his team would prove themselves. He was personally trained in negotiation and would use those skills if they were required.

Sam seemed as nervous as me. I knew it was stating the obvious, but we both wanted a good result tonight. We both needed Mel to be okay. Sam needed his hunch to be correct. His reputation was also on the line. If Mel wasn't being held in this cellar our raid would alert the gang, who would either move her to a new location or kill her. The risk was high.

The station had placed a couple of officers in a house opposite. They were reporting back to us every fifteen minutes. So far three men had entered and had already left. One of them appeared to have blood on his hands. My stomach knotted at this news. Within the last two minutes, fourteen men had entered. They were still inside. Shouting could be heard, but the officers couldn't make out the words.

Andy called his team together and asked for them to settle down. He praised them for their prompt response to action, despite the fact that many of them were not on duty. He gave a brief outline of Ashbeck's past before handing over to Sam, who gave an up-to-date profile of Ashbeck and his motivations as best we knew. He painted a very dark picture. Sam, with my permission, also spoke of the ordeal that Phil had put me through earlier and highlighted how Ashbeck had people in high places that were under his control.

Sam had given a description of the man he'd seen leaving the cellar, but the photofit hadn't done it justice. Instead he'd drawn a sketch portrait of the man himself. The detail of the image was outstanding and it humbled me that I didn't know of his artistic skill. How could I not of known this about him? Knowing that there was more to learn about this man filled me with such excitement, renewed energy and faith.

We learned that the journey from the station to the cellar would take just four minutes by car. Some officers would leave early on foot and wouldn't be in uniform. They would join the other officers from outside the area, strolling along the streets and making the place look busy. Hopefully this would restrict the movements of the gang during the raid. The more that were inside the cellar the better.

Sam's phone alerted him. Charlie had arrived.

"Excuse me. This is important and relevant," he announced and left the room.

Discussions continued, as did the banter, but nothing important was disclosed until Sam returned with Charlie in tow.

"Wait there," he said to his son at the doorway.

"Andy, can we have a word out here please? Lori, you too."

Andy and I left the room and I closed the door behind me. I gave Charlie a hug.

"That's for being a nosey brat," I told him.

Sam introduced his son to Andy, explained his contribution to the case and to the downfall of Phil Andrews. Phil was not in Andy's good books right now because of what he had just done to me. Charlie was not made aware of that situation. It was none of his business. None of it was, truthfully.

"The truth is, Andy, I just didn't know what to do with Charlie, so here he is."

"Right. I know exactly what to do with him. I'll get a car to take him to mine."

"Can't I stay here and help out?" Charlie protested.

"No, son, you cannot," Andy cut in.

"My wife and daughter are at home. You can keep them company. No argument. We appreciate everything you've done, but quite honestly, we need you well and truly out of our way tonight."

Opening the door, he leant in and requested the company of the two largest officers he had.

"Dave, Chris, I need you guys out here."

They leapt into action and joined us in the corridor. They towered over each of us.

"Take this young man to mine for us, will you. Don't listen to him bleating on about how helpful he'd be here, because we don't need him under our feet tonight. Make sure he goes into the house and my wife will make sure he stays there."

"Leave him with us guv."

"Cheers boys. Charlie, you'd be wise not to underestimate my wife."

"Or his daughter," Dave added.

The three of us returned to the briefing room, there was a definite buzz about the place now. We mingled amongst the men and women, getting to know a few names. The more time I spent with these people, the more I missed the job; the anticipation, entering the unknown, the adrenaline, the buzz in this room right now. It was like rediscovering a familiar friend that I was overjoyed to see. Holding on to the feeling, I peeled myself away from the crowd to take a moment.

Although my presence was required tonight, there was no real part in this plan for me because I wasn't one of them any more. No way could they ever let me be a part of this raid; if something went wrong, it would be an insurance nightmare. I understood this, of course I did. That's why Charlie had been packed off too. At least I had been denied that indignity and for that I would be eternally grateful.

I would help where I could, but I wouldn't be entering the building as I would have done in the past. As a spare part to the requirement of the raid, they would keep me at a safe distance from where they could access my extensive knowledge of Ashbeck. At least I had that. Despite wishing I'd never met him or that he didn't exist, I was needed for that. I was of some use after all.

"A penny for them," an unfamiliar male voice asked from behind me.

Turning slowly, I fixed a smile on my face.

"I'm Pete," he said and held out a hand.

"Lori," I said as we shook.

"We both know you're Kate," he whispered in my ear. "So does Andy. But you and Sam are only known to the two of us, so don't be too alarmed."

My eyes widened and it occurred to me that Pete and I were still holding hands. I broke free.

"How?" For I could see no use in denying it as my facial expression had very obviously given it away.

"Phil Andrews made a big song and dance about your arrival and threatened us with the commissioner. He sent images of you both. There were then these sensational stories that Lori Peterson covered about Katie-Anne Warwick and Samuel Cooper. Who the hell is Lori Peterson anyway? Where did she come from, all of a sudden? We put her photo through our image recognition software and your name popped up. Whoever changed your image did a damn good job sweetheart, but they can't change the shape of those cheekbones. You have great bone structure, by the way. All we did was change the eyes back to blue and replace your hair, and there you were."

I could feel my cheeks flushing and gathered my composure quickly.

"Sam. Sam cut and dyed my hair. Chose my clothes. Gave me this harsh look. I don't recognise myself. Does he know you guys are aware?"

"Not yet. But I'm having some fun with him now I know he's a hairdresser."

"Have to admit, all the years I've known him, I didn't know that about him either, or that he could draw so well. I'm rather impressed with his sketch."

"You and I are in the background together tonight. Make your excuses with Sam and Andy shortly, we have things we need to go through on the PC."

Pete winked at me and headed back towards a group of men.

One mixed group of officers left to a massive cheer. Heading out early in plain clothes, they would walk the streets in pairs, drink coffee and report back via text.

\*\*\*

Within moments a report came through that thirteen hooded men had just emerged from the cellar and entered the building above it. Andy, now deciding we needed to raid both areas of the building, needed to change tactics and warrants.

He was on to it. He had dialled the number before leaving the room, the hour was late and I expected he would speak directly to the local magistrate. I also imagined that he'd dined with said magistrate on many occasions and had already prewarned him, or her, that changes might need to be made last minute. I had every faith that this man was not going to let us down.

Approaching Sam, I touched him on the elbow.

"Hey, princess," he said, apparently forgetting where we were and sending my tummy into flips.

Smiling and blushing, I awaited the responses from around us.

"Get a room!" The banter began.

Our secrets were emerging, one by one.

"We need a quiet word, pumpkin," which created a huge outburst of laughter. He would forever be known as Pumpkin in this place.

Moving to the edge of the room, I am glad of his attention. I explained what Pete had told me and he seemed assured at the revelation. Like me, it gave him confidence in Andy's ability to manage the situation we were faced with. I also let him know that I would be working in the background with Pete and would not part of the team that would raid the building, and that I would be disappearing with him shortly to view some PC files and discuss our roles and expectations.

Taking both my hands in his and caressing them gently, not to hurt my bruises, he levelled with me.

"You be careful out there tonight, princess. Promise me you won't be taking any risks without me there to pick up the pieces."

"You need to make me that promise too, pumpkin."

"It's so obvious you guys are together. Hug it out, kiss, do something. Just get it over with. And Kate, sorry you can't be in on the raid, but you're not covered by the insurance. I hope you understand." Andy was back and being apologetic.

"I understand. I'm here to help in any way I possibly can. I ask just one thing, Andy. If Mel is in that building and she needs me, please let me get to her. I won't compromise your scene, but I will know more than anyone, because of my history with Ashbeck, what she might have experienced."

"You have my word. Has Pete caught up with you yet?"

"He has."

"Good. You will both be in the next street. You will be easily accessible."

"Thank you!"

Sam flung his arms around me and we embraced to the sound of clapping, cheering and stamping feet.

# CHAPTER TWENTY-SIX

Having been taken to a windowless room, I now felt trapped in a space with a man I did not want to be with because he had produced a file I did not want to discuss. He had closed the door to give us privacy and spread the contents of said file over the vast table. I did not need to look because I would never forget what I had already seen.

"The commissioner said to reveal the word 'Raven' to you, Kate."

"The commissioner asks too much. I don't work for the police any longer."

"The commissioner also said I would have trouble getting you to talk about this. I thought if you were reminded what Ashbeck did it might help."

"Reminded of what he did? Are you serious? I can pick any one of these photos up and name the victim and the position of her wound without looking at the reference number, even after all these years. I don't need reminding of what he did or how things could have been different in the investigation."

"I hope I'm about to earn your trust, Kate. What I'm about to tell you stays between us. You and me only. You must not tell Sam. Andy does not even know this."

I had no idea what he was going on about and nothing could have prepared me for what I was about to learn.

"Go on," I said.

"I didn't know this myself until yesterday," he said, as he walked over to the images. Picking one up he handed it to me. "What can you tell me about this one?" he asked, as he took two folded pieces of paper out of his jacket pocket: his hands were trembling.

"This lady was called Jane Gosling. The wound in this photo is to her inner thigh on her left leg. Jane entered the witness protection programme. She gave critical evidence in court against Ashbeck. She is a beautiful, brave lady."

Tears formed in Pete's eyes as he handed me the two documents. I unfolded them carefully. The first was a copy of Jane's birth certificate and the second was a photograph of him on his wedding day. Beside him stood his bride, it was without a doubt, Jane Gosling. He had my attention.

"She is an amazing, unique lady who does so much good. What's going on now, with Ashbeck escaping, has crushed her. She came clean and told me who she is."

"You never asked about her scars?"

"Of course, but she's a resourceful lady. She's had some amazing artwork done to cover them."

"You have my word, Pete. I won't share this information. You shouldn't have done either."

"The only reason I have is because I know you worked on the original case and you are personally invested in this case too. My wife is scared, Kate. We want this monster caught as much as you do."

"Have you told the commissioner about your personal situation?"

"No."

"Good. Keep it that way."

"Really, because?"

"Something I've learned in this case is we don't know who we can trust. Phil Andrews was my guv on that case and I guess you've learned what he's been up to. I'd have trusted him with my life until a few days ago."

"Point taken. My wife is petrified that Ashbeck will come looking for her though and she doesn't know what to do."

"She has a contact number. If she's worried she can use it. Hopefully it's only a temporary measure."

"Does she?"

"She does. Phone her and give her a gentle push. She probably needs your reassurance that it's okay for her to use it. They will take her to a safe house, but you won't have any contact with her until this is over."

"This sucks," he said, letting out a sigh.

Of all the places Jane could have chosen to move to I could not believe that she chose Norfolk. It wasn't lost on me that Phil may have had something to do with influencing that decision and I wondered if they had stayed in touch. I wondered if Jane featured in his book.

My mobile started ringing and I looked at its screen. Mandy Wiseman. I wonder?

"I need to take this, Pete. This is connected."

"Hello. Lori Peterson here."

"Lori, this is Mandy Wiseman. I've opened that envelope. You need to hear what it contains. This can't wait. Are you alone?"

"No, I'm not, but I can listen to what you have to say. I promise I won't react."

"Okay. It's lengthy, so I won't read it in full. I'll give you a summary. Basically, Mel states that she is suspicious that her boyfriend is mixed up in a gang. She has done a preliminary police search and has found links back to that escaped prisoner. Ashbeck. She has given this to me because she has discovered who I really am, it's why I recognised you. I'm one of his victims who gave evidence in court. She wanted to warn me so I could get the hell out of here. What should I do?"

Two women in the witness protection programme relocated to the same area, an area in which Ashbeck was known to operate from prison. That was certainly no coincidence in my book. Sam needed to know this. Perhaps Andy did too. I needed to discuss this possibility with Sam.

"Mandy, thank you for trusting me with this. Is there somewhere you can go for a few days? I am going to ask something of you now and you can say no if you're not comfortable with it. Would you trust me to share this with the other person you met with me? You can say no and I will keep it to myself. You have my word on that."

"I'm not sure. I shouldn't have told you."

"I know. But you have. And I've just asked you to relocate. Your phoning me has saved me a call because we need to reschedule our meeting. I can't disclose the details, but we have made progress this end. Can I phone you tomorrow evening to discuss when we could meet? That is if you remain in the area."

"I'm done with running. If he catches up with me, I'll shoot him. I have a gun."

"Mandy, no!"

"What more could he do to me, Kate?"

Before I could reply Mandy was gone. I took a moment before I turned back to Pete.

"Pete, what's your surname?"

"Allen. Are you in touch with my wife?"

"No. I thought for a minute I might have been. I can't give you the name. That lady was another victim, relocated into this area also. She has literally just come forward because she recognised me from her past. I need to speak with Sam. I will be back and I promise I will not mention your wife, despite the flack I will get if he eventually finds out."

"Can you trust Sam?"

"He is the only person I trust right now."

"Get him in here. I want to keep my wife safe and if that means taking a leap of faith in you two, then so be it."

"Thank you. That means a lot. But we can't disclose the other victim's name to you," I said, as I dialled Sam's mobile.

He answered immediately and agreed to meet Pete. I told him where we were and that I'd asked Pete to come and get him. I added that I'd spoken to our new friend and that I'd message him. I told him not to let anyone see the text, to delete it as soon as he'd read it, not repeat it and not to talk to me about it.

Within just a few minutes the three of us were staring at the images of the mutilated women. I was rearranging them in a way that made anatomical sense. Pete hadn't arranged them in any kind of order, he had just wanted to make me talk. But it hadn't been the images that had got me on his side, it was his personal connection to one of the victims. Once he'd finished explaining his situation to Sam, the seven women were arranged in the date order that the crimes were committed against them. Jane was the third. Missing from this file, it had just occurred to me, were the faces of these women. Despite me having the highest clearance on this case, they were also missing from the file that Sam and I had. This was what had been niggling at me from the beginning. These files were not complete. What else was missing? It had been years since I had seen the contents, how could I possibly remember what should be there? I shared my thoughts with the two men.

"Okay, Sam I know what's missing. It's been driving me mad. There's no faces. These women have no faces. Had they have not been removed from the file, I would have recognised one straight away. That's why they've gone. What else is missing? I am so angry right now!"Sam, Pete knows there is a second victim in the area, but not the location or the name, old or new. And, Pete, we don't know who she used to be either. Bearing this in mind, what to you both think to the possibility that all the victims were relocated to this area?"

"Ashbeck was operating in this area." It was Sam who had spoken out. "Why would they have relocated his victims into an area where he had been active?"

"Call me paranoid if you like, but what if Ashbeck wanted to keep his eye on them?"

"Jesus Christ!" Pete was beside himself and Sam shot me a look.

"Worst case. We know he's got a whole team of people on the outside and it now appears, on the inside too. Sam, Mel got kidnapped from her boyfriend's house – and we know he's involved. Pete, tell Sam where you live."

"Opposite the cellar we're staking out, we're using my house actually. My wife has gone to my parents."

"I don't believe in coincidences. Pete, I think it's time Andy heard at least part of this, don't you? Sam, our new friend isn't safe. She won't listen to me. Please try to get her to come here, or leave, or do something."

I walked out of the room and headed towards the briefing room. I intended to take control of this situation. I would handle it with tact and I hoped that Andy would too. I was about to put my trust in a man I had only just met and had never worked with until today. That was a big ask for me. By the time I reached the briefing room, I was astonished to see that it was almost empty: with the majority of officers already on the streets, the place had an eerie quietness about it. Checking the clock, I was taken aback to note that it was already half one.

"Andy, a word please. There's been a development."

"Nothing sacred here. Come in," he chirped.

"In private. This is a delicate matter, to say the least."

"Okay. My office then," he said, walking out looking displeased.

"Thank you."

We walked in silence the remainder of the way. I would not have this conversation in the corridors and Andy would understand once he'd heard what I had to say. Once inside his office, I shut the door.

"It's been quite a day already," I said, "and I'm about to shock you to the core."

"I very much doubt that."

"As you know, Mel was kidnapped from her boyfriend's house. Living opposite her is our witness, Mandy Wiseman. She reported Mel missing."

"That's hardly breaking news, what's your point?"

"Mandy described seeing Mel's boyfriend wearing a black hoodie with yellow eyes, linking him to Ashbeck, yes?"

"Yes."

"Mandy Wiseman entered the witness protection programme after giving evidence against Ashbeck at his trial. She came forward earlier today. I am going against her wishes by sharing this information with you. This is strictly off the record."

"Jesus Christ!"

"Are you aware who lives opposite the cellar and house we are raiding later?"

"Of course, Pete Allen. We are using his house to observe. Why?"

"I have had a private conversation with Pete this evening that leads me to believe you should visit him in your meeting room. Did he request to babysit me tonight?"

"Yes."

"You might want to ask yourself why he might have done that."

"He's told you something that you've promised not to repeat. His wife has scars, she's covered them well, but she has scars. Jesus fucking Christ! I don't need to go and see Pete and you don't need to tell me any more. If Pete wants me to know, he comes to me. We haven't had this conversation, Kate."

"That's two out of seven victims from Ashbeck's past that have been relocated to here. We need to find this man, Andy!"

"Let's do this. You two need to get into position. Pete knows where you need to be. Look after him. He might be a big bloke but he's got a sensitive side. If Ashbeck shows up, don't let him near him. That's an order!"

"Don't worry, he'll be behind me in the queue for that one."

Andy just looked at me, not quite sure how to react to that, unsure of my capabilities, my humour and my motivations.

# CHAPTER TWENTY-SEVEN

Pete parked the van and we both squeezed through the gap into the back. Our set-up looked like a delivery van that had been parked up for the night: with a magnetic sticker on each side fitting in with this scenario.

The reality was something quite different. Pete and I were busy in the back of the van in what could only be described as a mobile command unit. Apparently, I was the go-to person if anyone wanted to know anything about Ashbeck. Go figure. I could think of better uses, in all honesty, but I guessed, in this situation, nothing else was going to be of more use to anybody. I couldn't help with the raid so I had to play to my strengths. Pete, it was obvious, was very much into technology. From the back of this van he had access to various CCTV footage of local streets and I thought just how much Charlie would have loved this.

"Hey, what's this truck doing on this little street?" He hadn't taken his eyes off the monitors and nothing was going unnoticed.

"He's wearing a hoodie." I stated the obvious.

"Hooded figure approaching in four-wheeled box lorry. Heading south towards target street. Not behaving suspiciously. Just be aware for now. Out."

This message had just gone direct into the ears of the entire team. Just as Pete finished the message, the small lorry jerked to a standstill. The driver opened the door and jumped out. Disappearing from view briefly, he re-emerged behind the lorry and opened the doors. We were alarmed to witness a dozen hooded figures jump out and sprint along the street, six in each direction. Pete communicated this into his handset.

\*\*\*

A loud rumbling sound seemed to echo through the streets and it sounded as if it was closing in. Pete clicked buttons until the source of the sound filled a screen. A large lorry was closing in, two streets north of the target.

"Sure hope that's not full of hoodies too."

Pete communicated the presence of the lorry to the team and added that he would keep them posted of its relevance. I did not take my eyes off the monitor. Pete fiddled with the monitor adjacent and we suddenly had a view of the back of the lorry.

"Don't let this distract us from the other streets. They might be using this as a decoy," I suggested.

"Don't worry. Now I have the setting, we can flick from one to the other." He clicked back and forth from one street to the other with ease, leaving it on the original setting.

"Impressive," I said.

Before long, the lorry was attempting to turn into the target street from the far end. It was obvious to us on the monitor that it was too large and it soon became wedged between the buildings. Pete sent his communication through to the team. A message came back stating that an angry voice could be heard from behind its curtained sides. Pete pressed buttons and positioned monitors front and back on the lorry. He had a third covering the target properties and, of course, his own house.

We watched as the hooded driver opened his cab door, emerged and unclipped the curtain on the side, enough to let a man out. As he jumped to the ground and twisted, his hood caught in the wind and exposed his face for a moment. Pete pressed more buttons and when I looked at his computer monitor, I froze. The image that met me was the hooded youth that had bumped shoulders with me the night I should have been on the train.

"Talk to me Kate. You've seen him before?"

"Yes, I have. At Paddington station. The night of that train crash."

"Let's see if we can get an ID. Jackie is waiting back at base for any images I send her. I'll send this over."

"What about the driver? Do we have one of him?"

"Let's see. He's got his hood on, but you never know. Jackie is good, we might be able to narrow things down through association. Maybe not enough for a court, but enough to give us an idea."

"It would be a start."

"Exactly."

Men and women started to jump through the gap in the lorry's side. Their frightened expressions alarmed me. Each was tied to the person behind and I knew exactly what I was witnessing. Pete was stunned.

"People smuggling," I said quietly. "Make sure you capture every single one of their faces. They will need our help."

Ashbeck was back in town and he was being bold. He thought he was above the law. Part of me hoped he was in that building because it meant we'd have him, but for that to be the case I didn't want to think what might have happened to my friend.

A message came through that Andy had ordered everyone to hold back until the chain of people had cleared the street. There were two minutes until we were due to raid, but things had to change, again. There was too much going on that had possible links to Ashbeck. He was certainly making waves.

Pete started a random street search with one of the monitors, beginning with the street on which we were parked. There was some activity at the far end and he zoomed in. Three hooded figures were huddled. They seemed to be looking at something under a street light, but we couldn't see what.

"Keep your eye on those for me," he asked and started another scan with a different monitor.

It wasn't long until he spotted another small group doing exactly the same.

"That's it."

"Okay, there's definitely something going on. We need to start emerging from the woodwork guys. Three hooded figures on all surrounding streets, just hanging about. They seem to know we are here and they're causing a distraction. Close in on them and remove them. They will be unaware we are here in great numbers. We're going to start scanning the streets looking for more. Sweep in and make arrests. No noise. Are the vans in position?"

"We're in position."

"Excellent. Be careful out there tonight, guys."

The airwaves filled with static from radios.

The train of people were taken into the house next door to the main house and cellar we were going to raid. As soon as the door was shut the energy about the place changed.

Andy's voice filled everyone's earpieces.

"Go, go, go."

Men and women emerged from doorways and ran with purpose towards the cellar and the house. Pete and I watched everything unfold before us on the monitors.

"Don't you wish you were part of this?" I asked him.

"No. Not this time. I can't be in the same room as Ashbeck. Not knowing what he's..." He broke his sentence short and looked away.

I smiled and placed a reassuring hand on his forearm.

"I will recapture him if it's the last thing I do, Pete. If I have to rejoin the force to do that, then so be it."

"I texted my wife earlier and said I was working with you. She wants to see you. She said she knows you're not supposed to, but look where that's got everyone. Please Kate, would you and Sam come to dinner?"

"Pete, I'm supposed to be dead! I'm undercover!"

"I know. I'm sorry. I need her to know someone is looking out for her. She's so scared. She's lived with this secret all these years, not even told me. In fact, she's invented lies about how she ended up with scars that satisfied my curiosity. She can't have children, yet she has made the most fantastic foster mum imaginable. She truly is an amazing lady. Kate, I think it would do you just as much good to see how amazingly well she has done, as it would for her to see you."

"She sounds amazing. Of course, we'd love to," I said and hoped I was doing the right thing.

"She'll be made up." And, somehow, he seemed to be more relaxed. He had just pleased his wife and this made him happy.

"You guys will work through this, Pete. It doesn't have to change what you have. Your wife is still the same woman you married, she just has a different past. And it was a past that she wasn't allowed to tell you about. That choice was taken away from her. You do understand that, don't you?"

"Yeah, I know. I'm getting my head around it, slowly."

"What's taking so much time?"

"Don't know. There must have been twenty

officers enter the house and ten enter the cellar, but the communications have all gone quiet."

Pete flicked between streets on the monitors again. Our van was being approached by two uniformed officers.

"We have company."

"I'll go into the front."

"Leave the door open so I can hear what they say. It's Dave and Chris."

Climbing through the doorway, I greeted the two men.

"Hey guys, you okay?"

"Lori, we need you. We've found her. Mel is alive."

"Is she okay?"

"She's alive."

"Dear God, what has he done to her?"

"You go," Pete demanded. "Which one of you pretty boys are staying with me?"

"That'll be me," Dave said. "I drew the short straw."

# CHAPTER TWENTY-EIGHT

Approaching the scene, I couldn't quite believe what I was witnessing. I hoped Pete and Dave were viewing and recording this from the van. Phil Andrews was being dragged from the house, in handcuffs. Blood oozed from his shoulder and I wasn't sure if he had been stabbed or shot. I instantly thought of Sam and hoped he was okay.

"It's not what it looks like!" he yelled across the street at me. "I followed the same leads as you, I was negotiating. Tell them I'm a good person."

"Where's James?"

"He's about somewhere."

Chris's radio crackled, someone was requesting medical support. Two ambulances were required.

One was urgent, a matter of life or death. The second was for the walking wounded, someone who was losing a small amount of blood and giving attitude.

"You may want to take a deep breath to steady yourself. I know you've seen some sights, but this is your friend down here," Chris announced gently.

As we were about to enter the cellar, the door to the house opened and a familiar face was escorted down the steps. I hadn't met Mel's boyfriend, but I'd seen photos. Face to face with the man now, I was pleased he had been caught.

"He was armed. He ended up shooting your old guv," Chris said.

"We've never met, but Mel has shown me photos. He was her boyfriend," I announced.

"Seriously?"

"You might want to inform his arresting officers of that right now."

"Good as done," he said and rushed to relay this information to the relevant people.

I continued through the door and down the steps into the cellar. Temporary lights had been set up and I marvelled at how quickly this had been done and followed their path. The mood was sombre; the normal bravado and banter put aside. The bare minimum of people were here and that told me that Andy Preston was a respectable man. He met me outside a wooden box-like structure.

"Glad you're here, Kate. Sam is inside at Mel's request. There's also a female officer, who must remain. She won't let anyone touch her, only you. She's requesting that you to process her. Can you do that?"

"Will that stand up in court?"

"In all honesty, I don't know."

"I will collect fibres and bag her hands, feet and net her hair. I'll be doing it in the presence of two police officers. I'll swab her mouth, so she can have a drink, but she'll be going to hospital so the body and intimate swabs can be done there. Is the female officer trained in rape cases?"

While we chatted, I covered myself in protective clothing and put gloves on.

"No."

"Okay. I was, but I'm not a cop any longer, Andy. I'm not sure my contract covers this."

"Let's not keep her waiting any longer and we're going to assume that it does considering everyone that sent you and Sam here seemed to be in the know as to what Mel's situation was."

Andy opened the wooden door and I stepped inside. Nothing could prepare me for the stench that met me. Stale urine and faeces assaulted my nostrils and stung my eyes. Fighting the urge to gag, I made my way over to the mattress and to my friend.

"Hey, how are you doing, honey?"

"Kate?"

"It's me sweetie," I said, as I squatted beside my friend. I noticed the other officer for the first time. She was approaching me.

"We can't move Mel until we have collected fibres, right? Yet she won't let me touch her. She let him take off her gag and cover her with that sheet thing, but now she won't let anyone touch her."

"Mel will let me do what needs doing," I said with feeling. "What's your name?"

"Kirsty."

"Okay Kirsty, for a start, let's have some empathy. This beautiful lady is called Mel. She won't let anyone touch her because she doesn't want the scene compromised. Mel is a police officer, just like you and James here."

Turning to Mel, I smiled sweetly.

"Now Mel, you know how this goes. You know I'm not working for the police, but what you don't know is that I'm under contract, with James, to find you and I have permission, under that contract and from the guv here, to take your swabs in the presence of two officers. James and Kirsty are those two officers if that's okay with you, or I can request a second female officer if you'd prefer?" I look at her deeply and hope she does not call him Sam.

"You and Sam can process me, she doesn't touch me."

"She won't. I promise but I could do with her to label samples. Mel. Do you trust me to look for fibres?"

Mel nodded.

"Okay. Are you thirsty?"

"Yes."

"I'll get water." Kirsty now knew her place "Thanks. Mel, you're doing so well. First things first, we need to take photos of how you are before we remove the binds around your ankles and wrists. We'll do that, get you untied and then we can take swabs from your mouth so you can get a drink. How does that sound?"

"We usually use these sheets for the stiffs," Mel said.

"Come on sweetie, you know it's the only way we can preserve the fibres in a place like this. It's going to be far easier to collect them once we get to the hospital, once you've got the medical attention you clearly need."

"Hmm."

Sam and I started working because we wanted to collect as much as possible in situ. I held the torch for this part. He placed a ruler beside Mel's ankles, to give an accurate indication of scale, and then took images of the rope that bound her ankles. Removing a knife from his kit, he gently removed it and placed it into a bag for Kirsty to label. He placed each foot into a plastic bag to preserve any evidence and secured it. The process was repeated for Mel's wrists.

Sam now took hold of the torch and I started my process with the swabs. I chatted with Mel the whole time. Holding eye contact with her, I let her know my every move before it happened. She knew what was expected because she had done this so many times before. Opening her mouth, she allowed me to scrape the swab around her cheeks and tongue. I was as gentle as possible. Sam shone the torch carefully, so as not to hurt her eyes. There were fibres between her teeth. I looked at Sam and he nodded. He'd noticed them too.

Passing me tweezers, I plucked one fibre at a time and placed each in a tube that Sam was holding for me. Every so often Mel pulled away to swallow, before allowing me to continue. I reassured her constantly.

When I was done she started to gag and I gave her some space.

"Could we have the water please?"

Sam stepped up and helped Mel to drink. All the time we were sheltering her from Kirsty, who in all honesty had taken a step back unless she was needed.

"Gentle sips. I can't let you have much until you've been seen by the medics. Just enough to wet your mouth, okay." Sam was gentle but firm.

"Thanks Sam. I don't want her in here."

"I know, but we don't have a choice. Kate and I are the ones not supposed to be here, but we have special permission from her guv because we were sent to find you."

I could tell Kirsty was offended. Mel had absolutely no objection to Sam being there and he was male. It was obvious she couldn't work that out.

Kirsty held a second torch just above my hands and she was doing a great job. I gave her a reassuring smile, but wasn't sure it helped much.

"Get your hands away from me. Give that light to Sam."

"Kirsty, don't take this personally," I said, "and please stay. I need you to stay."

Sam took the light and held it above where I needed to work. We worked in silence, but I continued to chat with Mel as if nothing had happened and I wasn't processing her crime scene. She seemed comforted by the familiarity of Sam and I being there.

There was a knock on the door and it opened enough for Andy to be heard.

"The paramedics are two minutes away."

"Did you hear that Mel? We're getting you out of here!"

"Thank you, guv."

"Kirsty, Kate will ride in back with Mel, James in the front. You will be in the car behind with me."

"Guv!" Kirsty began her protest.

"That is an order. There is a bigger picture here that you don't understand. Don't fight it, Kirsty. Be humbled that you have been let in this far."

"Everything is going to be okay, Mel. The medical team are on their way. You will soon be out of this hellhole."

The fear in her eyes would haunt me forever. She grabbed hold of my arms with her bagged hands.

"I will be coming with you, I promise. I will stay with you."

From behind me I could hear Sam making demands.

"Get me blankets. Now!"

Mel fell asleep. The sudden burst of energy was too much for her body to bear. Tears filled my eyes and I fought them back. I hoped she wouldn't remember that Sam had seen her like this. The mind was a clever organ and had a way of blocking out what it didn't need to know and I hoped hers gave her that dignity.

It was an incredibly long two minutes and Mel was slipping into a deeper sleep. She was cold and dehydrated.

The blankets didn't seem to be forthcoming either.

"Kirsty, would you see if someone has one of those foil blankets in a first aid kit?  Someone must have something."

There was a sudden increase in activity outside the door accompanied by the clattering of metal which could, with any luck, only mean one thing.  The arrival of the paramedics.  Kirsty allowed them into the small space.

"The paramedics have arrived," she announced.

She allowed them into the small room and they weren't polite enough to hide their disgust at the stench that met them.  Someone should have warned them, perhaps they did. We'd never know. They both recovered quickly and approached Mel.

Mel was having none of it though and began freaking out at them.  I'm sure her screams could be heard from the street above. Sam stood and ushered the paramedics to the side of the room. I couldn't hear what he was saying but I knew Sam well enough to second guess what he might be suggesting.

And I was right.

Mel's outburst had proven too much and fatigue set in quickly: within half a minute she was in a deep sleep.

They introduced themselves as Lucy and Gail.  I was glad they were women, but after Mel's reaction to Kirsty I wasn't sure she would be.

"Hi, I'm Lori, this is James and Kirsty.  Our patient is Mel.  I've known Mel too many years put a number on it.

She's thirty-two. We know she went missing two nights ago and are led to assume has been held here since. Her condition confirms this. She shows signs of physical and mental abuse. I've taken preliminary swabs and collected fibres. I have allowed her to take on limited water, but only enough to wet her mouth to enable her to talk. She's exhausted. She has been awake and talking but as you can see her outburst has used the last of her energy. "

"Okay. Let's try and wake her. Kate, you know her, it may be best you try."

I moved close and placed a hand on her shoulder.

"Mel, sweetie. It's Kate. Mel. Mel. It's time to wake. Mel."

Mel groaned and opened her eyes slightly.

"Hey. Your ride is here. We need to get you on to a stretcher, honey. You have two paramedics who are going to do that."

I paused and waited for the storm.

"No way are they touching me," she screamed. "Get them away from me."

"She's in shock," I said calmly. "James and I have got this if it's okay with you ladies? We'll get her on the stretcher, strapped so she can't move in the ambulance and then you will be able to work on her."

Sam and I finished what we could with Mel in situ and helped her on to the stretcher, ensuring that her sheet was wrapped around her, preserving any fibres that remained on her body. We would finish our process at the hospital.

***

We strapped her on to the stretcher and the paramedics started to wheel her out.

"Hang on, just one question. Mel, I need to ask you something." I held eye contact with her.

"I've not seen Ashbeck," she said. "The 'artwork' was my so-called boyfriend. The rest were his mates. They all go about in these stupid hooded sweatshirts."

"We know about the gang and we know about your friend, and, so far, she is safe."

Mel knew exactly who I meant.

"Oh, thank God. Please let her know you've found me, Kate. Take a good long look at her, you've met her before."

"I know I have. I know who she is."

"Okay. We may have to sedate her. We'll see how she is once she's out of this place."

Sam and I worked together and made Mel as comfortable as possible. It was an impossible task really. When we emerged on to the street I was impressed that Andy had cleared most of his staff away. Mel didn't have an audience and this pleased me. I climbed into the ambulance and stood beside my friend. Sam got into the front.

"Okay Mel. This is how it is, sweetie. You need medical attention that I'm not qualified to give you. You need to allow one of these ladies to look at you: so, you choose which one. I am right here with you and am not going anywhere." I was firm with my friend.

"Kate, I don't want strangers looking at me."

"I know, but we need to make sure you're okay, don't we? We need to take your blood pressure. Can we at least do that?"

Mel nodded. It was a start.

"I'm a long way off okay."

You're not kidding lady, you have one hell of a journey ahead of you, I thought to myself. Of course, I didn't say this aloud. Instead I gave my friend a knowing smile of support.

Mel chose Lucy to take her blood pressure. We had lift-off. She had allowed someone else to touch her. It was a major start.

"Thank you," Lucy said sweetly and wasted no time taking Mel's blood pressure. She was on a roll now and wasn't going to let Mel back down.

"We need to give you some fluids, Mel. Is that okay for me to do that for you?"

Mel nodded.

"Excellent. I just need to give your arm a clean with this wipe, that's it," she said, as she carried out her duties.

"Brilliant. Okay. I need to insert this cannula now so that we can get the fluids in. Just saline to help rehydrate you. Is that okay?"

Again, Mel nodded. Now she was away from that place she was becoming calmer and compliant; more understanding of her own needs and I was glad. What she'd been through was so heartbreaking, I couldn't bear to see they'd taken her personality too. I knew she'd fight this and I knew it'd take time and that it would have changed her, but I wouldn't let them break her completely. I just wouldn't.

Arriving at the hospital, Mel was checked in swiftly and escorted into a private room. She had been assigned a nurse who was currently speaking with Andy. Sam and I continued with our physical evidence recovery kit and Kirsty labelled the samples. It was highly unusual for a man to be present during this process but Mel was having it no other way.

"You need to take more than one from there," Mel said in a deadpan tone, as I was about to swab her intimate area.

"Why's that, sweetie?"

"Just trust me."

"Okay. How many?"

"Do three."

"Okay."

I didn't ask why, but I trusted what she said. Mel had done enough of this work to know what she was asking of me. She wouldn't ask this if she didn't think it was necessary. I couldn't imagine what they might have put her through for her to have made this request. I knew she wouldn't say with Kirsty in the room. I wasn't sure if she would say with Sam in the room. Who knows, maybe she wasn't ready to say at all.

When I was done collecting evidence, Sam and Kirsty left the room. It was the nurse's cue to enter. She introduced herself.

"Good morning, Mel. I'm Sasha and I'll be looking after you today. Now that's over, I bet you really want to get in that shower?"

"Oh yes! More than anything."

"Your friend here has places she needs to be, but I'm sure she'll be back later. Am I right?"

"You are. Mel, I will pop back later," I said and took her hand in mine. "I'm so glad you're safe."

"Kate, thank you. I don't know how you and Sam came to be here, but thank you."

"That my friend, is a long story."

# CHAPTER TWENTY-NINE

Many things hung in the balance now Phil had been arrested. Sam had spoken with Charlie, who assured him that everything was under control his end. He was helping with the investigation from Phil's house. His detailed diaries and records were providing vital information and through them, the team were digging deeper into Phil's life. Andy's parting words, not to underestimate his wife, had been a message to Charlie. Charlie had, it appeared, kept the whole household up all night. So far, they had uncovered a whole web of deception that involved Phil in Ashbeck's businesses well before Ashbeck was known to me. Charlie was, apparently, in his element and was considering a change in career.

Having gathered his team back at the station, Andy was attempting to debrief them. However, sprits were high and adrenaline was still surging. There was a buzz in the room and, I had to admit, I really missed moments like this. There were coffees all round, because today was another day and duty called. Andy held his in the air and gave a loud cheer. Momentarily, he'd given up and had joined in the fun. The room erupted and it took a great deal of effort for him to settle everyone back down.

"Okay! Okay!" he began.

"What a night! Great teamwork guys."

The room erupted once again.

"Let's settle down now. We have things we need to talk about."

Banter continued, but it was growing quieter. Andy continued, his voice booming over everyone.

"First things first, allow me to introduce you to the people of the moment. You've already met them, of course, but they're not who you think they are. Stand up you guys," he motioned to us. "Sam Cooper and Katie Warwick." Andy announced our real identities to the room.

"Sam has extensive undercover experience and I think you'll all agree, it's paid off in this case." Again Andy's comments were met with more cheers. "Kate was the arresting officer first time round for Ashbeck. She made sure he went away for a long time and she came back to duty and went undercover, despite no longer working for the force for this case." The room erupted once more.

"Okay, okay. Mel is doing okay. She is ready to give her statement later today. She has built a good rapport with her nurse. Now, we need to tread carefully here. Mel was also an arresting officer in the original case against Ashbeck." Andy paused and let that information sink in before continuing.

He had everyone's attention now.

"On the matter of Philip Andrews, the guv in charge at the time of Ashbeck's arrest and the man who was shot in the shoulder at the scene yesterday, there will be an ongoing investigation into his involvement into the business dealings of Ashbeck dating back prior to the original arrest. We have found significant evidence, thanks to Sam's son, Charlie, which has enabled my wife to open an investigation into the matter."

"Yes!" someone shouted from the back.

Andy made eye contact with me. He wanted me to speak. I had already run this past Pete and he had spoken with his wife. She was done with hiding. I nodded.

"Andy has asked me to address a delicate matter. I need to inform you of this matter without disclosing any information. As you might imagine, that's not an easy task. It has, during the course of Sam's and my personal undercover investigation, come to light that this gang have acquired properties that are in some way connected to Ashbeck's prior victims. Now, these victims have been part of the witness protection programme and their identities have not been violated. However, two of their locations have been. We have not sought them out, they have sought us. They have come forward. It has not been lost on Sam and I that these two women have been relocated to an area in which we knew Ashbeck operated. We need to be attentive to the possibility that the other five women are also within the local vicinity. I will be making a formal complaint to the Home Office regarding this matter and will be encouraging the two women I am in contact with to do the same."

To my utmost surprise, Pete stood up. I made eye contact with him and gently shook my head. No, don't do this, I silently pleaded. She's been through enough. Don't do this to your wife.

"Some of you know Lisa. Her real name is Jane, she told me last night. She was one of his victims all those years ago. She's gone into hiding and I have no idea when, or if, she'll be back. The house you were in last night was mine. Right opposite where they were keeping Mel. Right opposite. How is Lisa supposed to live with knowing that?" Pete sat back down and the room was silent for a long time. No one knew what to do with that information.

Andy broke the silence.

"Phil Andrews will be released under surveillance later today. There will be a detail coming from London to do the honours. Kate, what he did to you yesterday was awful and we think he might confront you about it; try to get you to withdraw your statement. He is unaware that there is this a huge investigation going on. He thinks he's getting away with the rest of it.

"What we need is for him to lead us to Ashbeck. We haven't seen him yet, he is still on the loose. He appears to have gone deep undercover. We are hoping that Andrews can coax him out."

"It won't be as easy as that," I replied.

Andy continued to praise the key players in last night's events and my mind drifted. I was no longer paying attention.

# CHAPTER THIRTY

Mel awoke but felt foggy. As her eyes began to focus on her surroundings, she noticed a black lady in a light blue dress. Her smile was kind and she smelled beautiful.

"Well hello there, sweetie. Welcome back, honey. Do you know where you are?"

Mel's first attempt to speak failed. The lady offered a glass of water and helped Mel with the task. Mel took thirsty gulps, but the lady pulled the glass away.

"Slow, slow, slow. Take sips."

Mel looked her in the eyes and was touched by their kindness.

"Thanks."

"Now. Tell me where you think you might be."

"Hospital. It smells like a hospital and you look like a nurse. A very kind nurse, who smells a whole lot sweeter than I do."

"Okay. That's good, you know where you are. And don't you go worrying about smells. We'll get you cleaned up just as soon as we can."

"You can't clean me up until the police have taken a rape kit."

"You don't remember having that done already?"

"I used to work in that area. I am a police officer. I've not had that done yet."

"The team have done it already. Everything is already on its way to the lab. As soon as they left you fell asleep. You can shower whenever you're ready. I can stay in with you, or can leave the room. The choice is yours."

"Please stay. You are a breath of fresh air in my life right now."

The nurse smiled sweetly and Mel thought to look at her name badge. Sylvia. It suited her she thought.

"Here, when did you last eat? At least have a couple of mouthfuls before you try and stand."

Mel picked up a slice of toast and nibbled at it. She was becoming more aware of her surroundings. She had a private room. There was a wet room just through the door and she longed to stand under the shower. Despite all the rape victims she had supported over the years, the urge to scrub herself clean was overpowering. The grime and stench she carried on her skin would wash away. What she needed, though, was to not feel so dirty on the inside. She knew no amount of soap and water would make that go away, but the urge to try was intense. Protruding from under her bedding were varying tubes that were attached to various machines. Her blood pressure was a little high, but under the circumstances that was to be expected.

Her nurse, Sylvia, busied herself with monitors and making notes. She was quiet unless Mel wanted to talk. Two ladies knocked on the door and Sylvia went to speak with them.

Despite the lack of soap and shampoo, Mel stood under the shower. She didn't wait for the water to warm up. The feeling of the water on her body was fantastic. She didn't care that the cuts on her stomach were stinging. They were not deep enough for stitches. Mel heard a knock on the door and it opened a crack.

"Mel, there is a lady here to see you called Kate. She's brought you shampoo and shower gel. Could I bring it in for you?"

"No. Kate can bring it in herself please."

"Are you okay with that?" the nurse asked me.

Without replying, I walked into Mel's bathroom. The sight before me reduced me to tears. I so wanted to be strong for my friend but I am done.

"I know this isn't what you use normally, but it's better than nothing," I said, squirting a generous amount of shampoo into Mel's held out palm. I watched without staring as my friend scrubbed her scalp and rinsed. She held out her palm again.

"More please, Kate."

I obliged this routine until the bottle was empty. Next Mel started on her body. I opened the shower gel and wished I had brought two bottles. Perhaps limiting this routine was a good thing. Mel scrubbed and scratched at her skin until it was raw. She moaned that the water needed to be hotter. I was glad when the bottle was empty. Mel stood under the water for a further five minutes and I didn't know what I could do to help her further. The wounds on her stomach were bleeding from the scrubbing.

I turned and took a bath towel from behind me. Mel needed to stop now.

"Mel. Please turn the water off. I have a nice fresh towel waiting for you."

She looked at me and turned the water off without speaking. Holding the towel out, I wrapped my friend in it. With the smaller towel, I dried her face and gently rubbed at her hair.

When we returned to the bedroom, Sylvia has remade the bed with fresh linen. There were two mugs of steaming tea waiting too, one for each of us. I helped Mel on to the bed and Sylvia dabbed blood from her wounds and fetched dressings.

I took this opportunity to take a closer look. I was blown away at what I saw. I hadn't clocked what the wounds were through the water and soap, but now it was clear. Despite its crudity, the shape was definite. A thirteen-step pyramid with the top part missing; as if it was unfinished.

"Mel, would you mind if I took a photo of this?"

"Go ahead. It's going to cost me a packet to get it covered up. It's just awful, isn't it?"

"You know I can't comment as to why, but I need to show this to Sam right now."

296

"There are others. Oh God, no! He's always mutilated, Kate. But not like this."

"I know. This is definite change in MO. But *he* didn't do this did he? This wasn't Ashbeck?"

"No."

"Have you seen Ashbeck?" I knew I'd already asked her that, but I needed to be sure.

"No."

For that I was glad.

I took a few images of Mel's stomach. I viewed them, selected the best one and sent it to Sam with the caption 'Image of 13-step unfinished pyramid – Mel's artwork on stomach'. Within moments my phone alerted me to his reply. It wasn't polite.

Sylvia re-dressed the wounds and reconnected the monitors before fussing over the pillows.

"I will leave you two to drink your tea," she said. "Press the buzzer if you need me."

"Kate, please tell me what's going on."

"I will, but I need some answers first. I promise, I will tell you everything when I know."

"You know enough," Mel said and she has me there.

"Okay. This much I will tell you because you need to stay safe. Ashbeck has escaped. He was behind your kidnapping and I'm so very sorry to have to say this, but Mark helped him."

"That much I've worked out for myself. I've seen a lot of people, Kate, but not him."

"Thank God you didn't see him."

"The others were bad enough, including my 'so-called' bastard boyfriend."

"Phil's involved. Has been since before we were on the original case. I'm only telling you this because they are going to release him later today and I don't want him coming here and you allowing him to visit you. I will ensure you have a no visitor – unless approved by Kate and Sam – policy, if that's okay with you?"

She laughed, but I was being serious. It took her a moment or two to realise that and when she did, what little colour she had in her cheeks drained away.

"Oh hell. You mean it don't you. Okay. I'll make a list."

"The night you were kidnapped, Jen had a car accident and my train crashed. I missed my train and Jen has woken from her coma. Cutting a long story short, I've been working undercover with Sam. It was Sam that found your location while he was out running."

"Kate, be careful."

"We have been very careful. Sam is teaching me well."

"Where is he now?"

"Chatting with the nurses at their station."

"Please bring him to me."

"Okay, hang on."

Returning immediately with Sam, I was amazed at Mel's reaction.

"Thank you for untying me earlier, Sam. For covering me and for giving me dignity."

We looked at one another in amazement. We had decided not to let Mel know that he had seen her in that state and hoped that she wouldn't remember.

"Now, you can do one more thing for me please?"

"Anything Mel, name it."

"Make an honest woman of my friend!"

"How on earth did you know, Mel?"

"You're not the only profiler in the room."

Mel shifted in her bed. Her discomfort was visible for all to see.

"Is there nothing you can give Mel for her pain?" I directed my question at Sylvia.

"Are you in any pain?"

"Yes. Down there." Mel pointed with her eyes to her undercarriage.

"Okay. I can get you something for that," Sylvia said. She started to say something else but stopped herself.

"It's okay. You can speak openly in front of Kate and Sam. They are as good as family."

With an uneasiness in her voice, Sylvia continued, "Doctor tells me you have a lot of bruising and some lacerations. It's going to be painful for a while, my love."

Sam's cheeks flushed and he began to grind his teeth. He was not embarrassed that the nurse had shared that information, he was livid at what Mel had endured. I placed a gentle hand on his thigh and squeezed it. Calm down.

"Mel, I have placed an officer outside your door. Someone will be there all the time. We have a list, including photos, of the people allowed in to see you, so don't go worrying about your safety."

Mel didn't respond.

"Mel, we will be back soon, but we need to visit Jen. We haven't seen her yet."

Standing, I took a couple of steps towards Mel. I didn't know if I should hug her or not. Gingerly, I sat on the edge of her bed and placed a hand on each shoulder. She lifted her body away from the supporting pillows and I took that as my cue to embrace her. I was mindful of her wounds. Her body felt feeble in my arms and this shocked me. Sam leaned in and placed a kiss on her forehead.

"Anything you need, Mel. You only have to ask."

From his pocket, he produced a mobile phone and placed it on her bedside table.

"This is for you. It has all the numbers you'll need on it for now and, obviously, you can add more. You have unlimited texts and calls but only one gig of data."

We said goodbye and I was sad to leave. Sam had been clever. Mel was involved with a member of Ashbeck's gang, who it now appeared was high up in Ashbeck's hierarchy. He had just given us a tracking system – ultimately giving us access to Mel's network of friends and her movements when she left hospital – for as long as she used the phone. Additionally, we could keep tabs on her until Ashbeck was recaptured and I hoped that would give her a little peace of mind.

Andy had been kind enough to lend us a car from

his fleet. He had had it dropped off at the hospital and left the keys at the nurses' station.

Once on the road, I dialled Craig's number.

"Craig, it's Kate. Listen, we are on our way to visit Jen now. We are just leaving Norfolk and heading straight to you guys. How is Jen doing?" I listened to his reply.

I learned that Jen was fully awake talking and that Craig remained by her side. Her medical team were attentive, friendly and supportive. The accident had taken its toll on her body. She no longer had use of her legs, but her team were hopeful that this was temporary. They had been quick to add that they would know more over time and that they couldn't guarantee a full recovery. Her brain was allowing her to move her arms and this was a good sign. Despite this, she still had a way to go at controlling her hands, but each time she had physio there was improvement.

I let Craig know we'd found Mel and that she was now safe and in hospital.

***

Jen was holding on to a secret and it was eating away at her. She would share it with Craig, but he would just tell her she was being paranoid. He wouldn't understand. He hadn't seen the things she'd seen in her career.

"Craig, have we heard from Kate yet?"

"That was her on the phone. She is on her way to see you with Sam. They are just leaving Norfolk, so I guess they will be with us at lunchtime. Why do you ask?"

"Because I need to speak with her about a police matter."

"She isn't police any longer," Craig replied in an unconvincing way.

"Oh, you know something. What's going on, Craig? What is Kate up to? Why is Kate with Sam?"

"Whoa, back up with all the questions."

"Spill what you know."

"I don't know what's going on and that's the truth."

"But you know something. It's written all over your face and in the tone of your voice."

"Okay. Do you remember meeting Kate and Mel in London?"

"I haven't lost my memory, just the use of my legs."

"Well, Kate missed her train that night. She has been the lucky one, Jen. That train crashed and there were no survivors."

Craig allowed that to sink in.

"Bloody hell. What about Mel?"

"Mel is safe. But she hasn't been. She went missing, but Kate and Sam have found her."

"That's all you know. Where was she?"

"I honestly have no idea, sweetheart."

"Kate and Sam found her. Kate is working with Sam again?"

"Apparently so."

"Since when?"

"I assumed you knew."

"Okay. I haven't told you this because I couldn't listen to you telling me I'm paranoid. I saw Ashbeck after I crashed."

"I already know that, sweetheart. They are holding him responsible for all of this. Someone looking very much like him showed up on your dashcam."

"He's escaped? I had hoped I'd imagined it!"

"It's all over the news."

Craig was saying no more on the matter. He wouldn't be telling Jen that someone had tried to assassinate her while she'd lain in a coma. Maybe in time she could know, but not yet.

\*\*\*

Sam had driven so I could sleep. He figured I needed it more than him. When we arrived at the hospital I had no idea of our geographical location and quite honestly, there were more important things on my mind right now. We found Jen's ward with ease, but getting through the door proved more difficult than we'd expected. In a way, I was glad that they were now taking security more seriously. I phoned Craig, who met us at the door with security guards. We signed in at the nurses' station and Sam showed his badge. I was relieved that we were not undercover any longer.

Jen looked awful. I was taken aback by the way she looked. Bruising of varying colours covered every piece of bare skin. Her face was swollen. Upon seeing

Sam, Jen smiled. She then turned her attention to me. Staring for a long moment at a familiar face, but without recognition.

"How are you doing, Jen?" I asked my friend.

Jen's eyes widened in disbelief as it dawned on her who I was. Her smile widened and she held out her hand for me to hold. Moving around to her side, I took her hand in mine.

"Welcome back, gorgeous," I said.

Jen squeezed my hand.

"Can you talk?"

"I didn't recognise you, Kate."

"My sidekick and I have been working undercover. I needed a new image."

"You look tired."

"It's been a stressful time. I'm tired and grouchy."

"Can we ask you some questions, Jen?" Sam asked.

Jen nodded.

"We can't stop for long, but we will come back soon. Do you remember the accident?"

"I remember driving. I had just overtaken a lorry on the dual carriageway and pulled back into the inside lane. The car in front of me swerved to miss a parked car. I didn't have time because I was distracted. I saw Ashbeck standing with another man. Kate, I saw Ashbeck.

Craig just told me, literally after you called, that he's involved."

"He sure is. The other man. Can you remember what he looked like?" I am out with what we needed to know.

"He was wearing a hooded jumper with owl eyes on the hood."

"Did you see his face?"

"Yes."

"Start with his eyes. Can you describe his eyes?"

"They were dark circles. Small. Too small for the size of his face."

Sam drew this detail on his paper.

"His nose was long, but it was squashed at the end and rather crooked."

Again, Sam drew.

"His lips were puffy and he had bruising to his cheek."

"Which cheek, Jen?"

"To my right. So, it would have been his left."

Sam framed the image in a black hooded jumper and placed owl eyes where they needed to go. He turned the image around for Jen to look at.

"Not bad. The nose was crooked in the other direction though."

Sam redrew the image making the requested change. Jen nodded.

"Redraw it with the deputy commissioner's haircut," Jen added and looked pleased with herself.

Then it dawned on us all.

"Jen, you are a diamond," Sam said.

"We'll come back soon, I promise," I said, before adding, "but we need to get this information back to HQ."

"Jen, the information you have just given us is vital to our investigation. We are now able to move forward and make some waves. If Phil shows up to visit you, do not let him through that door. He is involved, right up to his neck. We are unsure of his motivations at this point. Something bigger than we anticipated is going on here and we intend to get to the bottom of it," Sam said, holding eye contact first with Jen and then with Craig.

Finally, it felt like progress was being made. Sam and I couldn't get out of the hospital fast enough and as soon as we were inside the car, Sam was on the phone to Andy. We had this information and we were not sure how to proceed with it. Finally, he answered.

"Andy, it's Sam. Kate and I have just seen Jen Jennings. She's awake and talking. She can positively ID both someone who she described as looking 'similar to' Ashbeck and one other at the scene of the car crash."

"Who?"

"I hope you're ready for a rough ride, my friend. Deputy Commissioner Smith."

There was a long pause.

"This is out of our hands now. I'll inform my wife."

"Who is your wife, if you don't mind me asking?"

"I will introduce you to my wife before you guys leave. Charlie is quite taken. She is quite something. We need you guys back here. Good work, by the way."

Sam insisted on driving. He had a list of people he wanted me to call during the journey. Top of his list was Charlie.

"Hello." His voice sounded into the car because I had put him on speaker.

"Charlie, it's Kate and you're on speaker."

"Hey Stepmum," he chirped through the loudspeaker. "How you doin'?"

"Charlie!" Sam laughed.

"Hi Dad. Update. I've been in your room at the B & B and installed cameras. Andy is convinced Phil will go back. He doesn't expect you to stay there, by the way. Just wants to catch him on camera."

"Listen Charlie, if you need a drink or some chocolate they're in the rucksack. Help yourself," I said.

"Thanks. I might just do that. Guess you're not going to be evil after all."

"Charlie, that's enough!"

"Come on Dad, I'm jerking you guys about. You know I like Kate."

"Listen son, make yourself useful. We should be about three hours. Could you order a Chinese and have it delivered? I'll pay you back."

"Sure. What do you like Mum?"

"I'm not fussy. I like it all."

"Don't buy her all of it. She'll get fat. Hey Charlie. Don't go out and about. There's a lot going on out there and you don't need to be caught up in the middle of it. And Charlie, I already have cameras hidden, so you don't need to worry about putting your own in. Andy already knows that, so I know you're on a hidden agenda."

"Oh, right. I just want you guys protected."

"Andy pretty much said the same thing. Don't worry, he's got me chaperoned."

"Listen guys, Andy has booked the three of us into another B & B. I'll text you the address. I've gathered some things for you both and taken it over there already. Hope you don't mind, Kate. I didn't rummage, I promise. I've left some stuff too, so it looks like you're just out and about. That way we won't put Phil off, you know?"

"Okay, son. We'll see you later. Text in English, I'm driving and our text talk thing…"

"Ha! Don't worry, I'll educate you so you can keep up. That's made my day!"

We ended the call and Sam took a moment to consider the conversation.

"Well, he's more supportive of us than he is of his mother."

"She cheated on you Sam and has made a lifestyle choice that Charlie's not ready to accept. That doesn't mean he holds prejudice views, it just means he's not worked out why his own mother has changed her preference. These things take time sometimes, that's all."

"You're right. You'll make a good stepmum if you'll have us." He turned his head towards me and smiled.

"Keep your eyes on the road. And you'll need to ask me properly."

"Let's phone Jade," he announced.

"Seriously? I didn't expect that."

"I am curious to know what side she is on. If she is with us, she will be fully informed. If not, she will be in a right panic. What she doesn't realise is that I know the location of the building in which she works. She's clever and resourceful, and right now I'm curious."

Dialling her number, I was surprised when she picked up on the first ring.

"Kate. I'm surprised to hear from you."

"Jade. You are on speaker. Sam is here too."

"Sam, hi."

"Hi."

"Have you heard that we found our target?"

"Yes. I am currently finishing all the paperwork now. It's a good result. Well done. It's not usual for us to have contact after the event, however. Is there an issue?"

"Plenty of them," Sam said.

"Do you need to come in for a debrief, or do you need an extension to the parameters of your mission? I could probably arrange that, but we should probably not talk about it over the phone. I will add that strategies have changed somewhat at this end and I suspect you might understand why that might be."

"We don't need a debrief, but perhaps the latter option might be of benefit."

"Okay. I'll send someone to you. I know you've broken cover, so I'll send your personal documents too. It's been a pleasure working with you both."

Jade ended the conversation. The dial tone filled the silence in the car until I turned it off.

"Cool, calm and collected," I said.

"When I think of all the missions she's sent me on, I'd hate to think she was somehow involved in all of this. I'm convinced she's genuine. I didn't like the way she reacted to you initially, but I don't think she's mixed up with Ashbeck."

We were reasonably quiet for the rest of the journey. If it wasn't for the occasional road sign read aloud, or for one of us pointing out something unusual, there would have been complete silence. I had placed my hand on his thigh and when the roads were quiet he held my hand. It was nice to be alone with one another.

My mobile broke the silence. It was Andy.

"Andy. You are on speaker."

"According to the reports coming in, the official stance is that Deputy Commissioner Smith is missing. His wife and children were found at home bound, gagged and tied together in their lounge. Apparently, the eldest daughter had made a good attempt at escaping, but that resulted in a broken arm and a dislocated shoulder. That didn't stop her delivering her mother's baby with the assistance of armed response. They are now safe in hospital, still under armed guard."

"Has he been kidnapped?"

"Unconfirmed."

"And are we suspecting Ashbeck?"

"Again, unconfirmed. If Jen Jennings saw the pair of them together at her crash site, they are in this together, right? She's not safe. She needs extra protection and I have my wife sorting that. I also know this: Smith's wife and his children were prepped for Ashbeck's arrival. There were three packs of playing cards left on the front doorstep. He planned to pay them a visit. Now, what I would like to know is if Smith is involved, did he know this detail?"

"That's a grim thought."

"Come direct to my house. I will collect Charlie. My wife has cooked a massive meal and has invited you all. I can't imagine you two have had any good food of late. I'll text you the address."

"That's very kind. Thank you."

"You're welcome. Charlie and Ruth get along just fine. Ruth is my daughter."

"We'll see you later and thank you, Andy."

Breaking the connection, I turned to Sam. He looked exhausted.

"What do we know about Phil before you met him?"

"Not much, princess. We grew up together. We went to uni together, joined the forces together, joined the police together and went undercover together."

"Okay. What about his father?"

"He wasn't about much until we'd almost finished secondary school. He served in various places, the Falklands, Ireland and Korea too, I think."

"What about the deputy commissioner? Is he ex-army?"

"Well he's about the same age. There's a question. I have no idea."

"Worth investigating don't you think?"

"Definitely."

We pulled up outside Andy's house. He must have heard us arrive because the door opened and he was waiting for us to park. He ushered us inside and introduced us to his wife, Kerry, and to his daughter, Ruth. Charlie entered and there was a hug for his father. Turning to me, we also hugged and he welcomed me to his family. I was touched to say the least.

"Are you two a couple?" Andy asked and let out a laugh.

"We've known each other for years, Andy. We reconnected when I missed my train and yes, it's all very new, but we are together."

"This isn't a great start to a new relationship, I'm sorry for that."

We ate, drank wine and chatted. Ruth and Charlie left us to it. When we finally joined them, they looked rather cosy. Andy had been right, they did appear to be getting along.

\*\*\*

"Andy, we have the need to use a computer at the station. We have had a thought about a possible connection between Phil and the deputy commissioner. It's flimsy at best, but we think it's worth considering."

"Go on, convince me."

We relayed our thoughts. Andy produced a simple Internet search and found a news article showing the DC in military uniform. Bingo. We had one connection, we now needed the reasoning behind Ashbeck's motivations. We needed to connect him to Vietnam.

"Let's take this to the station. Kerry and the kids can keep each other company."

"Don't you want to run this by her?" Sam enquired.

"She's already on it. Trust me, she's got a head start on this by several hours. Let's see what we can find out. Let's call it friendly competition."

I thought about what Andy was saying and understood that he might need to prove himself to his wife, whoever she might be. What I did know was we didn't have time for games. Our time would be better served focussing on another avenue. I put my point over to the two men before me.

"What I suggest is that we work with your wife and ask her how she thinks our time would be most beneficially spent. If she is already focussing her time on this, then our time would be of more use doing something else. How openly can we talk in front of Ruth?"

Andy looked momentarily deflated, but he knew I was right.

"You have a point. Ruth has an internship with her mother. She has a higher clearance than me. You can say what the hell you like to her. As for your son, Sam, despite him having absolutely no clearance, he seems to know more than any of us about what's going on."

# CHAPTER THIRTY-ONE

Not only had Kerry been working constantly with Charlie and Ruth, who she had set up at the kitchen table, she had produced a wonderful dinner for us all. A far nicer option than the takeaway we'd had planned.

Charlie and Ruth were tapping away at their keyboards when we'd arrived and had only taken a break to eat. They had soon returned to their makeshift command post. Kerry excused herself often to monitor their progress. Charlie had been let loose with a high-end computer, endless wires, printers, modems and no end of other technical garb. I hoped she knew what she was doing.

"How come you are trusting Charlie to work on one of your computers?" Sam asked.

"Oh, I'm not trusting him, Sam. Why do you think I've set them up where I can keep a very firm eye on them? I am using his incredible brain to my advantage. He can do amazing things with computers. I bet you've never had parental blocks on your Internet, have you?"

"Actually, I tried everything, but he always hacked around it. In the end, I gave up, it was one less battle

I had to fight. I figured it best to channel his energy into using his talent for something positive, rather than always trying to break the rules."

"You were lucky, he turned out an alright kid."

"Thanks!" Sam smiled. "How about Ruth? Do you trust her without the influence of my son?"

"Not even slightly. She doesn't get to use my equipment without my supervision. Tonight, they have a little freedom because you guys are here. This is rare. But they do have specific information they are seeking. Very specific information, with strict search boundaries. I will be alerted if they go AWOL in the system."

I revealed what I had found out about a possible army link between Phil Andrews and the deputy commissioner. But she didn't look convinced.

"He was definitely in the army. We joined up together. We were posted together, until I came home injured. He got posted once more without me. When he came home that last time he was different somehow. He left and we joined the police together. We went undercover together. We came out of that together too, but went to different stations. I can prove that but would need to go home to get the evidence."

"Okay. If you would give me your rank and number I could trace Andrews that way."

Sam obliged and Kerry excused herself. Within five minutes, she had returned with all the evidence we needed. Documents, photographs and articles linking the two men.

"Good hunch, Kate," Andy said.

Charlie appeared in the doorway.

"You guys have a visitor. Uncle Phil is sitting on your bed!"

"I think you need to stop calling him that, Charlie. Show me."

Charlie walked over and placed his monitor on the table.

"I'll leave it with you. Things are getting interesting in here.

You might want to join us, Mrs Preston."

Kerry excused herself again and followed Charlie back to the kitchen. We let them get on with it for about a minute, after all, her visits there had been frequent. Understandably.

"Jesus Christ, Charlie. How on earth have you got your hands on this?"

The three of us leapt out of our seats and ran to the kitchen. What had he done now?

"Charlie, what have you done?" Sam asked.

"It's okay. You guys need to see this. Gather round. I've no idea how he's managed to get hold of this without alerting the system," she said, giving him a playful punch on the shoulder. "Ruth, come look."This is a letter from a hospice requesting that Ashbeck visit his dying mother." She clicked another screen. "This is her DNA." She clicked another screen that brought up Ashbeck's DNA. "This is his DNA." She gave us a moment to compute what we were seeing. Ashbeck had been given permission to visit a dying woman who was not his mother. This was how he had escaped.

"Even to my untrained eye, this is not a match," she was saying.

"Charlie, you have just discovered the how. Where did you find this information?"

"Wouldn't you like to know. And if you're thinking of checking my keystrokes, I've turned that off already. It was the first thing I did. My knowledge of how things work is mine and I just can't share it. All you need to know is the results I can get you. There's more if you want it?"

"Seriously?"

"The ace of spades showed up on one case in America. But we are talking forty-four years ago. They'd given a name to Interpol, but nothing has ever shown up."

My rage didn't take long to surface and Sam knew exactly what I was about to say. He took my arm and shot me a look. He didn't want me getting upset in front of these people. If I spoke now that was likely, we both knew that. I was so angry.

"Kate made a request to Phil Andrews that he contact Interpol when they first caught Ashbeck. Her team concluded that the seven victims they had couldn't have been his first. He was too practised for that. Phil refused."

"It's not Ashbeck though. It's Alec Johnson. He was in Vietnam and he had a history with the ace of spades while he was there, so they say."

Sam and I exchanged looks. Could we now know a true identity for this monster?

"What else do they say, Charlie?"

"He left America on a return flight in the September out of New York. He never returned. His destination was the UK."

"Jesus Christ. What did we do to deserve him?"

"Kate, I need to speak with you in private. Please follow me," Kerry said.

I followed her through the spacious property and was impressed by the couple's taste. This wasn't the time to pass comment, so I didn't. She took me into what I expected was going to be her private office. She took a key from her pocket to unlock the door. I was amazed at what awaited us. Monitor after monitor lined one wall. Attached to each was a keyboard.

"You look shocked," she said. "Don't be. I am a private investigator with a very high clearance."

"I figured you were something along those lines. This is impressive, Kerry. What do you need to talk to me about?"

"I am aware that you know the whereabouts of two of Ashbeck's original victims. I've found all seven based on the information you and Sam gave us on Monarch Properties. It's frightening. I've gone right back to the person who assigned them their new identities. Andy has that person in custody right now. Eddie Sanders. He himself lived opposite one of the victims."

"Mandy Wiseman. Sam and I met her and have spoken with her several times over the course of the investigation."

"Are you aware that he befriended Mel and became her boyfriend? Are you aware that he was part of her kidnapping?"

"Yes."

"You do know that your friend will have to be investigated, don't you?"

"She's right in the middle of all this. Do you know that Sam gave her a mobile phone, so he can have her calls monitored?"

"No, I didn't. That's a smart move. Kate, I'm going to be frank with you. You're a smart lady, and correct me if I'm wrong, but I don't think you have any interest in returning to the police force but you've enjoyed – if enjoyed is the right word – getting your hands dirty again. How am I doing so far?"

"I am contracted for this case only, to work undercover with Sam. I'm no longer undercover but there might be a possibility to have my contract extended to continue working on the case."

"Excellent. In that case, I am offering you a position with me. As a private investigator. Take your time, think about it. Talk to Sam about it. I'd take him on too, but if he's half as stubborn as Andy he won't accept my offer."

"Will you tell me who you are?"

"No. If you agree to work for me you'll find out soon enough. Otherwise, you don't need to know."

"Fair enough."

"Come on. I've left that dangerous boy with my equipment for long enough. I seriously need to check on him."

When we returned to the kitchen there was more news waiting for us. It was Ruth's turn to bask in the glory and to show that she was just as clever as Charlie.

"Here, take, a look at this you two."

She had found an address for a man, dating back decades, given by the deceased woman from the hospice, claiming that her son had gone missing. He didn't reappear back into her life until Ashbeck was arrested and she started writing to him in prison. It was months before he answered. I would love to see copies of those letters and wondered if the prison ever kept copies of the letters that prisoners sent 'home'.

Time was passing quickly and none of us had slept since the night before the raid. Sam and I had both had wine, so Andy phoned for a taxi. It didn't take long to arrive. We left Charlie hitting keys with Ruth and had no doubt he wouldn't sleep. He was young and could handle the pace. We weren't and couldn't. What Kerry did was her choice. If I was her I would remove the electric from the house and ban all electronic devices for at least six hours to get some rest. But I wasn't her.

When the taxi dropped us off, we decided to take a walk along the beach. It had become a comfort to do so. We strolled towards the water, hand in hand. Our involvement in the case was at an end. We had found

Mel. It was over for us, but she had a long journey ahead of her.

The relief had lifted my mood. Spending time with Andy and Kerry had helped too, I felt we had made new friends there. For the first time since viewing the news that morning in Sam's flat, I felt that our life was our own.

When we reached the water, Sam stopped and turned towards me.

"Remember what I said the first time we walked on this beach?"

Sliding my arms around his waist, I pressed up against him. "Of course I do."

Sam wrapped his arms around me and we shared an intimate moment that reminded us of who we were. Each of us felt for the other's scar and remembered saving one another's life. This very act had jerked us back into the reality of our own lives and the moment felt good. Very good.

Sam pulled back suddenly, but I was not ready for the moment to end.

"We have company," he said quietly into my ear.

With a heavy sigh, I loosened my embrace and turned to face two men walking with purpose towards us. They are thickset, tall men and were dressed all in black. They were wearing black hooded sweatshirts. The hoods were down, but I had to wonder if they had yellow eyes on them.

"Boss needs to speak with you both," the stockier of the two men announced.

"He can wait five minutes," Sam replied. "Firstly, he is no longer my boss and secondly, I'm not on duty right now."

"Up to you. Come now voluntarily, or it will be under duress." The stockier man shifted slightly in order that we could see his gun. His double did the same.

"Our boss wouldn't send two henchmen, so we're guessing your boss is someone we don't want to see." Sam was buying time.

"You are supposed to be dead, Katie-Anne Warwick," the same man said, pointing at me.

"Who? I don't know who you think I am, but you seem to have me mixed up with someone else," I responded and I hoped I sounded sincere; because I didn't feel it.

"Good try, lady," the other guy said.

"Oh, you talk too. And there was me thinking you were the shy one." Sam took my hand as he spoke. "Come on, love. These two sweethearts need some alone time with their weapons." Walking away, he held my hand so tightly.

Sam had been tall enough to notice Phil approaching from behind the men. I had no idea. When they were in range, he made his move. The men were in Phil's sights and he fired two shots, hitting each in the back of the knee. They fell to the floor in turn, rolled and drew their weapons. Phil was faster. He shot both weapons from each of their hands. I wondered where he had learned to shoot like that and then remembered his army days.

Phil approached, gun poised. I glanced at Sam and the shocked look on his face was painful to see. Sam didn't hold my attention for long. Phil was firing again. Explosion after explosion seemed to echo over the water, like pebbles skimming. Phil was out of control.

During a brief pause in gunfire, Phil screamed at his victims.

"Where is he?" he demanded.

Each time they refused to answer, Phil made another hole in their bodies.

Sirens were approaching, getting louder and louder. Multiple cars stopped, but no one approached. They were not armed. I could see officers evacuating the area and I wondered how many of them I would recognise from the other night, from when we raided the house and the cellar.

Turning my attention back to Phil, I watched wide-eyed as he continued with his torture. I wanted to run away, but my legs wouldn't move. Sam's grip on my hand remained tight, he wasn't going to let me move.

Phil was becoming impatient with the men. His demands for information were being denied. He fired one last shot towards the larger of the two men, hitting him between the eyes. When the smaller man still refused to offer information, he met the same fate.

Phil turned and faced us. Sam and I were motionless and had no idea what to expect of this man. A man who we had respected once. A man who Sam had made godfather to his only child. A man we no longer recognised. My heart was pumping so fast I thought it might quit.

Phil allowed his gun to fall to the floor. Relief must have been visible in my expression because it made me feel light-headed.

"Don't move," Sam whispered.

"It was the only way!" Phil shouted. "They wanted to take you both hostage. I couldn't allow that to happen. None of this has been intentional. I hope you both at least believe that! All I ever wanted was to protect everyone from Carl and it blew up in my face. You need to know what he's told me. Kate, you need to speak with the Home Secretary. I have shared everything with him. He will send for you. For both of you."

We stood, listening.

"The prime minister is aware of what I have done for the country. It's not all as it seems in your eyes right now. When you requested the information it automatically alerted his office. I have information that is on a need-to-know basis. The prime minister now believes you need to know."

Looking at Sam for reassurance, I began talking. "Boss, do you have us bugged?" I asked of this man for whom I used to hold so much respect.

"I trust you guys more than any other people on this earth. No bugs. I promise," he replied.

Our faces were not convincing him that we believed what he was saying.

"Do you seriously think you are being bugged?"

"Yes." Sam answered for me.

"Whenever we make progress there is always some distraction to put us off track. The lorry last night. This scene today. We are being monitored and it's pissing us off."

"There's nothing I can do to make you believe me other than to let you in. What do you want to know?"

Sam and I looked at one another and nodded. There was a mutual understanding at the massive risk we were about to take.

"War crimes. Explain your involvement." I was out with it.

"My father was a spy. He shared something with me he wasn't supposed to and it led to an investigation. I was accused of spying for the other side and was cleared of those charges."

"The deputy commissioner?" Sam asked.

"Same."

"How does the deputy commissioner know Johnson?" I asked.

"Jesus, you really have done some digging. I'm impressed."

"What did you expect?" Sam asked.

"Okay. We met Carl during our mission, the one you missed out on Sam. He was involved in smuggling people over the border. After we left the forces we stayed in touch – he was making a lot of money and we wanted a part of it. In the beginning, it was just background stuff, but we got in too deep. Eventually, he started blackmailing us both. We allowed just enough information to be leaked in order for you to arrest him Kate," Phil pointed at me.

"How are the train crash, Jen's car crash and Mel's disappearance linked to him, to you?" I was out with it. The reason for our involvement.

"I have no idea other than because you were involved in his arrest, interviews and victim support for those he hurt."

"You mean raped and mutilated, and how did his victims end up living opposite members of his gang, Phil?"

"I know and I'm sorry."

"Where is he?" Sam asked.

"I don't know," Phil said. "And that's the truth. I promise."

"Then why kill these two? They could have led us to him."

"A warning. This will mean something to Carl, trust me."

"That's just it. We don't know if we can any more, Boss."

"You got us tangled up in this shit – I don't even work for you any more, for Christ's sake. We're getting out of here, Sam. Come on. I've heard enough."

As we walked away, one final explosion filled the air. As we turned to face Phil, he crumpled to the ground. Running over to him, we stopped in our tracks. Half his head was spread over the damp sand. He had committed suicide.

Dialling for the emergency services, Sam looked solemn. Whatever mess Phil was involved in they had been best friends. Charlie had just lost his godfather. Grief was evident and I could not find the words right now. Actions had to speak louder than words in this sad moment and my hand rested between his shoulders and I remained close by his side.

"Police," he said into his phone, then listened.

"Yarmouth beach. Three bodies. The tide is coming in so you need to get the officers that have just watched events unfold from the roadside on to the beach." He listened. "About two hundred yards south of the pier. The gunman has just taken his own life. The scene is safe now. My name is Sam Cooper and I am here with Katie-Anne Warwick. We can secure the scene, but we don't want to interfere with the evidence."

Again, Sam listened.

"We'll stay close to keep others away. I know the identity of the gunman, yes. You are going to wish you'd kept him in custody. It's Phil Andrews. The other two men are also armed. They drew their weapons, but didn't fire any shots. Andrews took his own life. Half his face is missing. Please hurry."

Within a couple of minutes two officers begin walking towards us. More sirens could be heard. Several more cars and three ambulances pulled up at the edge of the beach together. Both of us waved our arms to attract their attention.

"Do we let them in on what we've found out? We'll have to make statements and need to be speaking from the same place."

"Full disclosure. Do not hold back. Don't know about you, but I'm done with this shit." Sam was keeping eye contact with me. He was holding back tears. As I reached out to touch his arm he spoke. "Don't touch me, princess. I'll crumble and right now I need to hold it together," he said.

I nodded.

Finally, the officers arrived. They approached us, spoke briefly and patted us down. I didn't recognise either of them.

Turning us, they placed cuffs around our wrists and read us our rights. Unbelievable. We walked in silence up the beach and were placed into separate cars.

We were taken to Andy's station and escorted to separate interview rooms without being booked in. This wasn't official.

"Sit down."

So why was the guy being so cold and calculating?

He produced a file, slid it across the table and motioned for me to open it. I did and was astonished to see my own passport and other personal documents.

"How did you get these?"

"That doesn't matter. Yours were destroyed in the fire. My people have been working at providing you with new ones for when you broke cover. You have done what you came here to do, Kate. May I call you Kate?"

I was looking through the documents and was only half listening. I nodded.

"Sorry, yes. Of course. Sorry, I didn't catch your name?"

"That's because I haven't told you my name."

"Please thank Jade for me," I said, sure that she was behind this.

"I have no idea who Jade is and Kate, you look exhausted. When did you last sleep?"

"The night before last, but much has happened since. There just hasn't been time. It was where we were heading. Kind of wish we hadn't gone for fresh air now."

"I bet."

"May I ask why you arrested us at the scene, but haven't booked us in?"

"Okay. Kate, you have not been arrested. We have Sam under caution and he is currently being booked in. We don't have a choice. He was undercover with Andrews for years, we need to check it out."

"Jesus, no. Not Sam. He's not involved in this."

"We don't think he is. But we do have to check it out. You do understand why we would be concerned?"

"Oh, I understand alright. Phil is dead and you need someone else to focus your enquiries on. Let me tell you this about Sam, he is the most honest man you will interview. He has been livid with Phil over the past few days. I have been convinced that we've been bugged and if that has been you guys then you will know that he has not had a part in this conspiracy."

"We need you off the case. Let's face it, you're not even police any longer. Andrews had no right bringing you back in, despite your expertise on Ashbeck."

"That's a shame you feel that way. Am I free to leave?"

"You are."

"Goodbye then."

As soon as I walked free of the station's front door I was met by Andy. His cheeks were flushed.

"My wife wants to speak with you urgently. Apparently, you have her number?"

"I do. I'll phone her right away. Andy, you need to take a few deep breaths and calm yourself down. Your blood pressure looks like it's through the roof. I'm worried about you."

"Phone my wife now!"

I rummaged in my pocket for the business card Kerry had given to me and dialled her number. She picked up on the first ring.

"Kerry, it's Katie. Andy asked me to call you."

"Katie. You are not going back to your B & B. I have ordered a car for you and it is waiting in the car park. Come back to the house and I will explain what's going on, then you can sleep."

She continued chatting, letting me know the registration number of the car and once I'd spotted it, tapped on the window and climbed inside, she ended the call. The drive wasn't far but it was done in silence. Kerry greeted me on the doorstep and thanked the driver. No money changed hands and I suspected he worked for her. I didn't ask and she revealed nothing.

This woman held many secrets.

"You poor thing, you look exhausted."

"Have you heard what's been going on?"

"Yes. Charlie doesn't know yet. We thought it best that it came from you."

I nodded and walked towards the kitchen.

"Charlie, we need a quiet word."

"Hi Kate, I thought you guys left ages ago."

"We did, please Charlie. We need to talk right now."

"Hang on a minute, I might be on to something here."

"Charlie, I'll take over, you need to go and sit with Kate." Kerry was kind but firm.

Looking up from the screen, Charlie made eye contact with me and noticed how distressed I was.

"Geez Kate, you look awful. What's happened?"

"Please let Ruth know what's going on."

Kerry nodded.

Charlie followed me into the hallway and we sat at the bottom of the stairs. There was no easy way to break the news, so I was honest.

"Charlie, Phil has done some awful things and we are all finding out just how awful as time goes on. You have been an amazing part of that and we are all so proud of what you've uncovered." I took his hand and gave it a squeeze. "Now, I need you to listen carefully. Let me finish okay?"

"Okay."

"What's been uncovered has consequences. They are short-term consequences and I will do everything in my power to ensure that. Is that clear?"

"What's happened to Dad?"

"I assume you know that he worked undercover with Phil for many years?"

"Yeah. But I don't know what they worked on. I could probably find out if you want? Do you think that might help?"

"That's a question for Kerry. Please don't do that off your own back. Now, I need to tell you two things. The first is that the police need to investigate any connection your dad may, or may not, have had with Ashbeck. Now I am behind your father one hundred per cent, okay? You have my word. But, they have arrested him."

"Jesus Kate, he'll lose his job."

"Not necessarily. But, yes, it's possible."

"He'll lose his credibility."

"He will need us, Charlie. Now I have something else to tell you. This isn't police gossip or news frenzy. Your dad and I were witness to this and in his absence, I feel it appropriate that I tell you. Not because I'm his partner, but because I've known you for a very long time. Tonight, after leaving here, your dad and I took a walk on the beach to get some air. We were approached by two large men and then Phil joined us. The men were behaving in a threatening way so Phil shot them. He didn't kill them at first, he tortured them with gunshots.

332

He did kill them in the end. Charlie, he also took his own life."

"They are going to frame my dad for what he did because he is dead, aren't they? The selfish…"

"We don't know that. What I do know is we could ask Kerry to do a search right here, right now, to see if we can find any links. If we can't find any then we know they don't exist. How does that sound?"

"I've not been this scared since he got stabbed."

"And I was there to save his skin that time. I'm here this time too, for both of you."

"Thanks Kate, that means a lot," he said and gave me a hug.

"Come on, let's get back."

We walked back to the kitchen and Charlie was greeted by Ruth, who had a massive hug for him. They looked very comfortable in one another's arms and I wondered what else had been going on with them other than computer work.

"Does your earlier offer still stand?"

"It certainly does. Am I welcoming you into the fold Ms Warwick?"

"Yes please. I would be very honoured to be part of your team. I am most impressed with your set-up."

"Oh, this is only my home set-up. Wait until you see what else I have."

Charlie's eyes lit up.

"Mum. I'm not getting anywhere. We really need his help. He seems to jump through hoops I can't see."

"I know, sweetie. I think I need to get him on board too. I'm just considering the risks involved though."

"Better to have me on the inside, hacking out, than on the outside, hacking in."

"Don't think I've not considered that too. Charlie, let me level with you," Kerry was saying. "I have suggested that we try and find a connection between your father and Ashbeck. Let's hope to hell there isn't one, but I feel it will be helpful to us to find out one way or the other."

"He already suggested that to me, Kerry. I told him not to do that search without your permission."

"I'm going to time you. I've been working on this for ten minutes and can't find anything they worked on undercover. Go on, be a hero."

It took Charlie exactly two minutes and twenty seconds to get his first hit. Thirty more seconds to get his second hit and ten more for the third. I was astonished that it was that simple to obtain undercover documents so easily and was convinced that someone would bash on the door to arrest Charlie and Kerry within the hour. This was a security breach and someone would be in a whole lot of trouble. I had no idea Charlie was this clever with computers.

"Kerry, do you have clearance to obtain this information?"

"I do and I know it's a big ask, but you need to trust me on this, Kate. Time will reveal who I am, but in the meantime, have faith."

I took the printouts and started to read the classified information. Sam and Phil had worked on some long-term undercover details. They had joined a gang, two months apart. The initiation was for each to kill a man. Reading this sickened me to the core. I was learning things about Sam I didn't want to know and that he wouldn't want me to know. He was exonerated of the crime, but that didn't matter. He had killed someone in cold blood, outside war. I was having a hard time with that. Every instinct wanted me to protect Charlie from this, but he had found it.

The second document revealed details of drug smuggling.

It was the third that had me worried. The two men had gone undercover to infiltrate a gang who were suspected of smuggling people. Kerry and I shared a concerned look and decided we needed to concentrate our search here.

"Okay. Kate, I have put fresh towels in the spare room, it has an en-suite. Help yourself to the toiletries. I have also put a selection of clean clothes on the bed. We're about the same size. We all need to take a break and freshen up."

"Thank you and yes, it's been quite a day."

"Right. Scram you two," Kerry said to the youngsters and waited for them to leave.

She turned to me.

"If you hadn't noticed, there's something going on with those two. They think us oldies don't know. What little rest we have had since Charlie arrived, they have had it together. Thought you should know."

"Good for them, as long as you're both okay with that."

"They are both adults. We are fine with it. Come on, let me show you the way."

\*\*\*

The shower felt wonderful and I tried to clear my mind of everything that had happened over the past few hours. Easier said than done. Images of mutilated bodies, Mel's wound, Jen's words and her paralysed body, Phil firing at specific body locations and then half his face missing, telling Charlie that Sam had been arrested and the printed documents that now sat on Kerry's kitchen unit that might implicate Sam in horrors I didn't want to speak of.

Sam, Sam, Sam.

No amount of water could wash the past few days away.

Returning to the bedroom, wrapped in a baby pink towel, I looked through the clothes Kerry had selected for me. Choosing black yoga trousers for comfort and an oversized jumper because I was tired and prone to get cold when I felt this way, I dried and dressed. Running my fingers through my short hair, I opted for the scruffy look. That would have to do.

Emerging from the bedroom, I met Ruth on the landing.

"Hey, would you like to borrow my hairdryer? Come in. You'll have to fight Charlie for it though, he's a right ponce over his hair," she said laughing.

I dutifully followed her and hoped my astonishment didn't show as I entered. Andy and Kerry's house was beautiful. Ruth's room, on the other hand, was abysmal. I was sure Kerry would be embarrassed that I had seen it.

"I think it best there's no secrets between any of us, right? Mum will hate that you've been in here. And, for the record, I hate it in here too. It's just got to the point where I'm too busy to get on top of it. Charlie, you're done. Pass that to Kate," she ordered.

It took less than two minutes for my hair to dry. We left the room together. I was glad to be away from the mess.

Kerry was already in the kitchen when we arrived. Ruth was quick to make her aware that she had no secrets from me with regards to how untidy she was. The poor woman was beyond embarrassed. Changing the subject, she fussed over who wanted what hot drinks and tasked Ruth with making a plate of sandwiches to keep us going on the food front.

"Do a mixture of fillings, there's plenty of choice in the fridge."

Kerry picked up the three documents that were going to be the focus of our attention. One document particularly worried me beyond comprehension. It was damning as an individual document and we desperately needed to verify that there was no connection to Ashbeck and the case. I said a silent prayer and made a promise to go to church once this was over.

"Kate, I want your thoughts on this."

I moved over to Kerry and we huddled over the document and read in silence.

*Smuggling along an almost deserted coastline in East Sussex, this sophisticated gang operate a multinational, multilayered enterprise.*

This wasn't sounding good so far. I read on.

*Two specially trained officers will begin their covert operation three months ahead of joining forces with the gang. They will make themselves known, have dealings on the streets and work their way into the trust of the hierarchy of the group. These officers are highly skilled and will kill if that is what it takes.*

*They agree to revoke all contact with their former life for the greater good of society for as long as it takes to bring this organisation to justice...*

The brief continued for several pages, giving detailed descriptions of what Sam and Phil's expectations were, before giving details of the results that they got. There was no mention of Ashbeck or Johnson. Not that I would have expected there to have been. If Phil was mixed up with him during this case, I suspected he might have used a different name. There was no mention of Monarch Properties. None of the names mentioned in the report were familiar to me from the original case, or the case that Customs were working on when we were information sharing at the time. Nothing matched.

"Nothing is familiar to me. Not one name jumps out at me from my past case, not from other cases I have

338

had access to in the past, or from what we have learnt so far in this new investigation. Nothing."

"That's good. We can cross-reference that to confirm it. That's something I will do because these two kids don't get access to the code word, Kate."

"What code word?" I asked, making eye contact with her.

Both Charlie and Ruth span around simultaneously.

"What code word?" Ruth demanded.

"Never you mind, and Kate knows exactly what I am referring to."

Raven. How did Kerry know about that? Had Sam mentioned it to her? He wouldn't dare. This revelation had me on edge and she knew it. Was this woman playing games with me? Testing me? Pushing my buttons? Why wouldn't she tell me who she was?

I was putting all my trust in her, in a stranger I'd met last night. Please God, let her be genuine.

"How do you know the code, Kerry? At least answer me that."

"I assigned that code, Kate. I know this case inside out."

Giving Kerry a sideways look, my eyebrows raised, I was waiting for answers I knew she wouldn't give me now. Still, I wasn't playing this game. Kerry would actually have to physically say the word 'Raven' for me to believe she was as informed as she was making out.

"Kate, she's right," Charlie announced.

And from the look on Kerry's face, I instantly knew

he'd gone several steps too far this time. Striding across her kitchen, anger manifesting in her expression, she demanded to see his monitor. Ruth and I exchanged worried glances, before she continued with her own work. Charlie, oblivious to the upset he was causing continued to type, his fingers were flying over the keyboard.

"Charlie, stop what you are doing immediately. Show me what you have found. Explain your comment, 'Kate, she's right.'"

"Wait, it's not this monitor. This monitor's showing three searches." He pointed to the left. "All three are military, this one is attempting to link Dad to Phil Andrews and I'm obviously getting several hits as they served together. We already knew that. The middle one," he pointed again, "is attempting to link Andrews to Deputy Commissioner Smith. Again, I'm getting some hits. The third," again he pointed, "is attempting to link Dad to Smith. So far, nada. Good news, right?"

"Good work. And your comment?" because Kerry wouldn't be distracted.

"Your name popped up hours ago, even before I started to jump through hoops. One of my first searches produced a code word assigned to the Ashbeck case that only a handful of people were privy to. Kate, you were one, along with Mel and Jen. Others included Phil, the commissioner and his deputy, and the Home Office. The code word was issued by you Mrs Preston, because you were the head of…"

"Okay, okay. I clearly have no secrets. Kate, please accept my apologies. I hadn't wanted to let this out until after this investigation, for obvious reasons, but Charlie here is far too clever for his own good. At the time of Ashbeck's arrest I headed the National Crime Agency's human trafficking department. We, quite literally, continued investigating and monitoring where you left off. Ashbeck continued running his operation from prison with the help of some very high-profile individuals. My investigation led me here and, in all honesty, it was just easier to move and step out as an independent, and consult. That way I could focus directly on this case. I have expanded into other areas, but my priority is this one case; my staff deal with our other cases."

Turning to Charlie, she added,

"Remind me never to get on your bad side, Mr Cooper. Go on, we're all in this together. What's the code word, Charlie? Let's see if you really have sussed me out."

As Charlie said 'Raven' aloud, Kerry mouthed it to me.

In that very moment, I knew she was genuine and I knew I could trust her.

"Kate, come with me. Allow me to verify who I am. You have every right to be paranoid and angry with me, and I don't blame you."

I dutifully followed her back to the office, where she produced all the documentation to prove who she was. For the first time, I had faith that Sam would be okay. That his fate was in safe her hands, that we would get him out of this mess.

Moving back to the kitchen, I was keen to find out what the kids had established with their searches.

"Ruth, how are your searches going?"

"Well, I've established a few things. I've queued them up to print, but I think we need a third printer, to be honest, these two aren't keeping up with demand."

"Okay, I'll see to that," Kerry said. "What've you found?"

"Andrews has several guns registered to his name. I've printed the list, copies of the various documents, his licence etc. Mr Cooper also has one gun registered in his name, but no licence that I can find, which is a little off. I've printed a copy of the purchase document."

"I didn't know Dad had a gun, did you?" Charlie directed this at me.

"No way. He always said there was no place for guns in civilian life."

"Exactly. That doesn't sit right with me."

Having an idea, I voiced it.

"Let's cross-reference this evidence with the undercover work. The initiation murder Sam committed, what was the cause of death?"

"Hmm, good point," Kerry said, as she walked to the part of the kitchen worktop where she'd left that document.

"Stabbing," she announced. This revelation saddened me. I could not believe Sam was capable of killing another human being, outside war, whatever the motive or the means. My heart sank. Kerry seemed to read my mood and placed a hand on my forearm.

"We will get to the bottom of this," she assured me.

"Kate, I need you to sit down. There's something you need to know," Kerry said and repositioned one of her kitchen chairs, motioning for me to use it. "Firstly, Sam is being held at my request and is being interrogated by my old office, the National Crime Agency. This is for his own protection. He cannot be involved in these searches, it's bad enough that you and Charlie are. Sam is being interviewed at Andy's station while we carry out our searches. He's under caution regarding his associations with Andrews because we have to cover every single angle on this."

I was not sure how I felt about the information she was revealing to me and even Charlie had stopped typing to listen, his expression blank.

"Don't both of you look blankly at me. Is it not bad enough I have his son and his partner working on this? I can't also have the man himself working on his own investigation too. The both of you are not on my books, you were never part of this. Is that clear?"

We both nodded.

"Ruth, the two men shot by Andrews should have had their preliminary details entered on to the system by now. Please check for results."

Ruth's fingers flew across her keyboard as Kerry disappeared, returning moments later with a third printer in her arms. Within minutes she had it set up, Ruth had redirected her print queue and it had sprung into action.

Ruth had much to share.

"Okay, Sam's test for gunshot residue was negative, just so we're all clear on that."

"I've been with Sam for days, I could have told you that."

"You haven't been with him constantly, Kate. He went for a run without you."

I shot Kerry a look.

"How do you know that?"

"Come on. Two unknown reporters appear from nowhere, staying in a hotel owned by Monarch Properties. Vanessa gets murdered and you immediately move on. Do you seriously think I'm not going to have you tailed?"

"Did you have us bugged?"

"I didn't go that far. What makes you ask that?"

"Someone did. Phil swore it wasn't him."

"My second revelation may explain why you were bugged, especially with where you were staying. There's something else you need to know. Ruth and I have known for quite some time and Charlie has been told this evening."

Both Charlie and Ruth stopped what they were doing. This must be serious.

"This is going to be a bit of a shock, Kate, and for that I'm sorry. During this lengthy investigation, I've viewed much CCTV footage. Purely out of curiosity, I viewed several unsolved crimes that had very loose connections to Ashbeck: that included your stabbing. Now, we only had a partial face for an identity, but it went into my system none the less. Eventually we made an arrest and the image from your crime CCTV footage popped up. He was pressed at interview and admitted to stabbing you."

I was stunned.

"Now, there was so much pressure put on that young man, Kate, and eventually, he cracked. He admitted that Ashbeck had ordered the stabbing. We have it on record and he has signed a confession. Now that man remains in custody and he hasn't been charged with his crime against you yet, with actual bodily harm. It is up to you, now you know, what you wish to do with the information."

"Why hadn't I been told he'd been caught?"

"He's being processed for something else. You would have been, in due course. Ashbeck has a massive grudge against you that outweighed the actual facts that caught up with your attacker and a court found him guilty. First, Ashbeck ordered a stabbing, and now a train crash. Let's not forget, this is a man in his sixties. We are dealing with a highly organised individual with the means to, what appears to be, a team who can get their hands on whatever he asks for. "He is actively attempting to get the better of all of us and we don't need to be reminded that we still haven't caught him. We are closing in on his operatives though, as he likes to call them. His world is getting smaller, Kate."

I was stunned and had no words. How could I not have been informed of this? Perhaps if I'd have known

I'd have felt better sooner, you know, psychologically. Maybe I would have come to terms with the situation, knowing my attacker was behind bars. Every time I started to trust Kerry she threw me a curveball like this and I was back at the beginning, unsure where I stood with her. Right now, I needed Sam. I needed to know he was okay and, selfishly, I needed him here for me.

Without doubt it would take massive efforts from both of us to get us back on track after the things I'd learned about him, but I was prepared to make the effort if he was. I needed to hear his side of the story before I made judgement on what he'd done in his covert operations. We'd either work through it, or we wouldn't. Every cell in my body hoped we could. Time would tell, I guess. Right now, I needed the familiarity of him, of us, and knew deep in my heart he was the only person I fully trusted. That to me was a great place to start.

"Okay, we have news on the two bodies." Ruth was excited and set her results to print before she continued.

"Preliminary reports are suggesting a hit on the criminal records database. That means they've found a match based on fingerprints, because it's too early for DNA. The first one is… Charlie, are you ready to search this?"

"Yep."

I was amazed at the teamwork these two had going. There didn't seem to be any competitiveness between them and I found this encouraging in two people so young.

"Peter Armstrong, aka Hex. Forty-five, male, wanted for drug dealing, human trafficking and gun crimes. The second is Lucas Smee, aka Trunk. Thirty-eight, male, wanted for gun and knife crimes, and also rape." Looking up at me she added, "Kate, it would be some small consolation if these two were involved in your friend's attack and are now dead, don't you think?"

I smiled, for I still had no words.

"My daughter believes, with great conviction, that the death penalty should be brought back for some individuals. She includes Ashbeck on her personal list of potential applicants."

"Now there's a debate I'd like to have put to the prime minister," Charlie agreed.

"The two individuals were wearing hooded style sweatshirts, supporting yellow motifs resembling eyes on the hoods." Ruth continued, "They were linked to our investigation. Andrews knew exactly who they were."Oh, no surprise here. Ample gunshot residue found on Andrews' right hand. He has also been positively identified, by the way. His fingerprints were obviously on the system because he was a police officer."

"There's still no link between Andrews and Smith," Charlie said, "apart from their time in the army. It is literally the only thing I can find so far. I'll keep searching."

"Charlie, that may well be the only military connection they have. We need to think outside the box. It's obvious that's where they first met. If they'd met before, I'm pretty sure your dad would have shown up too. Correct?"

"I'm sure of that. They met after Dad got injured."

"Okay. Let's search for connections during covert operations. Can we do that, Kerry?"

"I need to make a call. Charlie, don't do that search. That is a direct order. Kate, handcuff him if you need to. Even I need permission to make that search."

Kerry disappeared and didn't return for ten minutes. When she did, she looked glum and was holding a printout.

"Kate, I have no doubt that you'll be of great value when you officially join my team. We have our link," she said, waving the paper at us.

"Phil Andrews remained undercover four months after Sam emerged from the people trafficking operation. We've already established that from scrutinising the printout. Two things, when Sam emerged he filed an official complaint against Andrews. I've queued that to print on printer three, but can't share the details as I've not actually seen the report myself. Second, and this is what we've been looking for. Two weeks after Sam emerged, Smith went undercover. We've got our link!"

All three of our mouths dropped open. We had him. We had just linked Phil Andrews and Deputy Commissioner Smith in a covert operation that had possible links to Ashbeck. It certainly had dealings with human trafficking. It was a good start. Two weeks was ample time to make new contacts that Sam would know nothing about. What we needed now were the names they had kept out of the investigation during their operation. The names they'd stayed in touch with over the years. The names that had earned them money, given them power and that had now landed them in some very deep and dangerous trouble.

We had enough to have search warrants issued and Kerry was on to that. Phil was dead, but Smith and his family were about to have their lives turned upside down.

"Mum, you need to take a look at this!"

Kerry moved behind her daughter and leaned in.

"Oh my. Kate, Charlie, you guys need to see this too."

"What are we looking at?" I asked.

"This is a message from the NCA. Basically, from the man who took over from Mum when she left. The PC I'm working on is Mum's and she's asked me to alert her if she got any messages. I have clearance to open messages relating to this case only. That way one of us is on duty twenty-four/seven. "The message is informing us that evidence has been found at Deputy Commissioner Smith's house that contains information linking him to Ashbeck's business dealings. There's already a search warrant in place and they are finding all sorts of other material implicating him. No wonder he's vanished. He's either in hiding, or dead."

"Who found it?"

"Er, hang on. It says armed response. One of the daughters was being protective over it, so one of the officers took a peek inside the bag. He called a backup team. Good call."

"Do we have an indication of content?" Kerry asked.

"Not yet. It's having forensic tests done first before being copied. It's then going to a handwriting expert. He wants to know who you recommend. He wants to go with your choice as this is your baby, his choice of words, not mine."

"Okay, I'll phone him, but I really don't mind who he uses. I'm sure he's got his own contacts."

Again, Kerry retreated to her office and I wondered if this household ever slept.

# CHAPTER THIRTY-TWO

Sam was ushered into a windowless room in Andy's police station. He was not used to being this side of the interview table. The cuffs had been removed because he appeared calm. He was not calm on the inside.

Less than half an hour ago he witnessed his lifelong friend torture, then murder, two men. Yes, they'd been armed with a firearm each, but not for long. What Phil Andrews had done was highly unnecessary. It was overkill. The men needed arresting for their part in Ashbeck's operations and, more than likely, in Mel's kidnapping, but they did not deserve what Phil had done to them. Kate had not deserved to witness what she had seen.

Sat opposite was a smartly dressed man much younger than Sam. He estimated he was in his early twenties. Smart, expensive suit. He'd carried in two coffees and passed one to Sam.

"Thanks."

"Mr Cooper, I don't usually conduct interviews in local police stations, but for you I am making an exception. Now, we can make this easy or difficult. The choice is yours."

"What do you need to know?"

"What are your links to Phil Andrews?"

"We met at primary school and were literally in every class together right through until we left secondary school. We went off to university together. He studied maths and me English, but the same uni. When we left there weren't really many jobs about, so we both decided to join the army. Again, we did that together. I got injured, so Phil went on one more tour than me. By the time he left I'd recovered and we joined the police. Our training was together. He'd changed though. Something happened during his last tour that he wouldn't talk about and I never did get to the bottom of it. We moved on from that and got around it. In the early days, we both went undercover. We'd depended on each other in war, covert operations were a doddle in comparison. When we came out of that we both moved about in the Met. Sometimes we were at the same station, but not all the time. When I got married he was my best man and he is, was, my son's godfather."

"Thank you. During your covert operations did you ever get married or father any children?"

"No, neither."

"Did Andrews?"

"Not to my knowledge, no. We went in, did our jobs and got out. You know I can't discuss them with you, don't you?"

"I know that. How come, after a prolonged break in undercover work, did you end up on the Ashbeck case?"

"Phil often sent me on refresher courses, so my training was relatively up to date. Any fool could see Phil was a panicked man. The only reason I took this mission was due to it being personal. Three close personal friends were at risk, their lives were threatened. Katie-Anne Warwick missed the train that crashed, quite literally, by seconds. Jen Jennings was run off the road in her car and has been in a coma. She's awake now, but has lost the use of her legs. Mel Sage was kidnapped and has been through an extremely traumatic few days where she has been raped multiple times and mutilated. I knew what had happened to the passengers on the train and I knew what had happened to Jen. I also knew Mel was missing and the likelihood of who was responsible for that. I also knew that Phil knew far more than he was telling me and seemed to know her rough location. He got me involved and I didn't really have a choice. How could I not have come here to find Mel? How could I have lived with myself had I chosen not to act on the information I had and ignored the fact that people I cared about were in danger?"

"Did you ask your son, Charlie, to spy on Phil Andrews?"

"Good God, no! Many years ago, I bought him a spy pen for Christmas. His obsession has progressed from that. I had no idea what he was up to until a few days ago and, even then, I had no idea what he'd discovered. In fact, I told him he needed to back off and grow up."

The questions continued for another hour. Sam answered everything with honesty. He explained how Phil had used body bags to remove Kate and himself from his flat, and that, for him, the routine hadn't been the first time he'd experienced that exit. Kate had been horrified, but had coped. The location of Jade's building and how the mission had been different was all explained. The fact that Jade suddenly knew Sam's real identity after working with him for so many years, had unnerved him.

"Who is Jade?"

"I have no idea other than she is the woman who has provided me with my undercover identities for my missions over the years. I only know her as Jade. I can't name the building, but I could drive you to it."

"That won't be necessary for now. Maybe one day though. The issue we're having, Mr Cooper, is the gun recovered near Mr Andrews' body has come back as registered in your name."

"That's not possible. I don't even have a licence."

"We're aware of that. Can you explain how you come to own a gun?"

"That's impossible. I've never owned a gun in my life."

"But you know how to shoot?"

"Of course, I was in the army and I've been to war several times. But there is no place for guns in civilian life."

"Okay. We have ways to look into that and we already have our analysis teams working on the documents."

"You can also swab my hands for gunshot residue."

"We will do that, but we have plenty of witnesses that say you didn't fire the gun on the beach tonight."

"Why are you holding me then?"

"We need to find out as much as we can about Andrews and the links he had in his past. You cover a great deal of his past. We are both in town, so here we are."

"And there's nothing more to this than establishing how far back in his history I go?"

"Put your trust in me, Mr Cooper. You cannot be where you want to be right now. I have you documented as being in this police station, helping me with my enquiries at a very precise time, for a very good reason," he said and tapped his nose.

Sam's eyebrows rose, but the man was not forthcoming.

"More coffee?"

# CHAPTER THIRTY-THREE

Kerry had spoken to Andy and insisted that Sam was kept in overnight. I'd overheard her side of the conversation.

"It's one night and what we're doing here is clearing his name. We're almost there. Trust me Andy, the computers are continuing to search, but we are all in need of a couple of hours' sleep. We have some fantastic leads, but none of this so far links Sam to any of it. He is clean. He cannot come here until these files leave the premises. Is that clear?"

Eventually, she'd insisted we all got some sleep. Four hours she gave us.

By the time we'd rejoined her in the kitchen, she looked energised and fresh.

"Oh, you realise she's found the energy to go for a run?" Ruth grunted. "I keep telling her she's going to crash and burn one of these days, but do you think she ever listens? No! What do I know?"

Four hours' sleep hadn't been nearly enough for me! I had no idea where this woman got her energy from, but she was looking as if she'd had the weekend off, looking refreshed and ready for the challenges that faced a new week.

It was toast and coffee all round, Even Charlie was up for coffee, rather than his usual herbal tea.

"Kate, I hope you don't mind, but I've arranged for one of my team to pop down to your place to have a poke about to try and find out the circumstances surrounding the fire. There's no reports filed, everything's so slow for some reason. We need to know if it is connected. He'll ask all the right questions, get them looking for connections they don't know they need to look for, because they won't be aware of them. An ace of spades for example."

"Oh, thank you. I've tried calling Cathy, but I can't get a reply. It doesn't help that everyone down there thinks I died on the train – I can't exactly leave a message can I?

What have your searches found while we were sleeping?"

"Nothing connecting Sam to anything. He'll be released shortly. Eat up. By the time you've finished, there'll be a car waiting for you outside to take you to meet him."

"Thank you!"

Eating in silence while the others chatted, my tummy started flipping.

\*\*\*

Sam stood in the car park when we pulled in and my heart melted. Rushing to him, we embraced; it didn't matter where we were. What I'd learned about him was gone from my mind for the moment. There were more important things in life than his past. Still holding each other tightly, I whispered in his ear.

"I can't discuss what I've been doing while you've been in there. If Kerry wants to tell you, then that's up to her."

"I think I'm in a whole heap of trouble, princess."

"Trust me when I say that you're not. Apparently, we're to go to the B & B to get our things. Andy and Kerry want us to be their guests. If you were in trouble, that wouldn't be happening. Our room is lovely. I slept there last night. Oh, and so you know, Charlie is sharing with Ruth and she has him drinking coffee!"

"Seriously? He didn't waste his time!"

We started walking, hand in hand, towards the bed and breakfast. I felt calmer than I'd felt in days, despite knowing that Ashbeck was still out there somewhere. Knowing that his operation was considerably compromised was a massive comfort, somehow. I knew he'd be annoyed and that it was likely he'd be focussing that energy towards me, but he had less people to rely on now. That could only be a good thing.

It must have taken us ten minutes to reach our room. When I turned the lock and opened the door, something didn't feel right. Sam sensed it too. He went to stop me from entering, but was too late, I was already inside. He was quick to follow. Everything looked in order and we allowed the door to close behind us. It was then we sensed we weren't alone.

***

Freezing on the spot wasn't something I was used to. Normally an action type of person, I felt trapped and needed time to think. I didn't have time. I willed myself to relax and for my heart rate to slow. Gradually, I began to turn around with a calmness I wasn't feeling. Being met by a gun pointed at my head did nothing to ease my fear.

"Don't scream." The voice was female and somehow familiar, but I was yet to place it. I couldn't see her face.

I held my hands up at about shoulder level.

"I won't," I said.

"Are you armed?"

"Neither of us are armed."

"Do you mind if I check?"

"Go ahead," I said.

As the woman stepped into view, recognition was immediate. Jade. Once she'd established we weren't armed she was more relaxed and lowered her weapon, but kept it in her hand.

"Who are you, Jade, because we both know that's not your real name?" I asked.

"My identity is irrelevant. I am here to help you through this mess."

"Why do you think we need your help?"

"Katie-Anne Warwick and Samuel Cooper. Undercover for Phil Andrews. You do realise that man has removed you both from society and you are now in limbo. You do not exist."

I nodded.

"Kate. May I call you Kate?"

I nodded again.

"You need me to establish you both back into society."

"No, we don't, Jade. We have our own contacts that will be more than happy to do that for us. In fact, they are working on just that already."

Suddenly it dawned on me. It was Jade who'd had us bugged.

"Jade, this meeting is over. You need to leave right now." Sam had had enough.

"I'm the one with the gun! I say when this meeting is over."

There was a knock at the door and Jade was distracted briefly. It was enough for Sam to make his move. He was on her before she knew what had hit her. She dropped the gun and I kicked it across the room. Opening the door, I was relieved when Andy walked through it.

"Charlie alerted me to a hostage situation on the CCTV he'd installed. I've come to make an arrest, but it looks like you are handing the situation between you."

"Be my guest, Andy!" Sam said.

# CHAPTER THIRTY-FOUR

Two weeks passed while we waited for test results. We'd spent them with Andy and Kerry. Sam had taken leave from work and was currently undecided if he'd return. Kerry had, of course, offered him an opportunity with her. He was undecided on that too.

We had, Sam and I, spent hours talking about his past and what he had been forced to do as part of his covert operations. None of it was supposed to be exposed, especially to Charlie and me. He now had to live with that, thanks to Phil. Hell, we all had to live with that. Placing some perspective on the situation, Sam had described the type of person he'd had to become to fit into his new role during the operation. He didn't try and justify the life he'd taken, but it had been an order. He'd needed to gain trust to get a foot in the door for the investigation to proceed: he did what he had to do. The man he'd killed, he'd explained, was very much like Ashbeck. He was into human trafficking and profiting from selling his cargo as sex slaves. Bodies were turning up on our beaches and it had been down to him.

The reality, Sam later discovered, was that this man was direct competition for the gang in which he'd been initiated. A gang that, all these years later, we were now discovering had Carl Ashbeck at the helm.

Sam's complaint against Phil had resulted in him being pulled from the investigation early and replaced by Smith. Phil was getting in too deep and becoming too involved. Sam had warned the authorities that the operation was going wrong and they'd ignored him. Someone else higher up in the chain was involved, he was sure. Corruption and politics. How could you ever win against that? Somehow, their friendship had moved past this.

\*\*\*

Rain sounded heavily against the kitchen window: the forecast for the next three days was torrential rain across the United Kingdom. Sam and I had our backs to it as we leaned against the worktop, sipping at our coffees. Kerry walked in waving papers at us. The results were finally here! I'd started to learn to read her expressions and I didn't like what I was seeing.

Sam poured a coffee from percolator – black and strong – and carried it to the table.

"Thanks."

The three of us sat in silence, Kerry apparently weighing up how she was going to approach the data she was holding.

"Whatever it is you need to tell us, just spit it out," Sam said impatiently. "Keeping us in suspense isn't going to change a damn thing."

"No, it isn't," she replied and placed a set of data printouts in front of each of us, print side down. "Before you look at these, please let me explain something. Had Mel not requested so many PERK tests, her results would probably have been disregarded as inconclusive. The results are astonishing. However, all three sets are identical and no court could ignore that – if this case gets that far."

Kerry allowed that to sink in before continuing.

"Now, I've had a few minutes to process this and have no personal connection to Mel. I need you both to remain calm – do you understand?"

Sam and I both nodded.

"Okay. All three sets of tests confirm that Mel was raped by thirteen different men."

Numbness overcame me and tears started to form in my eyes. Speechless, I just looked at Kerry before standing and walking to the kitchen window, where I watched raindrops run down the windowpane. There was nothing I could say that would ever make this go away for Mel and a feeling of helplessness enveloped me. Wiping tears from my cheeks I turned to face the others, just as Sam swiped at his coffee mug, sending it flying across the kitchen floor.

Always one for a reactional response, Kerry was lucky her table was still the right way up. Sam was not done and he stormed out of the back door and into whatever trouble he could find.

Kerry hurried to the door, but he was gone.

"Leave him. He'll come back with blood on his hands and alcohol in his system. I'll patch him up and we won't speak about it."

"How often does this happen?"

"It's rare. Just twice before."

"We have more results if you're up for it?"

"Let's get on with it. I'll be better if I keep busy."

"The DNA of the two men Phil shot on the beach showed up on Mel's DNA report." Kirsty looked up at me, removed her glasses and sighed. "We'll never know for sure, Kate, but just maybe Phil knew what those two had done. Just think about that."

It was certainly a possibility.

We discussed the forensics at length. There were plenty of DNA matches to past crimes, giving us names, possible addresses and a web of links that was astonishing. Arrest warrants were being issued and Ashbeck's net was about to get smaller. We were closing in on this monster and I hoped he could feel the pressure.

Ashbeck was, however, still at large. Sightings had been reported in their hundreds, but none had yielded any positive results. It was, however, obvious that he'd made the journey to Cornwall. To my home in Polperro. Thankfully, everyone had escaped unharmed. The fire crew had found three ace of spades playing cards on the bridge over the stream, each with a pebble on top. On each card was written a name; Mel, Jen and Kate. They'd photographed them and placed the items in evidence bags, but hadn't though any more about them until Kerry's investigator had shown up asking questions. Ashbeck had to be responsible: there was no other possible explanation.

In Sam's absence, Kerry and I added 'fire' to an Internet search about Illuminati symbols and got an instant hit. What was Ashbeck up to?

"This worries me, Kate – this connection he seems to think he has to this organisation. He's obviously spent a lot of time researching and adapting things to suit his own agenda. He's a dangerous man, with an outrageously dangerous mindset, that he appears to have fed with some sort of religious endgame. We seriously need to discover what his endgame is!"

"And we haven't caught him, Kerry. He's still out there, – wreaking havoc."

"Hmm. Okay, Andy and his team arrested thirty-six people on the night of the raid. They released Phil Andrews, who killed two more and himself. That means Ashbeck is thirty-nine operatives down. The manhunt for him and for the deputy commissioner continues, but it will be much harder for his operations to run with that fewer people. He might still be out there, Kate, but life just got very difficult."

\*\*\*

Sam returned, as predicted, with blood on his hands and up his arms. His knuckles were grazed and fingers bruised. Kerry sent me out of the room and, although I gave them space and couldn't hear what was being said, I could hear their raised voices. She was not best pleased with him – he'd potentially brought trouble to her front door and she was having none of it. Sam had met his match with this woman: this would either be the making of a beautiful working relationship, or it would send him back to London with his tail between his legs. Time would tell.

# CHAPTER THIRTY-FIVE

Rain pounded so hard on the windscreen it ricocheted off, making visibility almost impossible. The road twisted and climbed ahead of us, a mountain to our left and a sheer drop to our right. Metal barriers protected us from the drop and they glistened in the wet. We no longer had a clue what road we were on: the navigation system had given up over an hour ago – at about the same time that darkness had fallen. Headlights were making the conditions worse and surface water was starting to cascade beneath our wheels, like a fast-moving stream.

Common sense would suggest that Sam should slow down and find somewhere safe to stop, so we could wait the storm out before continuing with our journey – but our lives had become more complicated than that. Behind us was another car. Its headlights were on full beam and how its front bumper hadn't connected with our rear one, I'd never know. The faster Sam drove, the harder it pushed us.

We were without phone signal and in the Scottish Highlands, taking Charlie to his placement training. He had accepted a place on Kerry's team and his training started in three days. There was no doubt in any of our minds that Ashbeck was in the car behind us and our only chance of survival was to outdrive him. Sam was, by far, the more advanced driver of the two of us and I was so glad it was him at the wheel rather than me. We'd been driving over an hour like this already. At Sam's request, Charlie and I had remained silent so he could concentrate, which made perfect sense to me.

Suddenly, our car jolted forwards as the vehicle behind crashed into our back bumper. Sam had been expecting something like this and kept perfect control of the vehicle, but the same couldn't be said about his emotions. Words escaped his mouth and he punched the steering wheel in anger, as his foot pressed harder on the accelerator. We gained speed.

Gradually, the lights behind us faded into the distance, but Sam didn't ease his speed. He fell silent once again, but did not contain himself for long.

"Don't think for a second that bastard's gone. This isn't over!"

Glancing at both of our phones, I checked for a signal, still nothing. "He's playing games," I agreed.

Sam continued driving hard for another hour before he felt comfortable slowing down a little. It's only then we started to chat, trying to comprehend Ashbeck's next move. Unless he was working with someone else, there was no way he could get ahead of us. Although we didn't know the roads, or even where we were, our obvious remote location

– the fact that a mountain climbed to our left and a treeline dropped to our right – must mean that the roads didn't link up in a way that would enable Ashbeck to get ahead.

We started to climb a steep hill and Charlie spoke for the first time in almost three hours.

"Dad, when you get to the top of this hill stop the car. Trust me, it may just save us!" he said excitedly, as he started punching something into his phone.

Within three minutes we reached the top and Sam made the breaks scream as the car came to a standstill.

"Give me time. It's sending, hold on. Okay, go!"

Charlie had managed to get a signal.

"Who did you message and what did you say?"

"Kerry. I gave her our GPS location, an SOS call and I set a tracker up on my phone – fingers crossed it activated in time."

"We have headlights in the distance behind us. I'm speeding up again," Sam declared, as he gradually pressed the accelerator towards the floor. "Keep talking to me, I'm getting tired. Keep me awake."

I glanced at my phone, my signal was back!

"Charlie, I've got signal. Check yours. Phone Kerry. I'll check our location on my maps app. Okay, I think we've stopped climbing for now. There's a junction about half a mile ahead of us, off to the left. After that this road gets really narrow and climbs and falls, twists and turns. Oh Sam, you really will have to slow down!"

"We do need to consider one thing," Sam said. "If Ashbeck's got help, we might get company at the next junction. Smith is still missing, right. We don't know if he's kidnapped, or helping the scumbag. We do know he showed up at Jen's accident, but that could have been under duress. You know I love you guys."

"Don't talk shit like that Dad."

"He's right, Charlie. We have to face this for what it is."

"You still have GPS?"

"Yep. Almost on top of the junction."

"I've resent GPS to Kerry, but I can't seem to connect to phone her," Charlie said.

"At least Kerry will know our location."

Out of nowhere brightness filled the car and there was a massive crunch as metal struck something in the road. We were taken sideways and whatever Sam tried, he had no control. The car started to tip on to its side and we were airborne. When the car touched tarmac again, it did so momentarily with the driver's side, before we were flung into the air and then on to the roof. We bounced, as if the car was nothing but a cardboard box in the breeze, from roof to side, to right way up, uncountable times.

Momentum lessened and we seemed to have stopped flipping, but had settled on the roof, I thought. The noise of metal scraping along tarmac was overwhelming. Glass had covered me – it was in my mouth and up my nose. Water beat against my face. Finally, darkness overcame me: a blissful silence took me away from the horrors of the night.

# CHAPTER THIRTY-SIX

I was shivering when I opened my eyes. All I saw were bright lights: white, blue and orange flashes that were lighting up the blackness. Distorted voices seemed to be shouting at me, but I didn't recognise them, nor could I make out what they were saying. It was raining heavily, the sound of the falling water echoed as if it was falling on to a tin roof: and then images started forming and I remembered. The car. Scotland. Ashbeck. Sam and Charlie. Oh, God! Sam and Charlie!

Suddenly the sound of the rain faded, as something mechanical crunched against metal. Realisation that we were still upside down took a while, but it materialised as I got my bearings. The poor light and the fact I was dangling upside down in my seat belt weren't doing much to help my concentration. As I became more aware, I began to feel pain – it started to spread through my body, it was especially bad in my chest. Slowly, I dared myself to turn my head to face Sam. He was uncharacteristically quiet and that couldn't be a good sign: pain seared down my spine, but I needed to know.

Blood trickled from a wound somewhere on his body and was pooling around his head. I couldn't see how much he'd lost, but it looked like too much to me.

"Sam! Sam! Sam!" I screamed, but he didn't respond. Tears formed and escaped, and it felt strange that they should fall over my forehead rather than my cheeks.

Feeling light-headed, I tried taking a deep, steadying breath. Pain overcame me and I began to drift once again into an unknown darkness where there was no vision, no sound and nothing hurt any more.

The next time I came around a man was working on me and immediately shone a torch in my eyes. From what I could tell, I was in the back of an ambulance and we were on the move.

"Welcome back! You've been in an accident and you're on the way to hospital," he said in a Scottish accent. "What's your name, lass?" he added, lifting my oxygen mask.

"Kate. Where are Sam and Charlie? Are they okay?"

"You need to breathe, not talk. I'm not sure on their condition, but I can tell you three ambulances were sent to your scene, so they are in good hands."

I was not sure how long the journey took – if I'd slept or drifted in and out of consciousness – but what I did know was that by the time I arrived at the hospital I could no longer feel: there was no pain or emotion. Whatever relief I'd been given had sent me off into some euphoric place where nothing mattered any more.

Jumping straight ahead of the queue, I was booked in and wheeled straight around to X-ray. My paramedics remained with me, keeping me stable and insisting I stayed awake when all I wanted was to sleep. My body was pulled in different directions: I was transferred on to the bed and images were taken – then transferred back on to the stretcher and wheeled into a trauma room.

Eventually my care was being transferred to hospital staff. I reached out and touched the arm of the closest paramedic to me. "Thank you for taking care of me, both of you."

"Pleasure's ours, lass. We'll see if we can find ya fella. What's his name?"

"Sam Cooper and his son is Charlie. Thanks guys."

The nurses exchanged a grim look with each other and one followed the paramedics out. Immediately worried, I tried to sit up.

"You need to stay still. My colleague has probably gone to see if she can find Mr Cooper. He's walking wounded and desperately trying to locate you."

"And Charlie?"

"Not sure," she replied, a little too cautiously.

"Oh, come on. You know something. Don't you dare let Sam walk in here and me not know what's going on. At least tell me, is Charlie dead or alive?"

"Okay, I will level with you, Ms Warwick. I'm a nurse and I thought nothing could ever shock me. Never have I had to deal with anything like this. I don't know what you guys are involved in, but now I'm mixed up in something that scares me to death! This young boy you are asking me about, Charlie – whatever he's got to do with you – was dragged from the vehicle, tied to a tree and shot. Paramedics are saying there was no blood seeping from his wounds which means he was already dead. This whole department is buzzing for the wrong reasons tonight."

Lost for words, I turned my head away from my nurse and wished my bed would swallow me. Such a vibrant, intelligent and beautiful young man had gone: Ashbeck had claimed another innocent life. Consumed with heartache, I did not notice when Sam walked in until he took my hand. There were no words that could ever comfort him right now: instead I held out my arms and he collapsed into them.

Sam sobbed uncontrollably and I knew he'd never get over this. Charlie had become involved in all of this because he was living at Phil's – Sam would feel so utterly responsible and no amount of reasoning would sway him otherwise. It took every bit of strength I had left to hold him and to breathe. Whatever drugs I'd been given were wearing off and the pain was returning. Eventually, my nurse physically removed Sam from me.

"Mr Cooper, you need to allow Kate to breathe," she said. "We need to get her cleaned up and we need to get the doctor in here to talk about her injuries."

There was glass embedded in one side of my face, which my nurse – Penny – was now removing. When the doctor eventually showed up, he classified me as very lucky. I needed to stay overnight for observation: I'd broken my shoulder, both collarbones and a few ribs. My lungs were bruised, but not punctured. There was extensive bruising to my body, but no internal bleeding.

Ashbeck had had another good go at me, but I'd mend. Essentially, he hadn't broken me yet, despite having had a clear opportunity to take me out – instead he'd chosen to target Charlie. I didn't understand how this fitted into his plan, or 'endgame' as Kerry had put it: but was sure I would soon figure it out.

As for Sam, the sad truth was, I knew he was a broken man and that he'd probably withdraw from me emotionally. I also had no doubt in my mind, or in my heart, that he was about to go on a personal mission to hunt down Ashbeck with one goal in mind.

Revenge.

Printed in Great Britain
by Amazon